THE BRAND OF SATAN

Nancy was sure that her heart belonged to her betrothed, Peter Phenwick. She believed she was engaged merely in a harmless flirtation with the two handsome, inseparable strangers who appeared as if from nowhere to become her companions when Peter was away.

They called themselves artists, and introduced Nancy to a new world of sophisticated knowledge and pleasure. And now, on a picnic deep in the forest, they were introducing her to something else.

They were on either side of her, engaging her in what they called light-hearted play. They had stripped to the waist, Nancy felt their silken flesh under her fingers, her head was whirling as if with drink.

Then she saw the mark on the side of one of them . . . the black cross that was the sign of voodoo . . . and as lightning flashed in the darkening sky above, she knew too late the dark power that was taking her irresistibly as its own. . . .

#11
KATHERYN KIMBROUGH'S
Saga of the Phenwick Women

NANCY,
THE DARING

POPULAR LIBRARY   •   NEW YORK

PROLOGUE

I HAVE TO ADMIT from the outset that I admired Nancy Cox from the first time I saw her. I felt she was my kind of woman, the stuff that I wished some of the other Phenwick women were made of. In ways she reminded me of Joanna, with a great deal of spunkiness and aggressive enthusiasm. She liked to laugh, and I liked that. The difficulty was figuring how she could become a Phenwick.

I had always been especially fond of Patricia and was delighted to see that she had taken such an interest in Nancy. Patricia is a rarity and a person so pleased with earthly activities that it will be difficult for her to leave the physical plane. Perhaps she can will herself bodily earthbound as I have done spiritually. As you know, because of my will, I am held to the Phenwick women. And I will tell you now that I'm getting just a little bit bored with it all.

I hear of other dimensions, other levels of vibration beyond this which surrounds the earth, and I am becoming grossly curious to see what it is all about. And perhaps I will one of these days. I hear whispers. But apparently there is still much I must do as I am to superintend my precious Phenwick women.

It is ironic that the one child named for me, Augustus, was to marry a woman I could not accept—nor could Patricia for that matter. (Frankly, while I was pleased with the name, I was not overly impressed with Augus-

5

tus as a person, either.) Lillian Webb—something even annoys me about her name—was always the antithesis of the kind of female I admired. I knew from the instant that she married Augustus that he was doomed to a mediocre existence. My only prayer was that one or both or their sons might be worthy of the Phenwick name.

Souls, when they enter earthly form, choose the parents they are to have, the situations they are to experience. I somehow have faith in both Stuart and Gordon, despite their parents. But I wonder if Stuart would be a proper match for Nancy Cox. He is the only young Phenwick man—and he is still a youth—who would be a potential mate.

Yet I am determined that Nancy become a Phenwick woman. Perhaps— There is one other possibility. I wish I could see far ahead in time and know.

Chapter 1

LILLIAN PHENWICK was a meticulous housekeeper, a demanding wife and an exacting mother. Time had coarsened her. Grim lines cracked her face. Filled with Christian zeal and emotional religious concepts, she was a tyrant in the presence of any non-Christian person. She was ready to attack the heretic with her parasol or any other suitable weapon she might chance upon. She was also a bigot, believing that only the Caucasians were true Christians and eligible for the designs *she* had of Heaven. Her husband and sons tolerated her, but only her sons were sometimes moved by her enthusiasm about religion.

Young Stuart Phenwick, growing more handsome with each day, had inherited some of his mother's stoic qualities. He had a tendency to appear aloof and arrogant. Yet he was so enamored with his Uncle Joshua and his gracious personality, that the lad desired to change. If only there were a chance for him to spend time with Joshua, perhaps he would acquire some of the man's charm. And Stuart was bright. He realized that Joshua's charm was directly inherited from his grandfather, Peter. To Stuart, Peter Phenwick was still the most handsome man in the world, and there was nothing his grandfather could not do. And Peter, when permitted by Lillian, would get extremely close to each of his grandsons.

Now that Peter was a widower, he found himself inclined more and more toward Stuart and Gordon. But Lillian was determined her father-in-law would not have too strong an influence over the lads. Stuart was the first to realize that Peter was lonely. Lillian refused to let her son go live with the older man. Peter was only a lukewarm Christian, and she would not have that kind of influence over her son.

The wedding date had been set for Prentise and Harriet. Word was sent to London. Joanna returned a message asking them to postpone for a month, saying that she would return to America for the happy event. She had not missed the weddings of either of her other brothers, Augustus and Joshua; she felt it her duty as a loving sister to be present when Prentise took the marriage vows.

Joanna Phenwick was perhaps the most unpredictable member of the family. She was an actress on the London stage and extremely successful in her profession. Although she admired her Aunt Patricia and her cousin Susannah, Joanna with her rare exotic beauty was unconventional in every way she could possibly conceive. Therefore, when making the voyage from London, she did it with her usual flourish and her skill as a dramatic actress.

She arrived in Boston not on a Medallion ship but on one belonging to a competitive company so that her entrance would not be known to the family. Elegantly attired as she always was, she wore a bright red dress that spring morning. Over her shoulders draped a mink stole which set off her magnificent beauty, and there was no doubt that Joanna Phenwick was a beauty. An acclaimed actress in London, she had achieved much success and notoriety. She was the darling of the theater, and had many suitors and many more admirers who never got a chance to get close to her. She laughed at their frivolity. She teased men as a cat teases mice, and with all this, she was glamour and excitement. She was the epitome of what a lady of grandness should be. Twice she was introduced to the queen and on both occasions she received lavish praises from the monarch as well as from many of the gentlemen at court. It was not uncommon for her to be seen at the palace. When she performed, her performances were grandly attended by nobility. To say she was the toast of London would be putting it mildly.

The berth in which the ship docked was on a pier adjoining that to which the Medallion ships came for unloading. Hence, when she disembarked, she did so with as little fanfare as possible. However, every member of the crew, the captain included, was on hand to see her make her glorious exit down the gangplank. Her luggage would be sent for later. Catching the eye of a young stevedore, she asked him to secure a carriage for her, which he gladly did.

Her intention was to go directly to Edward House where Patricia Phenwick lived on Beacon Hill. But she was anxious to see her father. Almost as a whim, she decided to go to the adjoining wharf, sit in the carriage and scan the persons busying about. When she saw no familiar faces, she commanded the driver to take her to the Medallion office.

Medallion Enterprises Incorporated had long since moved from its waterfront address, and was now safely ensconced in a large brick building about three blocks away from the waterfront, a building which occupied an entire block. The carriage pulled up in front of this rather plain facade. The driver was instructed to go in and ask for Mr. Phenwick.

Patiently, Joanna sat in all her dignity and dramatic airs waiting while the middle-aged man grunted down from the carriage and went into the building. He appeared a short time later with a handsome young man who greatly resembled the reddish blond, electric-blue-eyed Joshua Phenwick, her younger brother. For a moment Joanna had a start, for the lad she was seeing could be no more than in his late teens, at best. Still she knew by his appearance that he was definitely a Phenwick. He had the features of her father and of her grand-

9

father both of whom had been extremely handsome. The boy looked perplexed. He wiped his nose with the back of his hand, then brushed his hands over his apron. Apparently, he did clerical work. He squinted up into the sun that haloed Joanna. A questioning look.

"Did you wish to see me, missus?"

"It's miss. If you are a Phenwick, as no doubt you are, I did wish to see you."

"I don't believe I know you," he said. "I am Stuart Phenwick."

"Stuart Phenwick?" A light ripple of laughter rolled from her throat. It was like a song. "My, yes, I can see that you are a Phenwick. Stuart Phenwick, the son of Augustus Phenwick, no doubt."

"The same."

"Pleased to meet you." She extended her hand as if she wanted to be helped down. The boy took it with a trembling gesture, uncertain.

"You needn't look so disturbed, young man. Allow me to introduce myself. I am your aunt."

"My aunt?"

"Yes, we've never met before. I'm your Aunt Joanna."

"Aunt Joanna; but aren't you supposed to be in England—I mean London—I mean overseas," the boy stammered.

"No. I'm supposed to be here at this moment," she replied. Again the music of laughter pouring from her. Her eyes sparkling, glistening in the sunlight. But there were always stars in her eyes. Always laughter surrounding her. She held his hand and bent herself slightly forward, offering her cheek.

"You may kiss me, Stuart," she indicated.

The boy swallowed and dutifully planted a kiss on the soft, smooth skin of the lovely face.

"So you are Augustus' son. I'm surprised."

"Surprised? Why should you be?"

"Gus was never the handsome Phenwick. He lacked the beauty of his brother Joshua. In fact, even Prentise

10

with his square jaw and his stoic expression had more—what shall I say—had more appeal physically than your father. Gus is my oldest brother, and as the eldest I looked up to him. However, I was never as close to him as I was to Joshua nor Prentise for that matter." She squeezed his hand. "Stuart, I do hope we will become good friends."

"We don't have to become friends, not if we are aunt and nephew," the boy answered, politely.

"Well, I suppose we don't; I hope that we do. I am only here for a short while. I'll be returning to London before long. I came for your uncle's wedding. I do pray he is marrying a sweet young lady."

"I like Harriet," he replied. "She's pretty enough, although sometimes she's a bit strange. I don't know that I'll ever get used to that funny way she talks. 'I d'clare, you-all, honeychile.' It's difficult to know how to take her at all times. And then she does have a rather bizarre way of going off into space. My mother said it was because of something that happened when she was a young girl, and that it has carried over into her adult life. Not that she is that much of an adult. Frankly, I don't think she's more than two years older than I am, if that."

"I'm anxious to meet the lady. What is her name?"

"Harriet Pettijohn."

"Harriet Pettijohn? That's a rather pretty name, meaning, of course, Harriet Little John."

"She does have a very attractive friend who is not at all, well, confused as Harriet is."

"A friend, a lady friend?"

"A girl friend," Stuart assured her. "Her name is Nancy Cox, and she is one of the prettiest young ladies I have ever seen."

"Aha, I detect the sound of admiration," Joanna said, putting her arm around Stuart's shoulders and heading him toward the Medallion office. "Is your father anywhere about?"

11

"No, Dad is off on business. He had to ride to Cambridge."

"I don't suppose your grandfather is here, is he?"

"He was going down to the wharf to see the *Augusta IV*."

"The *Augusta IV*? Is she in port at this time?"

"Actually, she's waiting to take Prentise and Harriet back to Savannah."

"Take them back to Savannah. You mean they're not going to live here in Boston?"

"You haven't heard of the office that is being opened in Savannah, then?" questioned Stuart.

"Well, I must admit I haven't been kept up to date on many of the Medallion Enterprises activities," Joanna said. "Then I suppose there is no need for us to go into the office, after all. I would know no one else, I am certain, and I did come to see my father."

Stuart freed himself from her hold and turned back toward the carriage. "It's very difficult for me to conceive of you being my aunt. You're such a pretty lady, yourself. It is even more difficult to conceive of you being Grandfather's daughter."

"Why is that?"

"I don't know, I suppose it's because, well, because you're so beautiful."

Joanna trilled laughter as she playfully patted Stuart on the cheek. "I thank you for the compliment. Now then, shall we walk to the *Augusta IV* or shall we take the carriage?"

"I'll ride with you in the carriage."

The curly blond hair was becoming rust-colored, increasingly getting gray. Brown eyes, crisp and sharp, pierced through everything they came upon. The large jovial smile illuminated a magnanimous disposition. The man, although he was fifty-eight years old, looked to be no more than in his early forties. Handsome. He was standing at the prow of the ship when the carriage came forward. Although his eyes had weakened a bit over the years, Peter Phenwick recognized the pretty lady riding beside his grandson. Like a man half his age, he ran from his position down the gangplank, reaching the carriage practically before the horses drew to a stop.

"Joanna, my darling! What in the devil are you doing in Boston?" shouted Peter, his arms open wide waiting for her to jump to them.

"As a matter of fact," Joanna said, as she hugged him, tightly, "I've come for Prentise's wedding. More important," she kissed him on the cheek, "I wanted to come to be with you at your time of bereavement."

"At *our* time of bereavement," Peter corrected. "I'm sorry you couldn't be at the funeral. Your mother would have been pleased to have you there, I am certain."

"Mother and I were never close. We were like strangers. Still I cannot think unkindly of her. My concern is for you and the loneliness through which you must be going."

"Let's not go into that," Peter said with a cheerful smile. He was not one to show a distressed face to anyone. "Come along, we must go someplace where we can have a cup of tea or a drink and chat."

"I would love to go to Aunt Patricia's house," Joanna said, folding her arm into her father's.

"Good, then we can drop Stuart off at the office and go on up the hill," Peter replied. "It's no problem at all. You've met your nephew, I see."

"Surprisingly, I'm most impressed with him. I would have sworn when I first saw him that he was Josh. You know how dearly I love Josh."

"The two of you were very close, always. You the big sister, he the baby brother. Well, come along then, Stuart, we three can ride together. I have no more to do here anyway. I was just having a look about."

Stuart was left off at the Medallion office. The driver was given instructions to go to Beacon Hill and the enormous, imposing mansion called Edward House built by Patricia Phenwick after plans used in the old Barrywell House as constructed by Augusta Phenwick prior to the Revolutionary War. The house was modern in all aspects, beautifully decorated, and complemented with works of art. Still an aura of mystery surrounded it. Neighboring houses were pushing in, and the once spacious yard had been sold to other residents who wished to live on the famous hill. The carriage pulled up the drive and the two alighted, father and daughter arm in arm.

Patricia Phenwick with all her majesty and grace had been observing from the rose garden at the side of the house as the carriage drew up. Once she had had flaxen blond hair that made her vivid blue eyes dance with excitement and anticipation of life. Now she wore a wig. She had many different wigs, but she preferred one that was tinted slightly red to the others that were more her old youthful color. Her heart-shaped face had not aged greatly. There were very few lines and she walked with the sweeping grace of a young girl. Her skin was firm, and she could easily pass for a person in her mid to late forties although she was now seventy. Upon recognizing her favorite nephew, she sauntered around the side of the house as Peter was connecting his fist to the door with a noisy knock.

"The servants will allow you in, Peter, but it's spring and the house is musty in the springtime. Why don't you join me in the garden?"

"Aunt Patricia!"

"Come along." Patricia held out her hand. "What is this? Don't tell me it is our Joanna, returned."

"Aunt Patricia," Joanna exclaimed, "you look younger than the last time I saw you!"

"My darling, I *am* younger than the last time you saw me, and the next time you see me, I'll be still younger. It's something I'm working on; it's all in the mind, you know," Patricia said, grandly. "I've decided that I'm not going to grow old like all these other old people. Why, when I look at some of my nieces, and I see them aging so fast, it appalls me. Helen in her last days, you'll pardon my reference, Peter, made me feel like a

14

youngster, and dear Jane Augusta, she's growing quite matronly. I suppose I've grown matronly, too."

"Never, you'll never grow matronly, Aunt Patricia," Peter exclaimed, "you'll always be lovely. The lovely lady I remember from my childhood."

"You can go on all day without saying that, Peter. Your childhood should have been my childhood, but, of course, it wasn't. I was married to your Uncle Edward, then later to your half brother, Elias, whom I loved deeply. I hope you understand that. They had a way of growing old faster than I did although they were a generation apart. Come along, let's go out into the garden. It's very comfortable beneath the trees with the new leaves just sprouting. There are some early crocuses, tulips, and daffodils. The tulips come from the Netherlands. I sent specially for them."

Tea was brought from the house and served to the three as they sat and became reacquainted. Joanna had never lost her admiration for Patricia, and the feeling was mutual. Although Patricia never aspired to being an actress, she was a poetess, and therefore considered herself in one of the arts, creative and talented. Perhaps she would never receive the notoriety that Joanna had received, yet she would be famed in her own way among her followers.

"I had hoped to get here for the funeral," Joanna said as if she felt it her duty to do so.

"Oh, I do hope not," Patricia said. "It was so dreary, funerals always are. But then she was your mother."

"Yes.

"I will make an admission to both of you," Peter announced looking down at his hands as he picked his nails. "I was only once briefly in love with Helen. I wonder if that wasn't simply biological, an emotional excitement, nothing more. By the time you were conceived, well, Helen and I had grown apart. It's a wonder Joshua ever came along. Yet I always wanted four children. The hope was two boys and two girls. We made do with three boys and one girl."

15

"Your father was a brave man," Patricia interjected, directing the statement to Joanna. "I admire his tenacity and stick-to-itiveness for remaining with Helen all those years." Patricia folded her hands together, gently stroking her fingers, her eyes focused down upon them for a few moments. Then she looked up at her niece. "My dearest Joanna, what about your love life? I thought by now surely we would hear that you had married someone rich and fabulous in London."

"Someone rich and fabulous, Aunt Patricia? No, I know many people and I have many friends. Perhaps I have been in love once or twice," Joanna remarked softly. Then she raised her voice as if she were on stage. "But when one has a career to think about . . . And I have become famous myself, I have many suitors, Aunt Patricia. That doesn't make me a bad lady; it simply makes me versatile, and I enjoy my sort of life, I really do."

"I have seen many of Joanna's men friends," Peter acknowledged, "and I must say that she shows good taste. Morally, I have nothing to say about it. I cannot be critical of the way she lives her life. She is in a profession filled with glamour and excitement. She attracts many men to her. My only hope is that she is happy." He reached forward and put his hand atop Joanna's. "Are you happy, my dear?"

Joanna smiled broadly. A swallow momentarily caught in her throat and the smile grew larger. Her eyes sparkled and all her beauty radiated at her father. "Yes, I am happy. Yes, indeed, for as dear Aunt Patricia says, happiness is a state of mind. I made up my mind long ago that I was going to be happy and remain happy for the rest of my life. I also made up my mind that I was going to be successful, and I will continue to be."

"And what of family, my dear?" asked her father.

"Family? Why, I have you, Daddy, and Aunt Patricia and Gus and Pren and Josh. Today I met a nephew who was extremely handsome, the likes of whom I haven't seen since I last laid eyes on dear Josh."

"You would be speaking of Stuart, wouldn't you?" Patricia inserted.

"Yes, indeed. He's quite a handsome young man. What are his aspirations? Is he to continue in the tradition of the Phenwick family and remain with Medallion?"

"Of that we're not certain, my dear," Peter replied. He was influenced somewhat by Helen. "His own mother, Lillian, is the one who exercises a great amount of force over his thoughts. Being a devoutly religious lady, she might try to persuade him to go into ecclesiastic endeavors."

"You mean become a preacher?"

"Preachers aren't so bad," Patricia concluded. "After all, Elias was a preacher. He and I got along quite well. At least, we did in the beginning, but let's not get into that."

At that moment a breeze of excitement moved like a whirlwind around the corner of the house headed in the direction of the wisteria arbor, a flutter of petticoats and skirts. Joanna glanced up to see the pretty girl who sped with dancing footsteps. Pretty, nearly black hair, flashing brown eyes, the girl was hardly more than seventeen, perhaps eighteen. She radiated the charm and the excitement of youth, the anticipation of looking forward to what lay ahead.

"Why, I d'clare," she said, bouncing to the three. "I didn't realize anyone was out here. I was determined to go find my fan which I left on the table beneath the wisteria arbor."

Patricia said, "I don't believe you've ever met my niece."

"I don't believe I have." The pretty young lady's big brown eyes grew bigger. Her smile was infectious. She could not hide the laughter that rippled in her voice.

"May I present Joanna Phenwick?"

"Th' actress. I d'clare, I was wonderin' if I would evah meet you," the girl replied.

"Joanna, may I present to you Miss Nancy Cox, who

17

has become a somewhat permament house guest," Patricia introduced.

Joanna placed her hand in the hand of the sweet young girl who had stretched hers forward. "I am very pleased to meet you, Miss Cox."

"Oh, lawsy, Miz Phenwick, you don't know how delighted I am to meet you. Why, I've heard so much about you, I could hardly keep from bustin' my, well, my whatever, until I met you. I thought perhaps you might be home before this. I mean for the funeral and all, but I can see you've come for the weddin', haven't you?"

"Yes, I have."

Patricia cleared her throat. "I think under the circumstances, 'Miss Cox' and 'Miss Phenwick' is a bit too formal. Why aren't you just 'Nancy' and 'Joanna' to each other? I have a feeling that you have much in common."

"Well, I don't know about that. Course, I haven't gotten to meet th' lady too well yet, but perhaps as the days go on, we shall become more friendly. Don't you think you would like that, Miz—that is, Joanna?"

"I think I would like that very much, Nancy."

"Now would you-all please excuse me. I've got to dash. I was just goin' to get my fan and run to meet Harriet at the dressmaker's. She's bein' fitted there. I, of course, am bein' fitted, too, for a new dress as the maid of honor. You-all will please excuse me. I do swear that we will get to know each other diligently, Joanna."

"That is my hope, too."

"I must dash." Nancy turned and with a broad smile flew toward the wisteria arbor, went in and in a few moments emerged, fan clasped in her hands. She flipped it open and closed to indicate to those watching that she had found the object for which she had been seeking. In another instant she had disappeared around the side of the house.

Joanna watched with some amusement. She instantly liked the girl, and she knew that she had potentialities of being an actress herself. There was something about her nature that told Joanna that. She could not contain a smile until she raised her eyes and observed her father still staring in the direction that Nancy had gone. She had never seen such an expression on his face before. It did not surprise her. Yet, she was a little amazed, and a little amused to see that he obviously took such an interest in Nancy Cox. She thought to herself, *That's a good and healthy sign.* At least, he had not died with her mother. She wondered what she might do to help her father.

Patricia observed both Joanna and Peter. It was not the first time she had seen that expression on Peter's face. Knowingly, she restrained comment. Yet she wondered.

Chapter 2

LILLIAN PHENWICK stood at the second-floor window, looking out at the warm spring morning. She had not had a special dress made for the occasion of her brother-in-law's wedding; instead she relied upon her good Sunday dress. Had she been able to work her will, she would not have gone to the wedding. Such things bored her. She felt no sense of family unity. In fact, although she had the name Phenwick, she did not consider herself a Phenwick woman or perhaps it was the attitude of others that caused her to have this feeling. Nervously, she cracked her fingers as she waited and watched the carriages in the street. Then on an impulse she turned to stare at the large four-poster bed in which she had occupied the nights of her married life with Augustus Phenwick. Gus, bald, paunchy, middle-aged before his time, had long lost interest in a passionate relationship with his wife, few exceptions. Lillian tried to tell herself that his austerity had nothing to do with the attitude that she had developed over the years of indifference, the cold exterior. Yet she felt something terribly missing in her life and her experience.

She moved slowly to the bed, tracing her fingers over the carved bedstead, glancing at the handmade quilt that covered the neatly arranged covers. Rarely did they touch at night. Rarely did he even bother to kiss her, and she never bothered to kiss him. Was it possible for two people to live a platonic relationship in the same bed? As far as Lillian was concerned, it was, and she did. The more she thought of it, the more she convinced herself that it was her choice.

The door to her room was slightly ajar. Footsteps approaching disturbed her thoughts. She looked up to see the handsome figure of her eldest son, Stuart, as he passed. The young man looked into the room and was about to move farther down the hallway to the stairs when Lillian called to him. Obediently, he answered her and entered the room.

"What is it, Mother?" Stuart asked. He was attired in a handsome outfit, blue-colored, which brought out the coloring of his eyes. It made him radiate a handsomeness that was both appealing and bewildering.

"Are you ready?" the mother asked, looking at her son with a terrible scrutiny as though he had done something amiss.

"Yes, Mother. As a matter of fact, I was just going now to get the carriage."

"I trust that you will not be reveling with the others after the wedding."

"Aunt Patricia asked us all to come up to Edward House. Naturally, I thought . . ."

"Naturally, you thought that whatever Patricia Phenwick said was law. Well, she may be matriarch of the family, but her words as far as I am concerned are not law."

"Mother." Stuart sounded shocked. "I don't understand your attitude about Aunt Patricia. I never have. Has she done something to you? You're so cold and caustic toward her."

Restlessly, Lillian moved slightly away from the intense stare from those vivid blue eyes that seemed to be glowing through her. "Patricia Phenwick has hardly been what I would call a Christian lady," she said. "In fact, I think she's a bit of a heathen."

"Mother, a heathen!" Stuart exclaimed. "How can you say that about Aunt Patricia?"

"Oh, do stop calling her Aunt Patricia. She isn't your

22

aunt, really. She's only—well, although she was married to your uncle, and he only a half uncle, she is no blood relation. She is a woman with designing tendencies. Tactfully or untactfully, she has wormed her way into becoming head of the Phenwick clan. Well, I for one think she is nothing but a trollop who has taken advantage of time. I don't care to have my children associate with her."

"I know that you have certain bitterness in you."

"Bitterness." Lillian bit her lip. "You mean Christian fervor, don't you? I know the type of woman she is, the type of harlot, the type of person that fraternizes with all those men of, as she calls it, artistic temperaments. But what kind of moral life could she possibly lead? She is twice married, and the stories I've heard about that would make you blush, my son."

"Don't let us go on about Aunt Patricia. I happen to like her very much. She has always been kind to me," Stuart remarked. "I will continue associating with her because she is a Phenwick."

"So am I a Phenwick by marriage," Lillian snarled, "but I am not considered a Phenwick by a long shot. No, I've never been that."

"Then you're not going to the wedding?"

"I did not say that. Of course, I will go to the wedding. Your father would be most upset with me if I did not attend his brother's wedding. I suppose it's the least I can do, but now that his sister is here . . . Well, I don't want to go into that either."

"Where is Father?"

"He has gone on to be with his own father. They're going to the church together."

"And Gordon?"

"I supposed he was going to the church with you."

"You mean with us, don't you, Mother?"

"I really thought that I would stroll over to the church by myself. It will give me time to think, to gather my thoughts."

23

"You are in a very strange mood today, Mother. Is there something I can do for you?"

"Strange mood," Lillian laughed. There was irony in her tone, cynicism. "No, no, there is nothing you or anyone else can do for me today, Stuart. I wonder if there is anything anyone can do for me again. I want to get to the church early to go to the chapel and pray. I feel that I must purge myself of the sinful thoughts that have entered my mind. Purge myself of the hatred or at least ask God for forgiveness."

"Hatred, Mother?"

"I suppose you can call it hatred. I hate—well, I hate the circumstances that life has thrown me into. I hate being—well, never mind, we'll talk about that another time, won't we, Stuart? You go along. I was just going to find a parasol and a light wrap to put around my shoulders. Then I will trudge off to the church."

"Wouldn't you rather ride?"

"Thank you, no." Lillian turned back to her son. "I would prefer that you didn't go to Edward House after the wedding."

Stuart gazed impatiently at his mother. He had always been close to her, at least as close as a person was allowed to get to Lillian Phenwick. But he did not understand her. He wanted to make a remark, but at that moment he heard the sound of footsteps in the hallway, and knew that it must be his brother, Gordon. He found a smile, but he could not find words to go with it. He merely shook his head and quickly dashed from the room.

The Ornbys, Dr. Theodore, Daniel, and their wives, as well as their sister, Jane Augusta Ornby-Clark, were the first to arrive at the church. Jane Augusta, impish and jolly, was always prompt. She gushed with laughter and found most things amusing. As a widowed lady, she was looked after by her two brothers, Theodore and Daniel. She herself was regarded as a kind of a matriarch on their side of the Phenwick clan. The Ornbys were the grandchildren of Jane Phenwick Ornby. Jane Augusta was the antithesis of her grandmother. She was plump and enjoyed a marvelous sense of humor. Her laughter rang out and was distinguishable even in a crowd of people. She was quite a social gadabout, talking here and talking there. Not going into the church, she wanted to stay outside to be a reception committee of one to welcome friends and acquaintances, family members she had not seen for a long while. A few of the Munsk family, who were really distant cousins, were present. Jane Augusta was the one member of the family who kept in touch with the Munsks.

Neither Dr. Ted and Daniel Ornby nor their respective wives were the socially prominent people that Jane Augusta pretended to be. They simply went inside and found pews. The ladies conversed in whispers. Dr. Ted and Daniel looked bored, cursing beneath their breath that they had arrived as early as they had as a means of pampering sister Jane Augusta.

In ten or fifteen minutes the church had filled with family, well-wishers and friends, many of whom felt obliged to pay homage to the Phenwicks; many of whom were also personal friends of Patricia Phenwick. Because they were socially prominent people, they attended out of respect for her.

Prentise Phenwick was never a particularly spectacular member of the family. As a matter of fact, he was usually considered dull by most of the neighbors and friends; but he was a Phenwick and so tribute would be paid to him. There was a great curiosity for those who had not met Harriet Pettijohn to see what sort of girl the awkward Phenwick boy would marry. Rumor had it that she was quite attractive, if not downright pretty. Rumor was more than correct. A mumble of anticipation murmured through the church before the affair was to begin.

Joanna Phenwick arrived with her father. They were greeted by Jane Augusta, who gushed, giggled, petted and kissed. She was always one to fondle men, not in a flirtatious way, but an individual who required physical contact with both men and ladies to indicate a closeness. Naturally, she kissed Peter on both cheeks, and once on the lips, showing how fond she was of him. Peter, who was always a little partial to Jane Augusta, particularly since the loss of her husband, showed the affection she seemed to be begging for.

"You remember your cousin Jane Augusta Ornby-Clark, don't you?" asked Peter as he put his arm around the rotund lady.

"How could she forget me?" Jane Augusta giggled. "Everyone remembers Jane Augusta Ornby-Clark, the widow lady with the sense of humor," and she giggled again. "This, of course, is beautiful, talented Joanne, isn't it?"

"Cousin Jane Augusta." Joanna kissed her on the cheek. "I have changed my name slightly to Joanna now. That is sort of a professional name, I suppose, but it is a little more European, I thought, and since I do live in London, I have taken it."

"Joanna, oh yes, of course, I remember seeing it in the papers, but to me I will always think of you as little Joanne. Dear girl, how successful you've become. To think that with all that success you've not married."

Joanna cleared her throat. "Well, perhaps there was no need for me to marry, Cousin Jane Augusta."

"You have no need." Jane Augusta's eyes widened, the puffs that hung over them seeming to go into her forehead. "Oh dear, I wonder if you're suggesting what I think you're suggesting."

Joanna laughed. "I rather imagine that I am."

Jane Augusta Ornby-Clark raised her eyebrows again. She tried for a giggle, but it came out as a cough. She quickly reached for a lace hankie to put over her mouth. "My dear," she said when she finally gained her composure, "you must come and have tea with me while you are here. I think we should get reacquainted. Besides, I'm terribly curious to know about your way of life."

"I thought you might be, Cousin Jane Augusta. It would be a pleasure," Joanna said. "That is, if you do not shock too easily."

26

"Joanna," Peter exclaimed, "what sort of ideas are you putting into poor Jane Augusta's head?"

"Whatever ideas she wants to put in there. You will excuse us now, Cousin Jane Augusta," and she kissed her again. "I'm really looking forward to having tea with you very soon. We, of course, will see each other at the reception at Edward House."

"Oh, of course," Jane Augusta managed to say, but she was still taken aback.

The elegant carriage was driven by a servant who was decked out in white, and the lovely lady who alighted from it was dressed in soft pink with red satin rosebuds trimming her dress. It was Patricia Phenwick looking grand and elegant in a lavish display as if she were the star of the show. But, of course, she was, as was always the case. With her were two men, Raymond Nelson and Arthur Townsend, both aesthetic, artistic young men with excellent features. They had long been part of Patricia's retinue, and often were seen with her in public places. Although an exhibitionist of sorts, she had a sense of propriety that made her want to appear with two or three men in public, lest others get the wrong notion. Most of Boston knew, of course, that she was a patroness of the arts, and that she did nurture the careers of many a prominent artist of one sort or another —musicians, painters, sculptors, poets, writers. They were always in her company. While Bostonian tongues wagged merrily when she appeared, no one knew for certain precisely what her arrangements were with these young individuals. For the most part, they believed that the relationships were strictly platonic. She was a widow content with her lot, and not in the least romantically inclined, particularly toward young men. That could not have been further from the truth. That was often the subject of their speculation; however, out of respect to the lady, they thought of her simply as an eccentric patroness and nothing more.

Jane Augusta Ornby-Clark gushed when she saw Patricia, and she even bounced down the steps to run toward the carriage to greet her as she stepped out, kissing her bountifully on both cheeks. Jane Augusta clung to the elderly lady's hands. "My dear Aunt Patricia, it is so good to see you again. How lovely you look, but then I've never known you to look not lovely."

"Jane Augusta, Jane Augusta, Jane," Patricia sighed, patting the jolly cheeks of her niece. "It is a pleasure to see you again. You know Arthur and Raymond, don't you?"

Arthur and Raymond bowed, each took the lady's hand and kissed the fingertips, their lips making the pudgy flesh tingle slightly.

"Oh dear, they're so gentlemanly, aren't they? 'Courtly,' I think is the word, isn't it, Aunt Patricia?"

"That's close. My dear, you *are* coming to Edward House for the reception, aren't you?"

"I wouldn't miss it for the world."

"And your brothers and their wives?"

"Yes, of course, we'll all be there."

"Then perhaps we will find a moment or two to chat, but I fear it is almost time for the wedding to start, and I want to get well situated before the bride appears."

"Oh yes, of course, Aunt Patricia."

Grandly, Patricia entered the church, her two escorts standing behind the crinoline skirt with the wide hoops so that it was impossible for anyone to stand really too close to the lady, at least from the back and sides. Her satin gown whispered as she walked down the aisle, and both ladies and gentlemen whispered as she did, their attention drawn to her, the entrance of the queen.

The small room in the basement was usually used for a Sunday School class, but on the occasion of weddings or other special events, it was used as a kind of dressing room. A large mirror was brought from another part of the church on this occasion so that the bride might see herself in the white satin gown she had chosen. Harriet had declined the assistance of any of the lady members of the Phenwick clan, including that of Jane Augusta

Ornby-Clark. There was hope that Lillian might step forth and offer to be of assistance to her future sister-in-law. She did not. However, Harriet did accept the help of Olivia, the new wife of Joshua Phenwick. Olivia was to be a bridesmaid, and because of her theatrical background and excellent taste in clothing, her assistance had been accepted from the earliest preparations for the wedding. Harriet's long, reddish brown curls were arranged in a style that was particularly familiar to her Southern background. Her remarkable beauty was accentuated by the white satin with the lace overlay. The gray-green eyes stared at her reflection in the mirror. There was that perpetual dream-fantasy quality about them. She eyed Olivia from time to time as the pretty actress helped her. Olivia's dark hair glistened in the beam of afternoon sunlight that shone through a tiny window high on the wall, and her attractive profile made it obvious that she, too, was a beauty. For an instant, remembering the loveliness of her attractive friend, Nancy Cox, Harriet wondered if she might not be upstaged at her own wedding by her maid of honor and bridesmaid. Still Harriet had a certain confidence in her beauty, a quiet inner assurance that she was a beautiful woman. Yet, there was that distant expression in her eyes that sometimes made her appear a little sad.

Nancy Cox came bubbling in, her light blue dress rustling with her movement. She was always animated and excitable. Having gone upstairs to take a peek at the congregation that had arrived to witness the rites, she came down with a flurry of excitement to relate the information to Harriet. However, as she was telling of all the people and of the singularly sensational entrance of Patricia Phenwick, she noted an expression in her friend's eyes, an expression that looked as if momentarily she was about to melt into tears.

"Why, I d'clare, Harriet, whatevah is th' matter with you? Why aren't you smilin' and happy?" Nancy exclaimed. "Wouldn't you know I would be if'n this were my weddin' day, and I was marryin' to become a Phenwick woman."

Olivia laughed. Her soft British accent was a quaint contrast to the Georgian accents of the two young Southern ladies. "Being a Phenwick woman doesn't make me feel any different. Prouder, yes, and perhaps more fulfilled, but I don't understand what all the excitement is about being a Phenwick woman."

"Honeychile, I'll tell you sometime. But you know, sugah, I don't really know myself except that it's supposed to be a great honor," Nancy said, her dark eyes wide as saucers. "You will excuse us, Mrs. Phenwick."

"Excuse you?"

"If you don't mind, I'd like to have a private word with Harriet b'fore th' weddin'," Nancy replied, shaking her head in such a way to indicate that she wished Olivia to leave her alone.

"Why, of course, I don't mind. I'll be just outside." Olivia observed Harriet's reflection again in the mirror, and realized that her friend must be interpreting her mood and attitude. Nancy moved to the door and closed it firmly, then turned around and leaned against it as she again observed her friend. "Do you want to tell me about it, Harriet, honey?"

"Tell you about what, Nancy?" Harriet replied. "I do d'clare, I don't know what you're talkin' about."

"Sugah, you and I have been friends for a long, long time, and I know when somethin' is botherin' you, and somethin' is botherin' you at this very minute. I can see it in your face, Harriet Pettijohn."

"It's that old thing, Nancy. I reckon it stems from th' past, and all the horrible things that happened to me," Harriet replied.

"Th' horrible things? You mean th' fact that you were accosted by a black man when you were a young girl, and that you had his baby? Is that what frightens you on your weddin' day. Oh, sugah, put such thoughts from your mind. It's ovah and done with. Th' past is all dead. That was down in Georgia. This heah is Boston,

30

you're a long way from home, and besides th' torment of that dreadful Elsworth Grayson which caused you so much discomfort and anguish, why he's no longer among the livin'. You wouldn't go, but I saw him swing by his neck, I'm happy to report. So what do you have to fear?"

Harriet moved away from the mirror after examining the strange expression on her face. "I wonder, Nancy, if I don't fear men."

"Fear men?" Nancy questioned in a whisper, startled at Harriet's statement. "You mean fear bein' made love to by a man? Is that what you fear?"

"I don't know, Nancy. I swear to goodness, I don't know. Honey, I am so confused at this moment. Mr. Phenwick has been kindness itself to me. He's nevah projected himself on me in an ungentlemanly way. I have a kind of fear that when he does, I may not respond proper-like. That I might be a disappointment to him, and that would be terrible, don't you think?"

Nancy went to her, placing her arm around her shoulder. "Oh, sugah, sugah, don't think that way. What is past is past. That was a black man who accosted you. He was no gentleman. He was a common slave. Mr. Phenwick, he is a gentleman all the way. I am certain he will do nothin' to hurt you. Why, he's told me what deep respect he has for you, and now he's lookin' forward to makin' you one of th' happiest ladies that evah lived."

Harriet swallowed and tried to smile. "Yes, Mr. Phenwick has told me that, too. I do want to believe him, but sometimes, there is this fear. I don't know how to react."

"If you like, I'll go back to Savannah with you-all when you and Mr. Phenwick go. I'll be right at hand to see that you're taken care of all th' time. See that you're properly looked after."

"That is not my fear, Nancy," Harriet assured her. "My fear is right heah deep inside of me. I don't want to be a frigid woman. I don't want to be cold to Mr. Phenwick's advances; but I'm afraid, I am afraid, Nancy. Oh, pray for me, will you?"

"Pray for you. You know that I'll do that, but you're not goin' to be frigid, you're not goin' to be cold. You're gonna be lovin' and wigglin' and excitin' and everythin' for th' man because you are goin' to be a Phenwick woman in not more than fifteen minutes from now. You got a legacy to live up to. You have to remember that. That you are a Phenwick woman."

"Not yet, not for another fifteen minutes, Nancy. Maybe I won't find the words to reply when the minister asks me."

"Harriet, Harriet darlin' sugah, don't evah think that way. You are goin' to be one of th' finest Phenwick women in the whole clan. Why, I know that for certain."

Harriet kissed her friend and tears had come to her eyes. She turned away and looked at herself in the mirror. The doubt would not leave her. She could only pray that her marriage to Prentise Phenwick would be successful.

Chapter 3

THE RECEPTION WAS HELD in the garden as well as in the ballroom at Edward House, presided over by lovely Patricia Phenwick. The family had gathered, the friends had arrived. Champagne punch was served and little sandwiches and cakes were passed around. It was a gala occasion such as was typical of parties at Edward House. Handsome young men and pretty ladies appeared. These were part of Patricia's retinue, those artistic people and artistic followers who surrounded the grand lady at her request. There were also the socialites, the cream of Beacon Hill and Boston society. At least, those who were on good terms with Patricia.

Prentise Phenwick had few friends in Boston, none who were close. His brother Joshua, handsome and dashing in appearance, had been his best man and as Prentise had feared, Joshua stole the show from him. At least, the whispers were about Joshua. Joshua, the handsome, the brother who looked like his father and his grandfather before him. Prentise was not plain, for he had his own aristocratic bearing, his square-jawed appearance. He nonetheless did not have the outgoing, gregarious personality Joshua had. Still Prentise was in no way as dull and drab as his eldest brother, Augustus, who attended the affair only out of duty and as soon as possible was imbibing from the flask that he often carried.

Gus Phenwick was an ordinary man who lived an ordinary life. It would be hard to think of him as being a namesake of the fabulous, often notorious, Augusta Phenwick, his great-grandmother. He was the antithesis of that elegant lady. In fact, generally he was considered a bore and not at all particularly pleasant to be around. His attitudes were simple. He was opinionated in a conservative way which was not unpredictable for him. It did not bother him that his brothers were better-looking or more appealing than he. In fact, he did not think much of his brothers one way or another. They were simply his younger brothers, and younger brothers had to be tolerated. He had little respect as far as that goes for his only sister, Joanna. She was his sister, born of the same parents, but from that point on they had nothing in common. Perhaps it was out of rebellion for family tradition or circumstance that he chose to marry drab Lillian Webb with her stoic disposition, her zealous religious attitude, her plain face and her unexciting character. She, too, of course, was conservative, but one who was given to expressing her opinions especially when it came to a matter of morals—all of which Gus ignored. Years before, he had learned to shut himself off to her words. He was pleased that he had become paunchy and bald and unattractive. It gave him reason not to perform husbandly duties. It also helped to rationalize staying away from the woman as often as possible, pretending to have business for Medallion Enterprises, or for staying out at the Tooth & Tail Tavern. It was a favorite haunt of his as it had been with other members of his family in years past. He kept a room in a small hotel near the waterfront where when he desired the company of ladies of the night, he would take them. Often, he would retreat to that place just to be alone and away from the tongue-lashings that Lillian was noted for giving. Yet, it is not fair to call him a henpecked man. He was far from that. He was his own man in his own way which was not at all like his brothers, or his father for that matter. If anything, he had his mother's tendencies in certain things, but his own individuality had become developed in childhood. He was proud of the fact that he was a unique Phenwick. Secretly, he

34

was happy that his wife had never been accepted as a Phenwick woman. There was something diabolical, cold and calculating in the man. Yet, neither of his sons, Stuart or Gordon, seemed to have many of his characteristics. Peculiarly Stuart, in particular, had the looks that had become known as the Phenwick appearance. Gordon was not quite the handsome lad that his brother was, but he possessed a kind of manliness and humbleness that was attractive and appealing. He also possessed an outgoing personality.

Lillian would have liked to have had her sons be anything but Phenwicks. But since they were, she put up with the family, especially with Patricia Phenwick, whom she did not like. Therefore, when she went to the reception, she took her usual attitude of being annoyed, of looking down her pious nose at the celebrating guests who had an inclination to imbibe a little too much, to be a little too jolly and frivolous at the occasion of her brother-in-law's marriage. Thus, she observed. The person who caught her attention at that time was strangely Olivia Phenwick, her sister-in-law.

Now, Olivia spent most of her time after arriving at the reception with her dear friend Joanna. The two ladies reminisced of days in England, the theater. They were perfectly happy in one another's company. Meanwhile, Joshua moved among the guests and was his charming self as if he were the host of the occasion. Many people had not congratulated him on his marriage to Olivia, which had only been a year before, and so they took that opportunity to praise him for having acquired so lovely a wife.

When Joanna left at Patricia's bidding to meet several of her friends, Olivia lingered back and watched. A peculiar expression came to her face, especially as she observed Nancy Cox flitting about, flirting with the young men, dancing, laughing, joking. What was it about the girl that annoyed her? Was she actually annoyed, or just perplexed? She had never known a

35

Southern belle before and she assumed that if there was a prototype of a Southern belle, Nancy was it.

"You are observing our little Southern friend, aren't you," Lillian said, coming to where Olivia was standing.

"What, oh, I say, you startled me," Olivia replied.

"Forgive me, I didn't mean to disrupt your solitude, your thoughts, whatever they were."

"I was admiring the guests. This sort of thing is quite different here than it is in England. Oh, we do have parties and things like that, and I must admit that when I was married, Joshua and I had a marvelous reception, but it was different. I suppose you know Susannah Phenwick, Susannah and Lex. They were the ones who saw to our reception."

"No, I've never had that opportunity. That side of the Phenwick family has never returned to the United States since I've been here. I understand Susannah is quite a celebrity."

"Oh yes, yes, she is quite that. Don't you know she's known throughout Europe? Why, she's acclaimed by crowned heads, she plays in all the palaces, beautiful places of the world. I admire her greatly."

"Admire or envy?"

"No, I admire her. She has vast talent. Anyone with a vast talent has the right to be admired. I hope someday that, if I return to the theater, I, too, will be as greatly admired."

"There is something about that young lady that bothers you, isn't there?" Lillian asked.

"I beg your pardon."

"That Miss Cox. You don't much care for her, do you?"

Olivia laughed. "I don't see how you can say that. I rather liked her. That is, I fancy her to be a rather cheerful person. She's very pretty, lovely."

"But you do find her annoying, don't you?"

"Should I?"

"Well, I don't know what your religious beliefs are, my dear," Lillian said, trying to assume a kind of grand-

36

ness. "I have always been one raised with moral responsibility and attitudes that differ greatly from what I observe in young Miss Cox. She's quite flirtatious and I don't wish to say unkind things about her, but I have the feeling—and it is just a feeling—that she might be—well, have tendencies to—you do know what I mean, don't you, Mrs. Phenwick?"

"My dear Lillian, can't we be on a first-name basis? After all, we are both Mrs. Phenwicks, and I do know what you mean," Olivia said. "I know the type of woman of whom you are speaking, but I hardly would say that Nancy Cox was of that nature."

"The potential is there, don't you agree, Olivia?" Lillian asked, biting the words.

Nancy, filled with life and joy, danced with as many men as she could, galloping about, skipping, hopping. Most notably, she danced with Raymond Nelson, the artist, or Arthur Townsend, the poet-writer. Both men were obviously attracted to her, and had been for some time. She flirted coyly with them, never once giving them the notion that she took them altogether seriously, but found them like playthings with which to be amused. When she was not dancing, she would mingle among the other guests, for everyone recognized her as the maid of honor. She attracted more and more attention as she moved about.

Peter Phenwick, who usually did not imbibe too heavily, drank his share of the champagne punch. For a time he had spoken with his cousin Jane Augusta Ornby-Clark, and even took the occasion to exchange several words with his son, Gus. The two had never been especially close so it was a strain. However, it was Gus's suggestion that his father dance.

"Dance?" asked Peter. "At my age?"

"Oh, come on, Father, you're not old. I see a distinct twinkle in your eyes," Gus returned. "Why don't you dance with Joanna or, for that matter, why not give your new daughter-in-law a twirl or two? I've noticed her kicking her heels up a bit."

"Oh, have you? So have I for that matter. I'm very fond of Olivia."

"What is your opinion of Harriet, Father?"

"I'm very fond of Harriet, too. I haven't known her as long as I have known Olivia. Olivia was one of the family, so to speak, before she married Josh since she was a close friend of Joanna's," Peter returned. "But now that you mention it, perhaps a dance or two wouldn't do me any harm. I've always enjoyed the activity. Certainly Olivia looks a little bored talking to your wife."

"I don't suppose you would care to have a dance or two with Lillian, would you, Father?"

"With Lillian?" Peter tried not to laugh loudly, but there was a tone of contemptuousness in his voice. "It's not that I dislike Lillian, Gus, your wife has always been kind to me, but I imagine she would be somewhat clumsy on the dance floor, isn't she?"

"I don't know, Father, I haven't danced with her in many years nor do I intend to. No, I think I'll excuse myself and go find some more to drink and leave you to your own devices."

Peter started toward where Olivia was standing talking to Lillian when he was interrupted by his daughter, Joanna, who came dashing at him as if she were making a stage entrance. He tried not to collide with her, but he did manage to catch her in his arms. "Joanna, my dear, have you been drinking too much?" Joanna laughed.

"Hardly a drop, Father. I don't have to drink to be gay and excited. I can be just as joyous without it. Besides, I'm rather partial to iced French champagne and French champagne is not being served. Won't you dance with me, Father?"

"I would love to, Joanna."

At that moment the orchestra had begun to play a lilting Strauss waltz. The tones themselves danced through the room, partners were taken and the dancing began. Peter held his daughter in an appropriate position. Soon they were gliding across the floor like a pair of professional dancers. Their movements were broad, flashy, perfectly coordinated to the point that others began moving back to give them room. Soon they were the only couple dancing while the others watched. Aware that they were the center of attention, Joanna played it to the hilt, throwing her head back and following her father to twirl her about, around and around the room, their footwork fancy, he with the form and verve of a young man, many years his junior, a smile of happiness lighting him.

Comments scurried around the room. They were all positive, pleased to see that Peter Phenwick had gotten over the remorse of losing his wife. What could be more appropriate than that he should dance with his only daughter, Joanna.

The second dance Peter declined, explaining to Joanna that he needed to catch his breath. "In that case, Father," Joanna replied, "I shall set you up for the following dance, and you will not say no."

"With you?"

Joanna laughed. "No, not with me. With my friend, your daughter-in-law Olivia."

"Olivia, why not? Why not, indeed?"

Peter danced as gracefully with Olivia as he had with Joanna, and again only a few couples remained on the floor while they were dancing. This time the tongues wagged a little more, not showing disapproval, for what could be more acceptable than a man dancing with his new daughter-in-law? But there was a great deal of chatter about Olivia Phenwick. The beautiful English-woman was a letdown to many Bostonians who felt that the handsome Joshua Phenwick should have married among them, should have joined with one of the better families in Boston. Here he was married to practically a pauper and a British pauper at that, and on top of all else she was an actress, like Joanna. Peter enjoyed the dance with Olivia. He enjoyed holding her, the feeling of holding a beautiful young woman in his arms created a titillating sensation in him. But knowing that she was, indeed, his daughter-in-law, he put any sort of untoward thoughts from his mind.

At the conclusion of that dance, a polka was announced which was far too lively for Peter. He was met by Joanna as he left the dance floor with Olivia. He was assured by Joanna that he could have that dance out to regain his breath and composure but that it would only be right and proper for him to have the following dance with his other daughter-in-law.

"My God, you don't mean Lillian?" he exclaimed.

Joanna laughed uproariously. "No, no, no, Father. I wasn't speaking of Lillian. That I think you can avoid, she is hardly the dancing type, but you seem to forget that you have a third daughter-in-law now."

"Oh, you mean Harriet."

"Harriet, indeed," Joanna replied. "I think it would be very nice and appreciated, Father, if you would dance with her."

"So it would," Olivia chimed in. "And he's a marvelous dancer, too. I have never seen a man dance as well, with the exception of Joshua, of course."

Harriet had been with Prentise greeting well-wishers, but she had tired of it. Her apprehension had built and she had become a little nervous. When she was approached by Joanna with the suggestion that her father would like to dance with his new daughter-in-law, Harriet found herself tightening, uncertain that she wanted to dance with the man. But she conceded. When Peter led her to the floor, she found that she was less tense than she thought she might be. Peter was charming, his disarming smile was magnificent. Soon he was twirling her about and she found herself enjoying the movement. His arm around her waist, his hand holding hers was a comfort. She felt pleased that she was dancing and was the center of attention until Peter danced her to where Prentise was standing and motioned for his son to take over.

Prentise had never really learned to dance gracefully. He was awkward, stiff, but he realized that he was center stage, he and Harriet, and that they must dance for it was expected of them. When they began everyone had left the floor to stand and watch. A light round of applause met their ears. Although awkward, Prentise still managed to put on a show.

Harriet was not at ease in her husband's arms, not as she had been in Peter's. Already she had become tight, that apprehension which had invaded her before the wedding had come back. Prentise's touch frightened her and she feared what was to follow in the hours beyond before this night was over. Still they danced and when they finished, everyone applauded.

Patricia Phenwick was pleased. She felt that her event was a success in most ways. She believed the bride and groom were perfectly happy and made a remarkable pair. Harriet had a way of complementing Prentise's appearance so that he almost looked dashingly handsome when he was with her. Then the matriarch's attention went from the principals of the afternoon to the maid of honor, lovely dark-haired Nancy Cox, who was outrageously flirting with all the men she could. Patricia squinted, frowned, she was not sure that Nancy was acting as she should or as she hoped that she might. Hence, when the opportunity arose, Patricia crossed to where Nancy was the center of attention, surrounded by six or seven young men—all with comely faces and handsome bodies. Among them, of course, were Raymond Nelson and Arthur Townsend, who eagerly pushed their way to be closer and closer to the major attraction of the day. However, as Patricia arrived in their vicinity, the gentlemen moved slightly back as they always did before the queen.

"May I borrow you for a minute?" Patricia asked. While Nancy was giving thought to her words, Patricia gave an all-inclusive look to the gentlemen which said retreat. They backed off.

"What is it, Mrs. Phenwick?"

"I've been noticing you, Nancy. You're charming, you're lovely, you're everything a debutante should be, but I fear that you are being a little overenthusiastic spreading yourself among too many men. Quite frankly, you're being far too flirtatious with everyone. There are some ladies present who do not have confidence in their —what shall I say—their relationships with their husbands and you don't help their confidence increase, if you know what I mean."

"Well, I d'clare, I'm sorry, I didn't realize I was doin' wrong, Mrs. Phenwick," Nancy replied, her eyes wide, her smile only slightly diminished. "I was only enjoyin' myself, you realize that, don't you?"

"Nancy, I know you are enjoying yourself. That is marvelous," Patricia returned, "but I think it would be better to curb your enthusiasm. Now with Raymond, Arthur, or some of the other young men, my friends, the artists, yes, fine. Oh, I don't mind that in the least. They are perfectly harmless, and they enjoy the excitement of being with such a lovely young lady. It's the married men I'm concerned about. There are one or two women who have raised eyebrows when you have gone past flirting with their husbands."

"I swear to goodness that I will not flirt with any married men here, if I only knew which were which or who was who."

Patricia could not contain her laughter. She found Nancy too amusing. "Very well, my dear, I didn't mean to reprimand you so severely, and I know it is difficult to know which is which and who is who," Patricia said laughingly, "but I do have a special favor to ask."

"A special favor? Why, I d'clare, whatevah could it be, Mrs. Phenwick?" Nancy asked. Again her eyes were wide and sparkling.

"I would like you to dance with my nephew."

"With your nephew? Whoevah do you mean?"

"With my nephew, Peter."

"With Mr. Phenwick. Why, I d'clare, lawsy me, I've nevah thought of dancin' with him."

"It seemed to me that you were eyeing him in a rather remarkable manner."

"Well—well, perhaps I was, just out of curiosity. He is evah so like Joshua, and I do find Joshua handsome,

42

ravishingly handsome," Nancy said, trying to contain her enthusiasm. "Well, I d'clare, Mr. Phenwick is practically a duplicate of Joshua."

"They're very much alike in appearance. Like father like son in this case, but not so with Gus or Prentise. Won't you consider a dance with Peter?"

"Why, Mrs. Phenwick, I'd love to dance with Peter. You must have been readin' my mind," Nancy said, trying again to appear nonchalant; at least that was the impression she hoped she was creating. She did not come close.

Patricia, locking her arm in Nancy's, led her to where Peter was conversing with Harriet and Prentise.

"My dear Peter," Patricia began, "you've been holding out on me. You declined coming to two of my balls, saying that you had forgotten how to dance. What I saw on the floor was definitely not a rusty old man or even a rusty middle-aged man for that matter, but a dashing young man with very attractive footwork, and the grace and ease of a gentleman."

"Aunt Patricia, you're making me blush, and I'm far too old to blush."

"Nonsense, you're not old, Peter. You're very young, I can tell that in your step and your movements. Therefore," Patricia continued, letting her large eyes move from her nephew to Nancy and back again, "I have arranged, or, that is, I have suggested, that you might like to have a dance with Nancy."

Peter looked a bit sheepish. "Yes, I think I would like that if Nancy doesn't mind dancing with the father of the groom."

"I d'clare, Mr. Phenwick, I would thoroughly enjoy dancin' with you," Nancy replied. "I've always admired you from th' moment I cast my eyes on you. I said to myself, there's a gentleman, there is a man of ease and grace and the epitome of what a gentleman should be. You are really an excitin' man to behold, Mr. Phenwick, if you don't mind my sayin' so."

43

"Nancy," Harriet exclaimed, shocked at what her friend had said.

"Hush now, Harriet, don't you 'Nancy' me. I do find Mr. Phenwick attractive. I wouldn't know that he was much older than your Mr. Phenwick, if I didn't know he was his father."

Patricia restrained a chuckle and twisted her lips to keep the smile from growing broad. "In that case, the next dance will be a waltz. Peter is quite adept at waltzing, as you have observed."

"So I have, so I have. Mr. Phenwick, it would be my pleasure."

One of the few times of the afternoon that Lillian and her husband, Gus, came in immediate contact with one another was when Peter began to dance with Nancy. Gus restrained comment, but he was a little surprised to see his father dancing with the one young lady who had aroused his fantasies that day.

Lillian, on the other hand, was not quiet in her reaction. The fact is she was quick to exclaim, "Would you look at that, Augusta. Would you just look at that!"

"Look at what, my dear?" Gus asked innocently, and drank from the glass he was holding.

"You know perfectly well what I want you to look at. Your father is making a fool of himself on the floor," Lillian replied. "That girl, that girl, do you know what she is?" Lillian asked.

Gus scratched his head. "She's a Southerner."

"Of course she's a Southerner. That's not what I meant," Lillian snapped. "That girl is nothing but a flirtatious opportunist."

Gus chortled. "A flirtatious opportunist! Whatever are you talking about, Lillian?"

"Do you know what I think, Augustus?" Lillian questioned, a determined expression lining her face. "I think that young lady has designs on your father."

"I beg your pardon."

"You heard me precisely, Augustus. That young lady is out to trap your father."

"To trap him, Lillian? Have you been drinking the punch?" Gus asked.

"I have not been drinking the punch. I have been observing, and I intend to tell your father that I think his behavior this entire day has been shocking."

"My father's behavior has not been shocking, Lillian," Gus replied, defending his father's honor. "My father is always himself. He's a lighthearted man who is always having fun. Just because you are a sterile old —whatever you are, doesn't mean that everyone must be that way. Now I'll not have you speaking to Dad in any way but kindly."

Lillian bit her lip. She had other thoughts. "Augustus, I think you should realize what's happened around here. There are suddenly two new Phenwick women, two women who will or might possibly be head of the Phenwick clan. I am speaking of Olivia, of course, and Harriet. I never considered myself a Phenwick woman because your darling Aunt Patricia doesn't consider me one, nor does your father for that matter."

"Nor do I, Lillian," Gus remarked. "I never have, I never will, and even if you dare assume the title, I will never admit to it. So if you're speaking out of jealousy, you might as well shut up. Harriet and Olivia are made of the stuff of what Phenwick women ought to be or are supposed to be. You're not, Lillian. I have no more to say on the matter. Would you excuse me, please?"

"Augustus!" Lillian called, but her husband had moved away, losing himself in a crowd of people.

Lillian brooded a moment, watching the dance. Within her an anger was mounting.

It was not until nearly an hour later that Lillian had the occasion to encounter her father-in-law. When she did, she told him precisely how she felt about his making a spectacle of himself with the young lady.

"My dear Lillian, you think I was making a spectacle of myself? Perhaps I was," Peter admitted. "I will tell you something. I have enjoyed myself. I have had a fabulous time and if I have made a complete jackass of myself in so doing, I have no regrets whatsoever. The fact is I enjoy what I have done and what I am doing. I'll tell you something else, Lillian, I have watched you this afternoon. You have stood here with your arms folded, looking down your nose at everybody. Every solitary person here. I know you are here out of duty to Prentise because he is your brother-in-law, but there is no reason for you to sneer, scowl and make derogatory comments about the proceedings. After all, Aunt Patricia has gone to a great deal of trouble to see that Prentise had a delightful reception and I enjoyed dancing with his wife. The bride, although not as graceful a dancer as Olivia, my other daughter-in-law, nor as my own daughter, nonetheless was delightful to hold, and I want to feel close to her. I want to know that when one day she has my grandchildren they will love me."

"Are you suggesting that my children do not love you?" Lillian snapped.

"No, no, I'm not suggesting that. I am very close to both Stuart and Gordon, but I feel it is no fault of yours. They are both beautiful young men, and I am proud of my grandchildren. My only grandchildren at this point. Although Stuart is in his teens growing toward being a man, I don't feel like an old grandfather. Today, for the first time since Helen's death, I have felt myself a young man again. A contemporary of Stuart's."

"You're demented. You've become senile."

"Oh, come off it, I am not senile. I'm not near senile. I am young at heart," Peter replied, "which is more than I can say for you. You are going to become an old lady long before I become an old man. I have no doubt of that. I even fear that Gus will become an old man before I do. It's funny about us Phenwicks, some of the men become old fast, others remain young. Do you know, I've heard it said from someone that my great-grandfather, the first Joshua, was a youthful man for as long as he lived. Perhaps that is only legend, but my own father would have remained youthful had it not been

46

for his unfortunate drinking habits. My father had problems. I don't. I have learned to live with life, Lillian, to accept it and to enjoy it. I am totally happy being as I am. Now, if you have any further criticisms of me or other members of my family, get it out. Don't let it smolder in your bosom like some cancerous disease."

Lillian swelled her breasts, sucked air through her teeth and pursed her lips, her hands clenched tightly at her waist. Words came to her mind, but she dared not speak them, for this man, no matter what else she thought of him, was her father-in-law and important to her and her future. However, there was a point upon which she could not resist making comment.

"Mr. Phenwick, I do not disapprove of your having fun if that is the proper word for it. I do not disapprove of your dancing with your daughters-in-law."

"But you *do* disapprove of my not dancing with you. Is that the situation?" Peter asked.

"I do not dance, Mr. Phenwick," Lillian replied. "I find it frivolous, besides I never learned. You know I am not a finished lady. I'm not what you might call a lady of class at all, only that I happened to marry a Phenwick. Very well, I accept that and that you dance with your other daughters-in-law and not with me because I don't dance. I know that I am not particularly pleasant to you, but as you observe, I *am* the mother of your grandsons, and we must remain on good terms, mustn't we?"

"What are you getting at, Lillian?" Peter asked.

"Just this," Lillian replied, now staring him directly in the face. "It's that girl."

"That girl?"

"Miss Cox."

"Miss Cox?"

"You were dancing with her, and I found it, well, my impression of Miss Cox is perhaps not as agreeable as your impression is."

"What is your impression, Lillian?"

She thought for a moment, her eyes shifted about

47

and she tried to look beyond the man. When their eyes met, she glanced aside. Finally, she looked down at her fingers, which were clasped tightly together. "Mr. Phenwick, I am of the impression that that young woman has—well, designs, motives that are—well . . ."

"Motives, Lillian?"

"I think she wants to be a Phenwick woman, Mr. Phenwick," Lillian said, "one of the notorious Phenwick women."

Peter laughed but only for a moment. "Well, you see, I've run out of sons, marriageable sons, unless you think she would try to get Gus away from you."

"No, that wasn't my thought," Lillian replied.

"What then? She is a year or two older, I suppose, than Stuart, yet that is a possibility."

"I would never want her for a daughter-in-law," Lillian replied. "Besides, Stuart is far too young for marriage. He's planning to go to Harvard, and I have— that is, he has other plans for his future. A woman would only complicate things at this time."

"Ah, then it is Stuart about whom you are concerned," Peter stated. "I think you're anticipating too much. Has Stuart said something about Nancy?"

"He mentioned a word or two, but it's not Stuart to whom I was referring."

Again, Peter laughed, but the laughter caught in his throat as Lillian glared into his face. A blank expression came as he seemed to lose color for a moment. "You're not suggesting . . . ?"

"Mr. Phenwick, you are a widower now, and there are whispers that you are now eligible for marriage again."

"Whispers about me?"

"Whispers about you and possibly about a certain young lady, Mr. Phenwick," Lillian said.

"But we're generations apart."

"A moment ago, Mr. Phenwick, you said that you were young at heart. I would hate to see you make a terrible mistake by marrying again—at least to a woman who is so much younger than you. One who would wear you out and put you in your grave long before your time, and one without seniority who could become the ruling Phenwick woman."

Again, Peter laughed, and laughed, but his laughter had a strange echo to it, both to Lillian and in his mind.

Chapter 4

Jane Augusta Ornby-Clark, the eldest daughter of the late Andrew Ornby, had become a kind of family matriarch in her own right. She had inherited from her late husband as well as from her father and was financially well off in her little house on Rachel Street in Boston. She refused to live with her brothers or any of the other family members, preferring to live alone in the house she had shared with her whaling captain husband for many years. Jane Augusta had a tendency to giggle or to pursue any emotion beyond that which anyone else would. Her soft brown hair was neatly coiled into a chignon at the nape of her neck. Gray eyes glistened in her round face and she had a double chin.

Although Patricia Phenwick was the undisputed head of the family, it was to Jane Augusta that many and various members of the family would come for special advice and assistance with problems and matters that needed a kindly ear and an understanding heart. She would always listen, always laugh, always cajole a person out of a bad mood, or sympathize. She was one who was looked upon by all the family as a beloved relative. Many urged her to seek a second husband, but Jane Augusta was content with her memories, with her recollections of days gone by and the romantic life she had pursued with her whaling captain husband.

Upon the death of old Rosea Hackleby, Jane Augusta fell heir to many of her mementos and memorabilia of the past. Significant among her inheritances from Rosea were the three books the old woman had written over her lifetime dealing with matters of the occult. Twice Jane Augusta thumbed through the ink-scratched pages. She had promised the old woman that she would one day have the books printed in a limited number of copies so that they might be kept for posterity. However, that day never seemed to materialize, and as was sometimes her wont, she procrastinated in carrying out the old lady's wishes.

Nearly two weeks after the wedding of Harriet Pettijohn to Prentise Phenwick when the young couple had returned from their honeymoon at Cape Anne, Jane had an urge to clear out and sort her belongings, going through the closets as she did at least once a year. With the beginning of summer she always felt it her duty to weed out the old and get rid of the things that were no longer necessary. Give clothing away, make room for new things to come in. She was in the process of doing that, having begun one morning just before dawn since she was an early riser. By nine o'clock she had her house fairly much in a clutter and was going through all the objects that she had collected, putting certain ones in a pile to be discarded; others would be given away, others returned to a secure place where they would probably lay dormant for another year until she brought them out and looked them over again.

A rapping on her door annoyed her. She was not presentable for company, yet appearances did not really make that much difference to her. She grunted as she raised herself from her position on the floor and with her quaint waddle-like walk, she puffed to the door. Surprisingly, Lillian Phenwick was standing outside.

"Why, Lillian, this is a surprise. I wasn't expecting anyone."

Lillian wore a stern expression as she always did, making an effort to create a congenial smile that quickly was whisked away as her somber expression returned.

"May I come in, Jane Augusta?"

"Certainly. However, I must explain my house is in a terrible mess. I'm cleaning, and things are everywhere. I'll have to remove some objects from a chair so that you can sit down."

Lillian entered and said, "I haven't come for a long visit, Jane Augusta, I simply wanted to have a few words with you concerning the situation at Edward House."

"Edward House, how could anything at Edward House concern you, Lillian?" asked Jane Augusta, sweeping her hand through her hair to catch a stray strand that had come loose from the chignon.

"It isn't Edward House in particular that worries me," Lillian explained, "but now that Harriet and Prentise have returned, I'm wondering how long they intend to stay living with Aunt Patricia."

"Why don't you ask Aunt Patricia?" Jane Augusta suggested, looking wide-eyed and innocently cherubic.

"As you well know, Aunt Patricia and I aren't on the best terms," Lillian explained, and cast aside one of Rosea's books from the chair in which she intended to sit. "Moreover, I'll tell you what my basic concern is."

"And that is?" Jane Augusta asked.

"It's that Nancy Cox person."

"Whatever should disturb you about her?"

"I figured matters out and she is all of eighteen, which is a good age for a girl. However, my Stuart, aged fifteen, has been eyeing her in a most curious way, and I feel she has designs on him, and wishes to lead him astray."

"Poppycock, Lillian, how can you think such a thing? Nancy is hardly that type of person."

"Oh, isn't she?" Lillian snapped. "Well, for all you know—and I don't believe you're much of a judge of character since you always manage to see only the good in people—she could be, well, a loose woman. And I don't want that kind of influence over my sons."

"I think you're imagining things, Lillian. Has Stuart shown any inclination of interest toward Nancy?" Jane

Augusta asked, her eyes now wide as she sat in a straight-backed chair with a startled expression on her face.

"Stuart has made some enigmatic statements lately, and I know he is coming to that age at which he will have an awareness of young ladies. It's an awkward age for a young man, I am sure, and one at which his curiosity is far too lively and aroused for his own good."

"Every young man goes through that, I understand. Just as every young woman passes through an age of curiosity, too. There's nothing wrong with that, Lillian."

"There may be nothing wrong with it. By the same token, I do not like the idea of my son being pursued by an older woman."

Jane Augusta laughed. "I would hardly call three years' difference an older woman. A girl three years his senior, yes, but not an older woman, not Nancy. Besides she's a very sweet girl. I've had several little chats with her. She is the type of girl that, had I had children of my own, I would have been pleased to have as a daughter."

"I thought I would find a sympathetic ear with you, Jane Augusta. I'm sorry to have bothered you," Lillian said and as she did, she inadvertently reached for and connected with the book that was beside her. She drummed her fingers on it, then out of curiosity looked down. Seeing the title and Rosea Hackleby's name, she almost dropped the book. "Why, Jane Augusta Ornby-Clark, whatever are you doing with this heinous thing in your house?"

"What heinous thing?" Jane Augusta asked innocently. "Oh, you mean Aunt Rosea's book."

"Rosea Hackleby was not your aunt," Lillian replied. "I know she was a longtime friend of the family, but she was no blood relation. As far as I am concerned, she was nothing but an old witch, a sorceress, one who delved in the evils of this world, if not a disciple of the devil himself."

"Pish and tish, Lillian, what a notion!"

"Don't pish and tish me. I know what it's all about," Lillian said, opening the book and happening to see a word which struck her as being significant. "See here, do you know what *voodoo* is, Jane Augusta?"

"I haven't the faintest notion. It probably has something to do with," she giggled, "something or other."

"It's the work of the devil! Satan worshipers, that's what these books are about. They should be taken out and burned, instantly."

"Oh, but I couldn't do that. I promised Aunt Rosea that I would keep them until one day I could have them printed."

"Print the work of the devil? Oh, Jane Augusta Ornby-Clark, what a curse you'll put upon yourself!"

"Do you really think that would happen, Lillian?"

"I have no doubt that it would happen," Lillian replied as she threw the book across the room, letting it sprawl open with its spine broken.

"Oh dear, I do hope you haven't hurt the book. After all, I made a solemn vow at Aunt Rosea's deathbed that I would see that her wishes were completed."

"Then I think it's high time you got yourself purged, that you saw a minister and confessed your sins."

"Confess my sins? But I have no sins that I know of."

"You don't think it sinful having these books in your house? Why, you're courting evil."

Jane Augusta laughed. "My dear Lillian, if I am courting the devil, it's been a one-sided courtship because I've not been aware of it."

Raymond Nelson, the artist-painter, was perhaps a little too handsome for his own good. His features were fine. A prettiness set him apart from other men. He also had an almost woman-like delicacy that caused other men to make comment. His handsome figure was aesthetic. He walked with lilt and an almost disjointed posture, casual, limp. At the same time, his dark hair and almost Latin appearance caused women to notice him, turn their heads as he went past, to get a better look. He always carried a walking stick and dressed immaculately in the latest fashion.

Though he came from a family of some wealth and position, Nelson lived in a small apartment above a hardware store near the wharfs because he found the atmosphere inspiring to his creative work. From his large window, he got a good view of the harbor and the bustling activity that went on within it. He liked the atmosphere. Although he was a dandy at heart, something fascinated him about being in an environment wherein seamen were known to be in large numbers. He never spent much time with these rough men of the sea; still he would often use them as models for his sketches.

His favorite haunt, as far as drinking was concerned, was the infamous Tooth & Tail Tavern, which had been a favorite for many of the Phenwick men for years and years. Regularly of an afternoon, when he had finished his work—whatever that might be, usualy creating some artistic rendering of one sort or another—he would go to the Tooth & Tail Tavern for a few drinks to chat with Pomeroy Belcher, the innkeeper, and with some of the habitués of the place.

On that particular day, the same day that Jane Augusta Ornby-Clark was cleaning her house, Raymond Nelson entered the Tooth & Tail Tavern at about five o'clock. Later that evening he would go to Edward House and chat with many of Patricia's friends who often congregated there. He also would have words or perhaps a private chat and a stroll in the garden with Nancy Cox, the young lady who had greatly attracted his fancy.

Pomeroy Belcher was a round man with not much altitude. Still he was muscular and strong as an ox, balding where once coal-black hair had been. Large, deep brown eyes were constantly scrutinizing those people who entered and left the tavern. He had a red nose and pink cheeks. He was troubled with perpetual sniffles. A man of good humor, a personable sort, he entertained his customers well. Because of his hospitality, he had a large clientele.

"How are things going today?" Pomeroy asked in his usual jaunty manner. "Draw any good pictures, did you?"

"Oh, I'm still working on that seascape I started two months ago. I do little bits at a time. The canvas is far too large to take to the shore. So I periodically go down and have a look, make a few sketches and a few notes, and return to capture the picture that I have retained in my memory," Raymond replied.

"That's an admirable way of working," said Pomeroy. "You ought to be commended, sir. Will it be the usual?"

"Yes, indeed. I need a little fortification before I go up on the Hill."

"You'll pardon me for asking, sir. Why does a man like you, a dandy to be certain, come into such a sleazy tavern such as this?" Pomeroy asked.

"Do you think of your establishment as a sleazy tavern, Mr. Belcher?"

Pomeroy laughed. "Well, I don't call it very high class, it that's any answer to your question."

"No, I suppose you couldn't call it high class. Sometimes I have a desire to associate with such surroundings to get the feel of earthy people."

"Seagoing people earthy?" Pomeroy laughed. "Perhaps you mean watery people."

Raymond laughed. "Perhaps I do."

While they were speaking, the door opened and a singular figure appeared in the doorway. Although it was summertime, the man was wearing a cape and a hat with a low crown on it. He walked in a deformed manner, not dragging his feet, but walking as one does who has a twisted spine. There was a lump on his back and his right shoulder. He pushed his way to the bar as if he were swaggering, yet moving with certain pain.

"I'll have me a mug of ale if you don't mind," the man said in an almost husky whisper.

Pomeroy served him. Then the man with the cape, who was standing beside Raymond Nelson, turned to eye him. The face was twisted, somewhat sinister-appearing. He sniffed and made a grunting sound as if appraising Raymond. Then he turned back to his drink,

57

which he downed in a single gulp. "I'll have another if you don't mind."

"You haven't paid for the first one."

"Never mind, Mr. Belcher, I'll pay for it."

"I don't think that advisable, Mr. Nelson. After all, you don't know the man," Pomeroy replied.

"Well, perhaps we will become acquainted. My name is Raymond Nelson," the young man said, extending his hand.

The other man, in his forties, looked at the hand, then glanced up into Raymond's face. "Do you think I'm some kind of palm reader?" the man asked. "Well, I'm not although I know those who do."

"I was offering my hand to shake. I'm buying you a drink. Pardon me, two drinks and perhaps more, if you would care to have a conversation with me."

"Why, what do you want of me?" the man asked.

"Simply to talk to you. You appeal to me. I'm an artist, and I would very much like to do some sketches of you. You have a most interesting face."

"A most hideous face, don't you mean? Ugly is the word for it. I make no pretense about being a beauty," he snarled. "I am what I am and I accept it."

"And I admire what you are," Raymond returned. "I find that you have an extremely interesting face."

"Hmm, very well, you may buy me drinks if you like, and I'll drink them. But I don't know that I'm anxious for you to draw my countenance. It's hardly a pretty thing."

"Ah, but beauty comes in many different forms. What I see is a kind of beauty, Mr., I don't believe I caught the name."

"For a good reason—I didn't toss it. If you must know, my name is Wartstone. Milford Wartstone."

"Do you live in Boston?"

"No."

"Do you travel?"

"I've lived in many places, travel many places, do many different things."

58

"And your means of livelihood?"

"For what reason do you want that information?" Wartstone asked. "You must accept me as you see me. If I wish to give you information about myself, I will do so. Otherwise, I prefer you ask no questions."

Raymond nodded his head. "Very well."

"Now, I suppose you live in Boston, Mr. Nelson?"

"Yes. My name is Raymond Nelson. I'm an artist. I have an apartment over a store down by the wharfs."

Milford Wartstone chuckled to himself. "An artist, oh, I could tell you about some pretty pictures all right. Some pretty pictures that would make your hair stand on end. Curl up into little tiny curls as it receded. Oh yes, I've seen many pictures, pictures of the macabre, the diabolical. Pictures—well, enough of that. I'll have another drink."

"Mayn't we go somewhere, back to my studio perhaps, and you let me sketch you?"

"Sketch me? If you like, Mr. Nelson, for a price," Wartstone said.

"And what is your price?"

"Well, shall we say four jugs of ale and two dollars, that's cheap at half the price."

Chapter 5

PATRICIA PHENWICK had observed Harriet when she returned from her honeymoon only to discover that she had dark circles under her eyes and a forlorn and distraught expression. On several occasions she tried to speak to her about it. The girl was close-lipped and would not confide in the older lady. Then too, Patricia had observed that Harriet spent a great deal of time with her best friend, Nancy, almost leaning on her as if she were some kind of crutch. That disturbed the old woman. She decided to take a roundabout route getting to the girl. Instead of broaching the matter with Harriet, she approached Nancy, asking her if she could discover what the problem was. Nancy agreed to do so.

"A problem?" Harriet asked her friend. "What problem?"

"I d'clare, sugah," Nancy replied, "you sure are not at your best since you returned from Cape Anne. What is th' matter?"

"Nancy,—Nancy—I don't wish to talk about it."

"Why, what did you do or what did Mr. Phenwick do for you to have such a sad look?"

"Oh, it was nothin' that Mr. Phenwick did directly, Nancy. It was what I couldn't do. I couldn't respond to th' man. Do you know what I mean? I was afraid of him, and yet, I knew he was my husband, and Mr. Phenwick is not a very strong man, not an aggressive man, and when he approached me, he was awkward, and

I was scared and I tried to participate, I tried to respond, but somethin' within me just ached and tightened up, and I know he was disappointed."

"Then you and Mr. Phenwick nevah . . . ?"

"Yes, after some time we were able to make love, and I realized how greatly I do love th' man; but I also realized that I'm not a very responsive woman. Fact is, I'd say I was close to bein' frigid. I didn't realize that about me, but I don't enjoy makin' love."

"Because it's Mr. Phenwick?" Nancy asked. "Or do you think it would be th' same with any man?"

"I fear it would be the same with any man, Nancy," Harriet confessed. "I really do. I'm scared I'm goin' to have to go through th' rest of my life pretendin', and that frightens me. I feel like a child havin' to hold out my hand to be switched, and just grittin' my teeth and lettin' my daddy slap a stick across my hand two or three times, and try not to cry when it hurts."

Nancy hugged her arms around Harriet and kissed her on the cheek. Tears had come to her eyes. "Ah, Harriet, Harriet, how can I help you, what in the world can I do? I feel perfectly helpless, sugah. I just don't know what to do."

"There's nothin' you could do. I want to go home to Savannah. I want to go home to my mama. I want to see Aunt Maggie and all th' folks at home. I'm tired of bein' in Boston."

"I thought th' intentions were to put a division of Medallion Enterprises in Savannah," Nancy said.

"Oh yes," Harriet replied, "and Mr. Phenwick is plannin' to go down there directly and get th' buildin' started."

"Then you'll go with him. That's settled. You'll be able to see your mama and Aunt Maggie."

"No, I think that while he's there, I'd rather be here. Do you know what I mean, Nancy?" Harriet confided.

Again Nancy hugged her. "Oh, Harriet, Harriet, sugah, what can I say, what can I do? I do d'clare you have put me in a strange state of mind. I feel so helpless."

Harriet got a distant look in her eyes. "You feel helpless? Hmmph," she laughed. "How do you think I feel? How do you think I feel with havin' to face th' rest of my days with this hurt inside me?"

Prentise had had several conversations with his Aunt Patricia, finally confiding in her his disappointment with his new wife. He was of the opinion that Harriet was too dependent on her friend, Nancy, and that if he could once get her away from Nancy's influence, he might be able to present himself as himself without someone to whom she could run to have a sympathetic ear. Patricia listened. As she took the matter under consideration, she decided that perhaps Prentise might be correct in his assumption.

It was then that Patricia decided to go into action in another direction. She sent word to her nephew Peter that she wished to see him. Joanna was planning a return trip to London. She had stayed away longer than she had planned, but there were things she wanted to do in the United States before she returned and she sent word overseas. She had wanted to go to Portland and to Greenfield to Phenwick House to see her cousin Rebecca, but that trip seemed a bit far and really unnecessary. So she was now making plans to return. It was July and it would be a pleasant time for crossing with cool ocean breezes. Although she did not find the prospect of returning to London in the summer a great joy, it would give her time to prepare for the fall season and a new play which she had contracted to do before she had left to come to her brother's wedding.

"What is it you wanted to see me about, Aunt Patricia?" Peter asked after the niceties of small talk were dispensed with. "I know you must have something on your mind. I can tell by the determined expression in your face that you didn't ask me here for a casual afternoon."

Patricia smiled coyly. "You know me a little too well, Peter, aware of my idiosyncrasies, my schemes. Very well, I do have something that I wish to speak to you about. I was going to wait for the arrival of your daughter."

"Joanna? Is she coming here, too?"

"I invited her," Patricia replied. "Perhaps it is well that we converse before she arrives so that you will know precisely what I have in mind."

"Very well, let's get on with it." Peter sat in a comfortable position opposite his aunt in her sitting room, overlooking the rose garden which was now in full bloom.

"It's about Nancy among other things," Patricia began. "I've noticed that you admire her."

"Admire her? How observant you are, Aunt Patricia," said Peter with a sly smile. "I didn't realize my emotions were showing that greatly. I suppose it is difficult to hide something like that from a practiced eye like yours, isn't it?"

"My dear boy, I've been around longer than even I dare admit. I have seen generations and generations of Phenwicks. Generally I like them. Mostly I like you. Of all the nieces and nephews I have, you are my favorite. Second is Joshua, and third Joanna. Of course, I do like Jane Augusta, she has her sweet qualities, but she's of a different ilk. The Ornbys were never the socialites that the Phenwicks were."

"Only because you didn't show a particular partiality to the Ornbys, I suppose," Peter joked. "Andrew was quite fond of you."

"Of course Jane Augusta's father was extremely fond of me. I was the matriarch. Even as a young woman, I was the matriarch. Jane Phenwick never once assumed that role. Who was left to do so? Margaret? Your mother was the only other Phenwick woman of our generation, and you know of her untimely death. It was left to me, and I played the role to the hilt. But although I don't like to admit it to others, I will admit to you I am up in years. I am much older than I look. And if you say I look much over fifty, I shall thrust a pin into your heart," she said laughingly.

"I wouldn't say you were over fifty for the world since I myself am over fifty. That makes you younger than me."

"Of course, you're right," Patricia laughed. "I will tell you my concern. I suppose it is something I inherited through legacy from your grandmother, but the Phenwicks are a strong family. They must remain strong because they are a very wealthy family. We have money, we have position, and we can be prominent for generations to come. Like dear Augusta Phenwick, I am aware that the strength of the family lies in its women. Unfortunately, the strong Phenwick women no longer reside in Boston. My daughter—not Rebecca, I don't think she has much strength—but Susannah has chosen to live in England. Of course, she's famous throughout Europe, crowned heads and all that sort of rubbish. And Joanna, I've had several conversations with her and she prefers to return to London. She likes the company of Susannah and Lex and all of her admirers there. Those are the strong Phenwick women. And I think of Olivia. I've had conversations with her. She has strength, too, but I know she wants to return to England. So who do I have left? Harriet, Lillian?" Patricia thumped her fingers on the arm of the chair, and chortled contemptuously. "No, Lillian has never been a favorite of mine. I don't particularly like her at all. I don't think there are very many people who do. Augustus married her out of spite. He is perverse that way, and now he is paying for it by having to live with her. All right, so I count Lillian out. Harriet—well, Harriet is a weak person. I don't believe she could ever be a strong Phenwick woman although I accept her as a Phenwick woman. She is weak. She doesn't have the social graces or the air of sophistication and glamour, excitement—"

"That you have, Aunt Patricia?" questioned Peter.

"Precisely. I think you understand what I am getting at."

"I'm beginning to perceive a little of what you have in mind."

"So you see, when I'm gone, when I'm beyond my prime, beyond my ability to reign at Edward House, there must be another Phenwick woman strong and capable of taking over."

"Do you really believe that, Aunt Patricia? Have you been persuaded to think that way by the legend of Augusta Phenwick, the first?" he said almost sarcastically. "Yes, I do. And I think you should consider it, too, Peter. You did not act foolishly when you married Helen. You must have loved her. She was hardly Phenwick woman material, but she was your choice. Now you're free again, and I think you should consider taking another wife. A woman with spunk and daring. A woman who is not afraid to become a lady of the Phenwick clan, to take my place, if you know what I mean."

"Aunt Patricia, nobody could ever take your place."

"But there must be someone here in Boston who can. Who is left? Olivia cannot be persuaded to remain, she wants to go back to England."

"Then I assume that what you are saying, directly or indirectly, is that you believe I should consider marrying?" Peter questioned.

"Yes, as a matter of fact, I do."

"Have you a likely prospect for me, Aunt Patricia?" Peter asked, a whimsical smile crossing his lips, knowing the answer before she said it.

"Yes. And you know precisely whom I mean."

"I thought as much," Peter said. "But don't you realize the difference in our ages? Don't you realize that I am fifty-eight?"

"Still in your prime," Aunt Patricia quickly interrupted. "And you look no more than thirty-eight."

"So be it. Still, I am beginning to think like a man of fifty-eight or at least a man in his fifties. I'm forty years older, forty years older than eighteen-year-old Nancy Cox. Do you realize that, Aunt Patricia?"

"My Edward was much older than I, and I loved him with an all-consuming passion. He was my life, and I was never so happy for anything that happened to me as

66

I was that I had married Edward Phenwick. I delighted in the fact that he was older. I could never have married a younger man first. Later when I married your half-brother, Elias, and he was younger than I, it was a beautiful thing, too, in a different way. But you have had a woman who was your age, and you lived with her all those years and happily. Now, while you still have years left and are not too old to father children according to what Daniel Ornby tells me—and I trust his word as a physician—you have the right to happiness, to loving a young woman. Perhaps you will have other children, another daughter who will not go to London, but who will become a Phenwick woman."

"You really think Nancy has the stuff it takes to be your successor?" Peter asked her.

"I do. I have had her under consideration ever since she arrived. Ever since I first saw you dance with her, I knew then. It was as if I were having a mystic flash. I was certain that she was the one for you."

At that moment the butler entered to announce that Joanna had arrived. A minute later, she came sweeping into the room.

"Father, Aunt Patricia," Joanna exclaimed, lavishing each of them with kisses, "I've been on a shopping spree. I've bought some marvelous things. I've just had a final fitting session with the seamstress. My clothes will be ready next week in time for sailing. I must admit I am anxious to return to London."

"Joanna, my dear," Patricia began, "won't you sit down? Would you care for a glass of sherry, perhaps?"

"Thank you, no. I'm too excited. Tea perhaps a little later."

"Very well." Patricia sat for a moment rubbing her fingers together, looking from Joanna to Peter and back again. "Joanna, you have definitely decided beyond a shadow of a doubt that you want to return to London, haven't you?" Patricia asked.

"There is no question in my mind whatsoever. I like Boston. I like my family, but I also am an actress and I love the theater. I love the admiring throngs who cheer me nightly, and I love all the excitement. That's where my heart is. I would never be happy in Boston. You must understand."

"Of course I understand, my dear. I have been among the artistic people too long not to understand," Patricia replied. "In that case I would like to ask your impression of Nancy Cox."

"Nancy Cox? I think she's a darling, very sweet girl. She has a flirtatious way, but that's nice," Joanna said, giving a quick glance to her father. "Nice as long as she knows how to handle it."

"Do you think she would make a good Phenwick woman?" Patricia asked bluntly.

"A Phenwick woman?" Joanna asked incredulously. "Why, whatever do you mean? How could she possibly be unless she married . . ." A gasp came from her throat. Wide-eyed she looked at her father. "Unless she married . . ."

"Joanna, my dear, I am a schemer," Patricia said. "I have long taken pride in arranging things. I arranged for my great-niece Harriet to marry your brother, and now I would like to arrange for Nancy Cox to marry your father."

"My God," Joanna exclaimed, "I don't believe it! And yet, why shouldn't I? It seems like a perfectly marvelous idea, that is, if Daddy is willing. Are you, Father?"

"I've given some thought to the matter, at least to the matter of having a liaison or an affair with her, but would you think it wrong of me if I took her as a wife?"

"Wrong?" Joanna rose and went to sit on the arm of the chair which her father was occupying. She kissed him on the cheek. "I think it would be very right for you, Father. I think it would be the best thing that could happen to you."

"And could you accept her as a stepmother? She who is a girl fifteen years younger than you are?"

"I could first and foremost accept her as a friend, as a

dear member of the family as long as I know that she loves you, Daddy. As long as I know that she is good for you, and that you love her."

"Then, dear Joanna," Patricia said, "I would like to make a suggestion. When you return to England, your father should accompany you along with Nancy Cox. You can act as a kind of chaperone for them; but give them sufficient time to be alone together to get to know each other. Perhaps I'm arranging things a little too much. Perhaps I have things down a little too pat in my mind as to how things should be. I rather hope so. Things should be arranged. I don't like them to just happen."

"Me, go to London with Nancy?" questioned Peter. "Don't you think that would cause a slight scandal?"

"So what. Besides, Joanna will be along," Patricia commented.

"But on the return trip?"

"Goodness knows, you're both adults. If something happens, it happens. However, I should think you would want to play your cards adroitly and not show your hand until you had captured the young lady. If you find by then that she is the woman that you want to marry . . ."

"I have a feeling that I will find that she is the woman I want to marry because you have found that she is the woman that you want me to marry," Peter said laughingly. "Very well, Aunt Patricia, I accept the challenge. It will give me something to do. Something to look forward to, and that will make life more interesting." He rose and kissed her on the cheek. "Aunt Patricia, you *are* a schemer, but I love you dearly. Well, Joanna, shall we begin making plans for our trip?"

"Father, isn't there one thing you'll have to do first?"

"What's that?"

"Won't you have to convince Nancy to go on the trip?"

Patricia cleared her throat. "My dear Joanna, I should think that might be something that you could do for him, don't you?"

Joanna's mouth sagged only slightly before a cunning smile came to it and she began to laugh. Then the three laughed. A jovial mood existed that could not be described had anyone walked in on them at that moment.

"Going to England," Lillian screeched, "going to England with that girl?"

"None other," Gus said. "My sister is going along. They'll be properly chaperoned. Besides, what is it to you, Lillian, whether they go to England or to Timbuctoo?"

"It's simply a man his age with a girl her age. She's just a child. I suspect he's getting senile."

"I suspect it's none of your business, Lillian. I also suggest that you keep your nose out of it."

"Keep my nose out of it? Augustus Phenwick, I have kept quiet about many things."

"Very few, my dear."

Ignoring his remarks, she continued, "But I do not see how I can stand by and watch this sort of thing happening in our family. It is disgraceful. What will my friends say? What will they say at church? The ladies will whisper behind their fans and goodness knows where else."

"Who gives a damn where they whisper, Lillian," Gus grumbled. "I don't. It's Father's business, none of ours. And that's all there is to it."

"But you're the eldest son. You must have some influence on him."

"Not an iota," said Gus. "I never had much bearing with my father. He has accepted me as his son, of course, and I work with him and I manage Medallion Enterprises, but I'll be damned if he listens to me. Besides, I rather think it's a good idea for him to get married again. Give him something to do. Keep him out of my hair."

"In that case, I have no more to say on the matter."

Unbeknown to Patricia Phenwick, at the same time the plans were made for Peter and Nancy to accompany Joanna to England, Prentise and his brother Joshua were making plans of their own to go to Savannah to situate

70

the branch of the Medallion office there. Prentise had convinced his brother that he wanted his help before Joshua returned to England. He wanted him to see the place he had chosen; he wanted his advice on the plot of ground he desired to purchase on which to build a home for Harriet. Also he wanted time with his brother to discuss his marital situation and the problems that had arisen from it. Joshua, being the kind and considerate brother that he was, gave the time to Prentise. In so doing, he had to leave Olivia behind in Boston.

There was more than one reason for her remaining in Boston. First, it was to let Joshua have privacy and time with his brother. Second, Olivia was pregnant, and she felt that travel, particularly at this time of the year, into the South might make her period of waiting most uncomfortable for her.

From the moment that Nancy consented to go to England with Peter and Joanna, a new happiness sprang over her, a contentment, a thrill of excitement and adventure. It never occurred to her that one of the reasons she was being transported from Boston was that she would be away from Harriet. Nor had it occurred to Patricia that Prentise would be gone a good part of the time that Nancy would be gone, but as circumstances would have it, it would give time for Harriet and Olivia to get acquainted and perhaps because of Olivia's condition, she might be able to help Harriet over a difficult period. It would be an advantageous opportunity for everyone. It would also give time for Lillian to get to know Harriet better, and perhaps she, too, could help her with her problems. Frankly, it was Patricia's hope that Harriet and Prentise would remain in Savannah, become buried there and never return to Boston unless it was for a visit.

On the day of departure for England, when the trunks were loaded and Nancy was busily going about her room searching for last-minute items she might have forgotten, she ran across an envelope that was left on her dresser. Her name was badly scribbled on the front of the smudgy envelope, and when she opened it, the message was simple. "Don't go to England! Don't marry Peter Phenwick! If you do, a curse will be put upon you!" At the bottom was a diagram that looked like two bones laid across each other forming a cross. Nancy took this to be some sort of prank. A joke, perhaps. A macabre sense of humor, but it frightened her. She instantly tore up the paper and burned the pieces, thinking the entire matter ridiculous. However, she could not put the incident from her mind. Periodically, over the next few weeks, it would pop up again and again.

In the meantime, when Peter came to get Nancy, she was all smiles and the silly note was forgotten, tucked back into the recesses of her mind. She was so filled with anticipation and excitement that all she could think about was the trip and the fact that she would be going with handsome Peter Phenwick. She, too, had had a talk with Patricia Phenwick and she was well aware of what was up, and that excited her even more.

When they arrived at the dock, they were met by Joanna. The three climbed the gangplank with excitement while Patricia sat in her carriage on the dock and waved. In another carriage nearby Lillian sat, her face a grim line. Jane Augusta Ornby-Clark sat in the carriage beside her, bubbling with excitement, too, for Jane Augusta thought it was a marvelous idea, much to the disapproval of Lillian.

As the ship pulled out of the harbor, Patricia's carriage was turned about and she caught a glimpse of Lillian and her stone expression. She wondered why Lillian had bothered to come. Then she saw Jane Augusta and her smiling-through-tears look of one who is saying farewell and loves it.

Patricia believed that whatever was going on in Lillian's mind could not be too disastrous.

Chapter 6

THEY WERE ABOUT THE SIZE of chicken leg bones, bleached, aged, brittle and somehow malevolent-appearing when Nancy arrived in her cabin and found them in a crossed position on her bed. They were similar to the symbols she had found at the bottom of the note she had received that morning. Seeing the bones, she became deeply alarmed, quickly running from the cabin to find Joanna in the next compartment.

"What is it, Nancy?" Joanna asked, concerned at the distraught expression written on the girl's face.

"Come see," said Nancy, connecting to Joanna's hand and tugging her forward.

Upon arrival in the cabin, Joanna examined the crossed bones and found nothing particularly remarkable about them. "It's some prank," she said. "Perhaps a little trick. I understand that chicken legs have some kind of connotation to insinuate certain things to young girls that might be of a suggestive nature."

"Perhaps. I received a note this mornin'. It was on my dresser, and there was a design at th' bottom of it that was identical to these crossed bones. I don't know why but I have a terrible feelin' of apprehension when I see it."

Joanna put her arm around the girl to comfort her. "I think you are letting your imagination run away with you. What did the note say, precisely?"

"I don't remember th' exact wordin', but somethin'

73

about not wantin' me to go to England and not wantin' me to marry Mr. Phenwick. Whoevah got that notion I'll nevah know. I nevah even entertained thoughts about that."

"Haven't you, Nancy?" Joanna said without trying to sound confusing.

"Lawdy, no. I do find Mr. Phenwick attractive. He is a very gentlemanly gentleman," Nancy replied, "and I do find him very distinguished and handsome, but I certainly wouldn't have designs upon him. I'm just not that type of lady. Besides, that note said if'n I were to do so, I would—well, there would be some kind of curse put upon me. Lawsy me, I have no idea what that's all about. Why, I swear I don't."

"Some kind of curse? Nancy," Joanna confided, "there is a strangeness that happens to Phenwick women. It's like a trial we all go through some time or another. Somehow diabolical. I don't know from where it stems. I suspect it has something to do with Augusta Phenwick, my great-grandmother."

"Augusta Phenwick? Oh yes, I do recall hearin' about her. She's that lady in that picture in Edward House, isn't she?" Nancy commented. "She's a very pretty lady as I recall. Why would she have anythin' to do with anythin' diabolical?"

"My great-grandmother had a very strong notion about the Phenwick women. Her successors, all of us, those of us who have been classified as Phenwick women, have had our trials, our moments of terror as if some supernatural force were causing it. Perhaps—and this is only my speculation—perhaps Great-Grandmother Augusta has some way of contacting us from the other side and has means of testing us. She doesn't do it herself, although there are one or two persons who swear they have seen her materialize. Somehow situations are set up wherein we find ourselves in temporary jeopardy."

"Lawsy me, if it has anythin' to do with ghosts and that kind of carryin' on, just count me out! I don't want to be a Phenwick woman. I nevah had my mind set on it in th' first place," Nancy declared. "Why, I'm not one to put up with that sort of thing. I'd faint dead away."

"Yet, Harriet had her moment of trial, didn't she?"

"Why yes, but that was somethin' else. That had to do with hangin' that nigra down in th' South who up and raped her when she was just a little girl. It was all just a crazy plot by a man who was deranged."

"That well may be, Nancy. But how do we know that some supernatural force wasn't behind that?"

"Lawsy me." Nancy's eyes grew large. She stared forward.

The first day at sea was otherwise uneventful. The bones were thrown overboard at Joanna's suggestion. That night at dinner, the matter was mentioned to Peter. He simply laughed it off, saying, as Joanna had said in the first place, that it probably was some sort of prank and nothing to be disturbed about.

Joanna excused herself early, complaining of a slight headache and desirous of getting an early sleep. She enjoyed watching the dawn come up over the water, quite contrary to her routine back in England where she was in the habit of sleeping late, sometimes into the afternoon. Perhaps it was a ploy that would allow Peter to be alone with Nancy.

This ship was especially designed for the luxury of the Phenwick family in their travels. Peter took Nancy above-decks to see the immense starry sky their first night at sea. He pointed out various constellations. The moon had not yet risen.

Nancy was overwhelmed. "I d'clare, Mr. Phenwick, I've nevah in my life seen so many stars. I nevah realized in all this green earth that there were so many stars."

Peter laughed. "They're not on this green earth, they're around it, Nancy. As a sailor I learned to navigate a ship by the stars."

"Howevah could you do that?"

"It takes a bit of learning, but after a while you get so that you discover the stars are your friends. It is only the foggy nights and when there are heavy clouds that one has a difficult time of it."

"I d'clare, I suppose there are all kinds of things in this world I haven't even heard about and that's one of them for sure," Nancy replied. "I must be innocent about so many things that it just makes my head spin to think of them."

Peter laughed again. "How could your head spin over things you don't know about?"

"I don't rightly know, but I'll think about it. I suppose what I mean is that my head spins when I discover them. I nevah knew so many things went on," she commented with animation in her voice. "It's so phenomenal —I mean to say there's so much a person doesn't know about till they get out and see th' world. Th' thought of me goin' to England, why, that's th' most excitin' thing that's evah happened to me in my life so far."

"Do you think you will enjoy it, Nancy?" Peter asked. "Being in London in the company of an older man like myself?"

"I d'clare, Mr. Phenwick, why do you call yourself an older man?"

"Because that's what I am, Nancy, quite a few years older than you."

"What does that have to do with anythin'? After all, you are a gentleman. I don't think of you as anythin' but a gentleman, any more than I would think of Stuart Phenwick as a gentleman: a young gentleman."

Peter laughed again. "And I'm an old gentleman, is that it?"

"No, that is not what I meant in th' least. I d'clare, you are puttin' words in my mouth. What I mean is that it wouldn't matter if you were a hundred and fifty years old. You would still be you, and I would still be me. If we enjoyed bein' together—I mean—what I mean to say is —you do kind of know what I mean, Mr. Phenwick, don't you?"

"Nancy, do you like me?" Peter asked simply.

"Why, of course I like you. How could I not like you? You're such a sweet gentleman."

"I see. Do you like me more than just a little?"

"I d'clare, I don't know how much more 'than just a little' is, but I think I could like you an awful lot."

"I was married for a long time to a woman who didn't understand me," Peter said. "She was an ordinary woman, a good woman. The woman bore me four children. I was always good to her. I confess that she was always good to me. But there was something missing in our relationship, and I think that something was love."

"Love? Why, howevah could two people live together so long and not have love?"

"I was devoted to Helen in my way. I gave her as much understanding as I could. She tried to understand me, I am certain. I'm a man of the sea, or at least, I was as a younger man. An adventurer. To be perfectly frank, I was madly in love with my cousin."

"Why, lawsy, in love with your own cousin? What a curious situation," Nancy exclaimed.

"It was a one-sided love. I admired her. She was slightly older. You'll meet her in London. Her name is Susannah, Aunt Patricia's daughter. My brother married her. I don't begrudge Lex. I know he loves her. I never revealed how I felt. Then Helen came along. I knew her father, he was an associate, a merchant. We carted his goods. I ultimately absorbed his company into Medallion. It was a profitable marriage and we had four fine children."

"Why are you tellin' me all this, Mr. Phenwick?" Nancy asked, playing her finger along the railing as she gazed out over the sea. The wind disarranged her hair.

"Because I want you to understand me, Nancy."

"Why is that?" Tiny lumps of excitement had already begun to form at the back of her neck.

"I find you very attractive, Nancy. I'm physically affected being in your presence." Peter tried to stare deeply into her face, then looked away. "I confess I've known other young ladies while I was married. It was a way of expressing myself, of compensating for having married

77

Helen. I used to think if I were free, I wouldn't marry again. I realize now that if I were to marry again, this time for love, that I would be so happy that I would never want to have clandestine dalliances. I don't like being a philanderer, that's not my nature. I'm basically a very loving man."

"Why are you confessin' all this to me, Mr. Phenwick? You don't have to tell me about such things," Nancy said, turning to him to gaze into the shadowed face, handsome in profile.

"I want you to understand me, Nancy. I hope you will."

"Did you say anythin' to anybody else, I mean about me?"

"I've mentioned my feelings to Joanna. She's my daughter, my confidante."

"No one else?"

Peter silently remembered the conversation he had had with Patricia. "Why do you ask?"

"I didn't tell you all that was written in that note I found back at Edward House. 'Don't marry Peter Phenwick,' it said. 'If you do, a curse will be put upon you.' "

Again Peter laughed. "Whoever got the notion you might want to marry me?"

"I d'clare I don't know. Someone."

"I don't intend to ask you to marry before we return to America," Peter said lightly.

"Lawsy me, I never thought in all th' world that you might. I might have hoped and mentioned it in a prayer or two, but . . ."

Peter put his arm about her. "Nancy, I think it time we said goodnight. We'll have time to get better acquainted."

Nancy returned to her cabin. Goose bumps rose on her skin as a twittery feeling moved through her. As he left, she turned with a graceful spin. Dreamily she entered the cabin. *Peter Phenwick,* she thought, *wouldn't that be a catch? I d'clare whatevah has come over me? Fact is, what's come over him?*

Nancy had prepared herself for bed and was about to

pull back the covers when she saw a large spider, a tarantula, creeping over her pallet. She screamed, became hysterical for a moment, and ran from her cabin screaming more. Joanna was the first to enter the hallway, pulling on a peignoir. As she did, she caught Nancy in her arms. "What is it, Nancy, what is it this time?" Joanna asked.

"I d'clare, there's a terrible creature in my bed!"

"A creature?"

"I think it's a spider, probably a tarantula. It's that big."

Peter was summoned by the steward, as were two of the deckhands. The men went in, caught the tarantula and threw it overboard. Then Peter said goodnight again, leaving the distraught girl with his daughter.

"Would you like me to sit beside you for a while, Nancy?" Joanna asked. "I might recite you a speech or two that I have done from a play."

"Yes, I think I would like that," Nancy replied. "Would you mind holdin' my hand? Maybe th' image of that dreadful spider will go away. I hope I nevah see another one of those in my whole life. Why do you suppose someone is tryin' to frighten me?"

"I don't think anyone is trying to frighten you, Nancy. It's probably an accident that the tarantula appeared. It must have come aboard on some of the cargo, and inadvertently found its way to your cabin. Put it from your mind."

Joanna sat in the chair, took Nancy's hand in hers and began to recite a speech from Shakespeare.

Alexander Phenwick was sixty. His once dark hair had turned gray and his flashing brown eyes were beginning to look weary. The philanthropist, benevolent employer and generous giver of parties *was* tired. Life had presented its challenges, he thought, and now it was a matter of downhill, of reliving events that had once been exciting to anticipate, doing the same thing over and over again. Still Peter's older brother was not one to give up easily. He looked for things to amuse him while his wife, the still

79

lovely Susannah, was off on her concert tours throughout Europe. Even when they were home together in England at Merrihew Manor, they were a little bored, childless, and terribly used to each other. The prospect of Joanna returning gave them rise to anticipate parties and celebrations. Having received word that Peter would be along with her, they decided to make a gala event of their arrival.

Both Susannah and Lex were at the boat dock when it arrived. Beautiful blond Susannah with her dancing blue eyes watched with eager anticipation until she caught sight of her cousin Joanna and her brother-in-law Peter. The man whom she had secretly loved all those years. For some mysterious reason unbeknown to herself, she had chosen to marry his older brother. Then she beheld the lovely dark-haired girl between Peter and Joanna. Instantly, she knew that she was more Peter's friend than she was Joanna's. She intuitively discerned that this girl was romantically interested in Peter.

When the greetings were over, and introductions made, Lex hustled them all off in a carriage to his town house in London near the theater district, an apartment which had been his private place to get away for so many years. Susannah often frequented it. She, too, had her own apartment in London where she gave intimate little parties for her friends in the artistic world. Like her mother, Patricia, Susannah was given to celebrating the genius of promising artists, writers, composers, actors. She even coached gifted pianists, more and more devoting time to developing their talents, to polishing them and preparing them for concert tours of their own.

Susannah suspiciously eyed Nancy on several occasions that first afternoon. Although she had suspicions, she could not help but admire the young lady with the flashing, almost black eyes, with dark raven hair, and a personality that bounced with enthusiasm and a certain *joie de vivre*. She would make an attempt to become friendly with the girl. Deep within her heart, Susannah wept for Peter's unhappiness and knew only too well the difficulties he had

had during his marriage to Helen and the discontent that emanated from that union. If he were attracted to this younger girl, then by all means she would give her blessing and swallow whatever emotion she felt about the situation.

Lex, too, observed Nancy and an old emotional tugging came within him: the envy he had for his younger brother, Peter, and the fact that he always managed to attract delightful people, persons who were happy and carefree, beautiful people—people who liked to laugh. True, Lex had Susannah and his love for her was as deep as any man's love could be for a woman even though she led a somewhat private life of her own. He had his own club and little activities on the side. Lex had grown staunch, a little stodgy in his attitude, terribly settled in his ways. He had taken on a British disposition which seemed to settle him into a different person than he had been in younger years, a person who no longer twinkled at the sight of beautiful young ladies. Yet when he saw Nancy, that old twinkling began to emerge. He, too, was happy for his brother.

Joanna went immediately to the theater, where she renewed old friendships, picked up the manuscript for the new play she was to do and got things in order businesswise. She promised she would return to Lex's town house for a party that evening.

The party that evening was a small soiree with about twelve guests selected from more intimate friends of Susannah and Lex. The dinner party was for the purpose of welcoming Peter and Joanna home, but it turned out to be a time of introduction of the interesting Nancy Cox.

After dinner, the ladies went into the music room, and the gentlemen into the library where they smoked and had brandy, a custom which the Phenwicks had maintained from as far back as Augusta Phenwick, who thought it a nice tradition to establish.

In the music room, Nancy was the center of attention. The ladies, most of whom were contemporaries of Susannah, fired questions at the girl with the interesting accent.

Susannah said, "I understand you are from the South, from Savannah, isn't it?"

"I'm from Savannah, Georgia, yes, ma'am," Nancy replied, "I suppose there is a distinction between the North and the South, but I hardly think about it myself."

"You come from a large plantation: cotton, tobacco?"

"My daddy does have a small plantation and some cotton, mostly."

"Then I suppose you have slaves working for you," one of the ladies stated.

"We-all have some slaves, we've had more on occasion, but economic conditions are such that we've not had as many as we used to have. Things are changin' and with th' cotton gin, things are goin' to be different throughout the South. There's a lot of slaves who are not bein' taken' care of properly because of it."

"Then you believe in slave owning?" questioned Susannah.

"It's not so much a matter of whether I believe in it or not, it's an actuality where I come from, if you-all know what I mean," Nancy said. "I don't rightly appreciate seein' people misused, I mean, there are some very sweet darkies whom I like very much, and there are those who aren't quite as nice. But I've nevah seen any badly abused like I understand there are stories about."

"Why do they keep the slaves?" asked another lady. "Why don't they just let them go free?"

"I don't believe you understand the situation where I come from. What would happen to them if they were to be set free? Would they take them back to Africa?" Nancy asked. "I don't know if they'd want them back there either. There would be nothin' for them to do. They're used to livin' on th' plantations. It would be very difficult, I should think. I know there's a lot of rumblin's and talkin's about slavery and abolishin' it. I just rightly don't know how they would take care of somethin' like that."

"Well, I should think that your government would find a way to handle the situation," another lady said.

"Perhaps they-all might, again they-all might not," Nancy said, perplexed, scowling slightly. "I do wish we would talk about somethin' else. I know so little about it. I just know that I was raised with a mammy and that I grew up with the little pickaninnies, and we were all like good friends. I nevah felt hatred or malice toward any of them. They were just people. Maybe that's why I like bein' in th' North."

"If you like bein' in the North," Susannah said, "why don't you do something about losing that accent of yours?"

"What accent is that, Miz Phenwick?" Nancy questioned innocently. "You-all think I speak with an accent?"

A titter of laughter went through the music room.

"No, Nancy, we don't think you speak with an accent," Joanna defended, putting her hand to the girl's and clasping it gently. "The ladies are just curious. They've never met a person quite like you." She turned to her cousin. "Susannah, darling, why don't you play something for us? Poor Nancy doesn't want to be bored with all this quizzing and interrogation."

"Whatever you say, Joanna, I would be delighted to play something . . . Chopin perhaps, or Liszt." Susannah went to the piano. After a moment's hesitation, she was quickly flying her fingers over the keys.

Nancy sat listening to the music enraptured by the glorious sounds of the great artist that Susannah was. Her fingers made the piano speak as if by magic. The ladies sat around the room gently fanning themselves, straight-backed and elegantly postured as they admired the glorious tones, and when the selection was completed, they applauded. Susannah was persuaded to give a second rendition.

During the course of the next selection, Nancy began to feel a peculiar sensation come over her. First it was like a hot rising of temperature and her face flushed, then she had a chill to the point that her hands were trembling together and she noticed her teeth clicking. She placed a finger to her mouth to hold the teeth apart to keep from making a noise and hoped her gesture did not appear obvious. A cold sweat burst forth on her brow. She managed to contain her feelings until Susannah finished playing, then she rose as the ladies were applauding, a stark expression of fear upon her face.

"I d'clare, I do believe I'm goin' to be sick," Nancy managed to announce before a dark cloud enshrouded her brain and she fell forward in a dead faint.

Excitement followed. The ladies rushed to assist her. Joanna was first to get to the floor beside the fallen girl, lifting her in her arms.

"Quickly, get a cold cloth," Joanna ordered.

One of the men present was a doctor, Dr. Sedrick Wellington. His wife, Martha, ran from the music room into the library to interrupt the gentlemen from their tobacco and brandy to summon her husband to look after the sick girl.

Dr. Wellington was a man nearing fifty, a proud man with a large moustache and muttonchops which ran together, making a gray line around his face. He adroitly went about his business, immediately examining the girl. He suggested that she be taken to a bed, all tight clothing removed from her, and that she be then left for him to examine.

Some time later, Dr. Sedrick Wellington returned from examining Nancy. He had a concerned expression on his face, perplexed. "Quite frankly, I have no idea what's wrong with the young lady. She has several symptoms of which none are complementary to one another, they're all conflicting. I really will have to call in a colleague for consultation. I suggest that she be kept in bed and cool compresses put on her forehead whenever she seems to run a fever and heat applied to her when she gets the chills. This is most unusual. I've never seen the likes of it."

Lex did what he could, making all the arrangements and turning the town house guest room into a hospital room for the stricken girl. Peter Phenwick was beside himself with concern. He spent many hours sitting at her bedside. The girl was unconscious for long hours on end.

When she showed no sign of improvement within a

week, the best physicians in London examined her, and reached no concrete conclusion of what was disturbing her. Peter became desperate and suggested that he might go to Vienna to find a doctor who would look after her. The consensus of opinion among the medical men was that in some way Nancy had been poisoned; but it was not food poisoning nor were there traces of any kind of known poison about her. It was a peculiar illness to say the least. They had never seen anything like it.

After she had been in a coma for nearly a week, the doctors had virtually given up hope of bringing her out of it. One morning as Susannah was sitting beside the girl's bed, her eyes suddenly popped open and flashed a look of recognition. Then came a smile, and Susannah noticed the color had come back to Nancy's face. For some reason completely unexplainable, she had been miraculously cured. Although a little weak, Nancy was her old self again. Susannah quickly summoned Peter. When he arrived at where the girl was resting, he found her sitting up, her arms open to him. He embraced her, with a tender, overwhelming compassion, for he knew that his prayers had been answered. He had made a promise to the Divine Intelligence of the universe that if Nancy was saved, he would love her with all his heart and soul, and marry her that she might become a Phenwick.

Chapter 7

ARRANGEMENTS WERE MADE for the return to America when Nancy was strong enough to travel. A Medallion ship was scheduled the following Friday morning. Special care was taken and a room prepared for Nancy that was as luxurious as any stateroom could possibly be. Lex spared no expense in seeing that all the comforts were provided. The adjoining room was equally as well prepared for his brother. Plans were made and the packing had begun.

Peter had lunch with his brother at his club on Wednesday afternoon, prior to the sailing. The two men played a game of billiards before lunch, afterward they relaxed in the lovely old oak-paneled dining room in the club reserved for gentlemen of nobility and class. Since Lex had an honorary title, he was considered to be in both categories, and hence, a very valued and honored member of the club.

The table was in a quiet corner. A white linen cloth, lovely crystal stemware, bone china plates, and silver utensils that were especially designed for the club with its crest on them.

"So you're returning to Boston, are you, Peter?" Lex began the conversation awkwardly.

"Nancy is well and Dr. Wellington assures me that she can travel now. I think it best that I get her back to Edward House and Aunt Patricia, whom I am sure has deep concern for her."

"And your concern for her, my dear brother?" Lex asked.

"You know my concern, Lex. I have discovered during her illness that I am very much in love with Nancy Cox. I intend to ask her to marry me once we are back in the United States," Peter confessed.

"What of this illness that came on so suddenly, and disappeared as mysteriously as it came?" asked his brother. "What if it recurs?"

"If it recurs, I shall see that she has the greatest care in the world. Suddenly this child, this person means more to me than even my own children. You know how deeply I love Joanna and Josh, even Prentise and Gus are close to me. I'm a doting father."

"Yes, and for that I envy you," Lex replied, looking down and playing nervously with a fork. "You have always been a good father, and I am proud that you are my brother. I am equally proud of my brother's children. I wonder though if you will be doing right by marrying a girl so many years younger than you are."

"Is age that important, Lex?" Peter asked, then sipped from a glass of water.

"It is in some senses," Lex replied. "I don't know about you, but I have, now at sixty, lost interest to a large extent in the old physical pleasure of making love. Oh, occasionally, yes, but only occasionally. Perhaps I'm peculiar."

"Is this a confession, Lex?" Peter questioned, a light smile on his face. "That is not a family trait; at least, not so far as I am concerned. The fact is, I have found the last few years that my desire for such expression has increased. That may be, of course, because of the situation with Helen all those years. Again, it may be because we've lived different lives, you and I, and have different outlooks. At any rate, I find that I am eager in my anticipation of making love to Nancy."

"I am happy for your sake then, Peter, that you have this nature," Lex commented. "In a sense I wish that I were so endowed. I think that Susannah would be happier with me if I were. However, since I'm not, I'm not. I can only give you my blessing and welcome Nancy as a Phenwick woman."

The next day, Peter had lunch with Joanna, who was able to take time away from rehearsal to spend a few hours with her father. First they took a carriage ride through the park and ended at Joanna's favorite restaurant, a place where she was well known and treated as the reigning theatrical queen that she was. They were shown to a private booth, where they had lunch together.

"I'm happy for you, Father, that you've found Nancy Cox, and happier still that she is well again. I do love you, Daddy, and I do want to see you content. If Nancy pleases you then I am delighted for both of you."

"Thank you, my dear."

"What about the difference in your ages?" Joanna asked.

"Don't you remember the difference in Uncle Edward's age and Aunt Patricia's? They had a beautiful life together. I want the rest of my life to be beautiful, too. What would you think of having half brothers and half sisters?"

"It would be perfectly marvelous, Father, and if I get my hands on any of them, I'll spoil them rotten."

"Of *that* I am certain. Thank you for the warning."

"Daddy, Daddy, I want you to dive into the situation head first. I want you to have Nancy in sickness and in health. After talking with Aunt Patricia, I know her feeling only too well. Nancy is to be a chosen Phenwick woman. I suspect she will ultimately take over where Aunt Patricia leaves off with the American side of the family. Who else is there? Harriet? She's a sweet girl, and I have a fondness for her. I'm proud that Prentise has her, but I don't think that she will be a strong Phenwick woman, not as Aunt Patricia is, not as Susannah or—" she hesitated.

"Or *you* are, my dear?" Peter suggested.

"Well, I'm strong in my own way, but I'm not the head of a dynasty nor will I ever be. I will be supportive of anyone who is. If Nancy is to be the matriarch, then long live the queen!" she exclaimed, raising her glass as if in a toast.

Peter laughed joyously. "My darling, my darling. Thank you so much. Now I am certain of what I must do."

Joanna said dramatically, "Be certain that you love her, that you are not just marrying her out of pity for her illness or out of a lustful desire for her, but because you love every part of her. What she is deep within. There is time."

"Time, Joanna?" He chuckled softly. "How much time does a man my age have? Not forever."

Joanna put her hand on her father's. "Do you really want to marry again, Father? Not because Aunt Patricia has coaxed you into it?"

Peter paused a moment reflectively. A concerned expression crossed his face and he scowled slightly. "How I wish I had known Grandmother Augusta. I wish I had understood what motivated her desire for such a strong line of descendants, particularly women. Aunt Patricia didn't know her well, if she knew her at all. Yet, she has the same fervor."

"You've never seen any indication of your grandmother, have you? I mean, any sort of manifestation of her? There are those who say she makes occasional ghostly appearances."

"No, I don't believe I have, yet I often think of her, and I see a picture in my mind's eye of her portrait. When I do, it is as if I hear her speak. She tells me how much she loves me. Always that's the way it begins. I don't know why. She tells me that I am the favorite son of her only child who lived. My father had a terrible life. The heavy drinking over, the unhappiness, and God knows the torment he went through both with mother and with Rachel when she—well, when she died so young. Yet, somehow I feel Grandmother Augusta is pleased with me because I have been what my father was not. No doubt, she is pleased with Lex, too. I don't think she was pleased too greatly with Elias, not because he was a minister, but

90

because of his confusion stemming out of much of his background. But I feel she will be pleased if I marry Nancy. I don't think she, like Aunt Patricia, approved of your mother, not as a Phenwick woman."

"I never thought of Mother as a Phenwick woman. Therefore, why should have Great-Grandmother or Aunt Patricia?"

"Of course," Peter admitted, drinking from his glass. "I'm pleased we have had this talk. I think you understand me."

Joanna rose from where she was sitting and walked around the table to put her arms around her father, press her cheek against his, kiss him gently. "No matter what you do, I want you to always know that I will understand, no matter what it may be, because I love you that much."

Farewells were made that Friday morning. Lex and Susannah saw Peter and Nancy to the ship and aboard. Nancy was still weak but she had regained some of her strength. A joyous attitude prevailed. She eagerly looked forward to the trip as much as she had looked forward to going to England. Within she felt the voyage back would be different. Without Joanna along, she would be alone with Peter.

That evening while they were on the high seas and the ship was swaying gently with the current, Peter and Nancy sat on the deck bundled in blankets and stared up at the stars.

"I have had a lot of time to think, Mr. Phenwick," Nancy remarked after a long period of meditative silence.

"To think of what?"

"Of you and me," Nancy said, "of how I feel toward you. I couldn't feel any differently about a man closer to my own age than I feel toward you. These past days bein' confined to bed and not quite myself, I realized I could love you even more than I could love a younger man. I never was close to my father. He was always busy, and I was one of many children, if'n you understand what I

91

mean. Consequently, I believe you will be many things to me."

Peter took Nancy's hand. "Nancy, my dearest, I was going to wait until we had returned to the United States, but I'll ask you now. Will you marry me and become Mrs. Peter Phenwick?"

Nancy gasped, hesitating only a moment. "I d'clare, I would be most honored to, Mr. Phenwick, most honored and delighted."

Peter raised her hand to his lips. The excitement that ran through the girl and through the man was like electricity. Somewhere music seemed to be playing. The angels seemed to be laughing. Nancy leaned forward in her chair and allowed him to kiss her lips. She knew at that moment what Heaven must be like.

Chapter 8

THE THREE BOOKS written by Rosea Hackleby, an accumulation of her life's study and investigation into the occult, were left in the safekeeping of Jane Augusta Ornby-Clark upon the demise of the writer. Because of certain things included in the texts, the contents were to be protected. Jane Augusta had been sworn to secrecy to see that they were. Herself quite intuitive in many ways, Jane Augusta was more than sympathetic to most of the writings in Rosea's books. However, when it came to matters of witchcraft and other peculiarities, she was not knowledgeable. She looked on them with a curiosity and an open mind. At the same time, she was a good Christian lady who went to church regularly, to prayer meetings during the week, and from time to time had even taught Sunday School classes. She was devout in her spiritual nature. Yet she knew that there were certain things she could not explain and certain things that were not clarified through the teachings of Christianity as dictated by the Fundamentalists' doctrine and creeds imposed on parishioners. The churches were becoming stronger and stronger in their organizations.

She read the books Rosea had written. The scribbly writing in places was difficult to decipher. Yet these recorded mysteries, many of them legends handed down to the enigmatic authoress, fascinated Jane Augusta.

Although many members of the family knew Jane Augusta was in possession of the books, few had interest in them. Thus, she kept them well hidden, intending one day to speak to Patricia and suggest that arrangements be made for them to be published. Others of the family might like to have copies of the books. Jane Augusta had accepted an awesome responsibility from Rosea.

Intuitively Jane Augusta picked up many and various vibrations about members of her family. On more than one occasion, she was certain that she had communicated with the spirit of her late husband, Eustace. On many other occasions she was convinced that she had been in the presence of the spirit of Augusta Phenwick. She did not consider herself mediumistic or to have particular supernatural powers, yet she realized she was a receiver for vibrations that came from another plane of existence, another level of life. Such did not worry her, but she had accepted it. Yet, there were times when she felt burdened by the responsibility that was hers.

Lillian Phenwick, well aware that Jane Augusta was in possession of these books, believed it was her moral and Christian duty to destroy them, if only she could get her hands on them. On at least four occasions, she had come in contact with the books, but at the same time Jane Augusta had been present, her jolly face watching as Lillian eyed the books suspiciously and scowled. She believed them to be the work of the devil and made caustic remarks regarding the books, and the character of old Rosea. The only account she actually had read in the books was that of the possession of Rachel Phenwick many years before. Lillian was convinced the child was not possessed by discarnate spirits, but by the devil himself and that such an account was erroneous and glossed over. Furthermore, when she read of Rosea's suspicion that Rebecca Phenwick was the reincarnation of Rachel, Lillian was beside herself with rage, declaring that such things did not happen. When a person died he went either to Heaven or to Hell and that was it. There was no such thing as returning to earth.

Jane Augusta did not argue the matter with her for she was not too well informed about such things; still from the evidence that she had seen, and she knew Rebecca Phenwick quite well, she could see where there was a very distinct possibility that the girl was a reincarnation of that tormented creature. Fortunately, Rebecca was not plagued with the discarnate spirits who had perplexed Rachel and driven her to madness while still in her teens.

Lillian, although she had a household staff of a housekeeper, Mrs. Muldune, two maids, Hanna and Sylvia, and a butler, Winston Hayward, regularly took charge of the housework. She saw that the modest mansion in which they lived was well kept and spotlessly clean, overseeing the maids, reprimanding the housekeeper whenever she found anything out of place or not to her liking. She harangued the butler when the silver showed the slightest tarnish or a teacup was broken. A stern woman, Lillian permitted only perfection in her house, perfection according to her standards. The only imperfection she felt in her life was the presence of her husband. Yet, without him she would have been nothing but a poor farmer's or a tradesman's wife at best, scratching out a living in some sort of humdrum existence, probably in a house with few rooms, crowded and overrun with children. She did have to thank Augusta for raising her from the mediocrity of her humble birth. Why he had ever been attracted to her, she would never understand. It was not so much attraction on her part as it was a realization that she was making a worthy catch. If she made life miserable for Augustus, he made life miserable for her. They were like strangers in a house with two sons who pretended to be at least cordial to each parent, but who basically disassociated themselves from both Augustus and Lillian, hating to admit that such mismatched people were their parents.

"I intend to find those books of Rosea Hackleby," Lillian declared one afternoon when she was speaking with her eldest son, Stuart. "I wish to locate and destroy them. I will not have Satan's instruments in the family."

"But they are not your books to destroy, Mother," Stuart argued, "they belong to Cousin Jane Augusta. She

95

is the possessor of them. They were given to her by Rosea. What right have you to them?"

"I have the right as a zealous Christian to see that they are destroyed, that they do not contaminate the minds of other generations to come. If you were to read them, Stuart, you would know precisely why I want them destroyed. The things that they go on about are disgusting. Why, I understand that the rituals performed by witches —and there were those in Salem and other places throughout Massachusetts—were absolutely disgraceful, disgusting. Dancing around naked in the moonlight in front of a fire, calling down curses and calling forth Satan from Hell. That's what's included in those books! I believe the world needs to be purged of them and *we* must destroy them."

"*We,* Mother?"

"Yes, we. I insist that you help me in this matter."

"And if I refuse?"

"Have you sold your soul to Satan as well?"

"No, Mother. I have no idea who Satan is," Stuart replied, "but should I meet him one day, I at least will talk to him and find out what his terms are before I sell myself to him."

"Oh, God in Heaven, I pray for you, my son! I pray that the Holy Spirit will come and purge you of all this sin!"

"Purge me of what sin, Mother?"

"Of what you've just said. You've glorified the devil, Satan himself, with your tongue."

"I said nothing wrong, Mother. I do have a modest curiosity because sometimes I wonder if all that I hear in the church is correct."

"On your knees, boy, on your knees!" Lillian commanded. "Get on your knees and pray to God that you be forgiven for what you have just said, for such blasphemy!"

Stuart shrugged his shoulders. "What blasphemy? I simply made a perfectly normal observation. Am I to be condemned for that? Is that blasphemy? I have not taken the name of the Lord in vain. I have simply said that I have a curiosity. I'm not so certain that everything I hear spouted from the pulpit is the truth."

"Oh, God, God, forgive him! He is a transgressor," Lillian said dramatically, "and he knows not what he is saying."

"I know perfectly well what I am saying, Mother, and I don't think I am such a transgressor. This is a land of free speech and if a person can't inquire about what is being taught here, then he doesn't have freedom at all. Maybe many of the things that you believe in are nothing but legend, fables, allegories passed down by word of mouth. Maybe you don't understand the truth, understand the way things really are."

"On your knees, boy, on your knees!" Lillian shrieked. "How dare you say such things to your own mother?"

"Am I to be stifled because I have a mind of my own?"

"A Phenwick, that is what you are! They are all, every last one, prompted by Satan himself," Lillian screamed and ran from the room.

Stuart scratched himself and stared in the direction in which his mother had gone. A feeling of antagonism moved through him and he wanted to follow her and say more, but basically he was a controlled young man who kept his thoughts mostly to himself, confiding secrets only to his brother, Gordon.

It was the following afternoon that Olivia Pritchard Phenwick went to call on Cousin Jane Augusta. The British actress, newly a Phenwick woman, was still uncertain of her role in the family. Although she had had several encounters with Patricia, and seemed to be accepted, she only saw one side of the situation, the very grand and opulent matriarch and her points of view.

Joshua was in Savannah with Prentise, looking at land and possibly purchasing property. Olivia was alone. She had tried on several occasions to become friendly with Harriet, but Harriet had become withdrawn and quite moody since Prentise was gone. Therefore, Olivia felt it was time that she made acquaintance with the second leading lady of the family, and made a special effort to get to know Jane Augusta.

They visited for nearly two hours while Jane Augusta filled in many of the details of the family history, going back to the time of Augusta and her son, Daniel; to how Augusta had adopted Jane and Edward Munsk as her own children and raised them as Phenwicks, which meant in reality that Jane Augusta was no blood relative to Peter Phenwick and his children. However, they were brought together through the bond established by Augusta and were basically a close-knit family.

"I was speaking with Lillian the other day," Olivia commented, "and I was concerned with the strange attitude she suddenly reflected."

"I fear, my dear, that you will find Lillian Phenwick is a singular person," said Jane Augusta, "with many eccentricities and terribly set in her ways. I love her, of course. She is a member of the family. But I find it difficult to get close to her. She has such strange opinions."

"That was my feeling precisely, Jane Augusta. It seemed to me that Lillian was almost abstract in her thinking."

Jane Augusta chuckled. "Abstract is not really the best word for her condition. I would say that she is jealous. I'm a Christian lady myself; I go regularly to church, but I don't have the fervor and the imagination which Lillian possesses. Rather I think I am not necessarily naïve, but conservative and more understanding. Lillian is, I am afraid, intolerant of anyone and anything that does not agree with her philosophy."

Olivia sat a moment contemplating the lovely parlor with the old relics and antiques that had been handed down through the family, many of which had belonged to Jane Augusta's father and some from Portland and Falmouth House.

"Lillian mentioned a peculiar lady, a Rose somebody."

"Rosea Hackleby?" questioned Jane Augusta. "She was probably the one. Lillian, who knew Rosea only briefly in her declining years, was not at all sympathetic

98

to the old lady's attitude toward life and death and such things."

"I understand that the lady wrote some books," Olivia said.

"Oh yes, she has written three rather sketchy notebooks, I would call them, about the occult."

"The occult?"

"Yes, Rosea was deeply immersed in the occult, the mystic and the mysteries of life," Jane Augusta explained. "She was a searcher and believed that what she was seeking was a higher form of truth than is found, shall I say, in orthodox Christianity. I listened to her, and I had long conversations with her. Several times I tried to puncture her arguments, but never was I able to, for the old woman was strong in her opinions. Then before she died, she made me promise that I would keep the books safely and one day have them published, at least in a limited edition."

"Have you had them published?" Olivia asked.

"Not yet. I simply haven't found the time."

"I should like to see them one day," Olivia commented. "Joanna had spoken to me of Rosea Hackleby while we were in England. I understand that there are many cults and groups formed in and around London. I even encountered a medium once who quite accurately told me about myself and even predicted my marriage to Joshua. Since then, I have become, not necessarily a believer, but curious about the entire matter."

"In that case, my dear, I think I should make a confession to you," Jane Augusta said. "I am quite intuitive myself. Oh, most of the family is completely unaware of this. They don't realize and I don't want it told about because there is intolerance—not only with Lillian but with other members as well. My own brothers, Ted and Daniel, are not altogether sympathetic to my predictions even though they see them come about as I have seen them happening."

"How very interesting," Olivia said. Then with a laugh, she asked, "What do you see for my future?"

"I'm not a fortune-teller, my dear, but I do seem to have the ability to tune in on some people and see where they are headed," Jane Augusta replied. She closed her eyes, pausing for nearly a minute before she opened them again. "I believe that you and Joshua will return to England where he will ultimately succeed Alexander as head of the Medallion company in London. I also foresee that you will have several children and that you will be happy; but you will not be truly happy until you return to the theater. Fortunately, you have Joanna as a very close friend, one who loves you dearly and who will see that you are successful in that endeavor, too. Joanna will also be a second mother to your children. I don't want to make too many lavish promises, because that is all I see. But I do envision you again appearing on the stage with Joanna."

"How many children do you see?"

"That I don't care to disclose, my dear. Some matters are very private and I'm not that accurate."

"I see." Olivia changed her approach. "There is another situation about which I would like to ask, if you don't mind. I have tried to be friendly with Harriet, but she is a strange girl in that she seems to confide only in her one friend, Nancy. With Nancy away, she has become morose and despondent."

"Harriet is a disturbed child," Jane Augusta said, closing her eyes and looking into the crystal ball of her mind. "She will never be content in Boston, nor will she be happy until she returns to Savannah where Prentise will be most successful."

"She seems ill. Is that the case?"

"My brother Ted tells me that she is not well. As you know, she is pregnant, which is causing her to experience depression and unhappiness. It is unfortunate that Prentise is away, for a woman needs a man during this particular period, especially with the first child." Jane Augusta suddenly gasped. "Oh dear, oh dear me! I had hoped I wouldn't see something like this."

"What is it?"

"I fear that Harriet will lose her child; in fact, I see no way that that event can be avoided."

"We must do everything we can to help her," Olivia said. "I wish that I could be as close to her as Nancy is, but she seems to have some sort of suspicion of me. Perhaps it is my accent, or the fact that I am British."

Jane Augusta's eyes were still closed when she gasped again. Her eyes popped open. "Oh dear, I have a feeling that Nancy, too, has been quite ill over the past few weeks. I get this strange piercing sensation as though— no, but that could not be . . ."

"What could not be?"

"I don't like to speak of it. It is like a pin being driven into my upper chest on the left side. I feel a stabbing as if something supernatural has been performed to cause Nancy to have this illness. Ah, now she is temporarily better. I must get out Rosea's books. Perhaps I will find a clue. My intuition tells me the answer I am seeking may be found in those books."

Olivia looked surprised, yet she smiled pleasantly. Her desire was to see the books herself, to examine them; then she could make up her own mind which of the two Phenwick ladies she wished to believe, Lillian or Jane Augusta.

"Gus, I had a dream," Lillian announced the following week, "and the angel of the Lord spoke to me."

"A pipe dream, no doubt," Gus grumbled, uninterested in his wife's imaginings.

"It was no pipe dream. It was a very vivid experience. I was told that I must purge the world of Rosea Hackleby's books, destroy them once and for all."

"Do what you like, my dear. However, I think it's none of your damn business," Gus said to find an excuse to leave.

Lillian fumed for nearly a half an hour. When Stuart arrived, she started to broach the subject with him, but recalling his most recent reaction, she let it pass. However, when the younger of her sons came to where she was busying herself in the kitchen, she felt she had a better opportunity since he was the baby and the one whom she most favored of her children. Husky and corpulent, Gordon was not always aware of what was happening around him. He had a tendency to live in fantasy and to dwell on abstract thoughts. A dreamer, he was often lost in his imagination.

"What is it, Mother?"

"I want you to do a favor for me."

"What is that, Mother?"

"I want you to go become better acquainted with Cousin Jane Augusta and, when the occasion is right, to ask her about Rosea Hackleby's books. Then observe from where she gets them. Later, when I have arranged a time for Jane Augusta to be away from her house, you will go back, get those books for me and bring them here."

"Isn't that stealing, Mother?" the boy asked, his eyes wide.

"There are some things, Gordon, that we must do in the name of God and for the sake of Christianity. One of those is to destroy the work of the devil. Those books, I am thoroughly convinced, are nothing but the handiwork of Satan dictated to that addled old lady who believed in the most preposterous things."

"What if I am caught?"

"You will not be caught. Besides, you are also a Phenwick. Since the books were left to the Phenwick family, you have as much right to them as anyone. Should Jane Augusta say anything, tell her that you merely want to look through the contents, but of course, you won't. God forbid that you should!"

Gordon left after promising his mother that he would see what he could do about the situation. Lillian stood in the kitchen, staring off into a vague nowhere as a plot conjured in her mind.

Chapter 9

DURING JOSHUA'S ABSENCE in Savannah, Olivia spent a great deal of time with Patricia, getting to know her and the family much better. She also got to know some of Patricia's friends, particularly Arthur Townsend, the writer. When he showed a particular friendship to her, she began to confide certain things about herself and her aspirations as an actress. Arthur Townsend was impressed. He had known one or two young ladies who aspired to the stage, but never had he met one who was an accomplished actress and had herself been in the theater, that is, with the exception of Joanna Phenwick, who really had no time for him at all.

Taking a book of poetry to read, she and Arthur Townsend sat in the rose garden enjoying the warmth of the summer day.

"Arthur, I would like you to do me a favor if you would."

Eagerly, Arthur responded, "Why, whatever is it, Mrs. Phenwick?"

"There are three books which when edited down and put in concise form would make one book that I would like to see published. If you would go over the material and see that it is in proper form, I will arrange for that publication. I fear if Jane Augusta procrastinates any longer, she will not see the book in print within her lifetime."

"What book is this?" asked Arthur.

"A book which has been inherited by the Phenwicks.

I would like to have a copy of it to take back to London with me when I go. I think it would be rather nice if you go over it and make any corrections necessary, edit it, as it were."

"I would be pleased to do anything for you, Mrs. Phenwick," Arthur said, a look of admiration on his face. He was a romantic sort who seemed to be moved to express his feelings to any lady with whom he happened to be in company. Because he had spent so much time with Olivia, he was beginning to have amorous thoughts about her. This was not at all her intention; rather, she wanted to become acquainted with his creative talents and have him work on the book.

Arthur Townsend took Rosea Hackleby's books and diligently set about putting them in order for publication. Olivia went to Patricia and told her of the project, explaining that she would like to have copies of the book for both Joanna and Susannah in London as well as having a copy of her own.

Patricia, who had never read the books, agreed that such a venture should be pursued. After all, Rosea Hackleby had been a longtime friend of the family and one whom she had known as long as she had known the Phenwicks. Thus, Patricia consented to pay for the production of the publication, and also to pay a handsome salary to Arthur for his work.

With money promised and an early deadline desired, Arthur worked around the clock until he had the book in condition for the printer. The thing was in the works and soon there would be more than one copy for Lillian to attempt to destroy.

Prentise and Joshua returned from Savannah by mid-August about the same time that Nancy and Peter returned from their ocean trip. Naturally, Patricia planned a homecoming party for everyone. Before that event, she called Prentise and Joshua together to find out what progress

104

had been made in Savannah. She wanted a further word of her sister and her nephew, Patrick McGregor.

"In the first place," Joshua announced, "we purchased the property for the Medallion Enterprises building, and construction has already begun. We hired an architect to design and a contractor to see that the work was done. Naturally, Prentise will have to return again in a month or so to supervise the building."

"Furthermore, I acquired a piece of land," Prentise informed her, "from your nephew, Patrick McGregor, about five hundred acres of very choice land, once a tobacco plantation. There is a dilapidated old house on it ready to fall apart. I have ordered it demolished and have drawn up plans for a new mansion to be built to which I can take my Harriet."

"Moreover," Joshua interrupted, "we have purchased an old shipping firm and the wharf that it is on in Savannah. The buildings are quite adequate to be used as storage warehouses and in time can be replaced. Prentise can go at any time and begin setting up the Medallion industry in Savannah."

"Sounds like you had a productive trip," Patricia mentioned, admiring her two nephews with an appraising glance. "Your wives, no doubt, were happy to see you on your return."

"I intend to spend a week in the country with Olivia away from everyone," Joshua said, "to catch up on all the things I have missed while I was gone."

"Moderation is always a good policy, Joshua."

"Perhaps for you, Aunt Patricia. When one has abstained for so long, one has much catching up to do." He poked his brother, "Eh, isn't that so, Brother?"

Prentise straightened, cleared his throat, a strange expression came to his face, tinged with fear. "Yes, I suppose one should."

"What is it, Prentise?" Patricia asked. "Is there something wrong?"

"It's Harriet. I don't quite know what to make of her attitude. She seems different, strange."

105

"Well, I'll tell you for one thing, according to Dr. Ted Ornby, your wife is with child and that is enough to make any woman slightly strange or at least different for the duration of her pregnancy."

"I know that. But Harriet seems as if she's, as if she has not gotten over the old fear that she had. I at times am afraid to touch her because she winces and pulls back from me."

"You've got to become master, Prentise," Joshua said. "You've got to let her know who is the husband and what he demands."

"Well, that's all very bold and bullying of you," Patricia stated, "but I think that Harriet needs a different type of handling, more gentle and considerate. After all, she has gone through much in the past. There have been many unfortunate circumstances. Prentise knew this before he married her. Perhaps he could not anticipate what her moods might be or how she might change. Still there is no doubt in my mind that she is haunted from the past."

"What does Dr. Ted have to say about her condition, Aunt Patricia?"

"I think you had best ask him. In the meantime, tomorrow evening I'm having the entire family in for a dinner. That would be a good time to corner your cousin and find out exactly the problem. I do know that the advice given both by Ted and Daniel Ornby is that Harriet be returned to Savannah as quickly as possible. She is homesick, among other things. Yet it is ill advised that she travel until after the child is born. Now, that may mean that you will be apart from her again. I can only try my best and I can only hope that the others of the family will also help to make her feel that she is loved and protected."

"Might it not be wise to return Harriet to Savannah, risk the perils of traveling on the sea, and get her home to her Aunt Magnolia's house where she may rest the last days of her waiting period in familiar surroundings?"

"Dr. Ted seems convinced that that would not be wise

at this time since she is under a severe emotional stress, and feels that she has not escaped the curse that was put on her."

"What am I to do?" asked Prentise.

"Again, I advise you to speak only with Ted. He's the doctor, he's the man who would know."

Joshua put his arm around his brother's shoulder, "Come along, let's go see Ted now and have the necessary conversation with him."

The party that Patricia planned was elaborate, including not only family but friends as well. The evening was to begin early with supper on the lawn at large tables that the servants had erected for the occasion. All the Ornbys and Phenwicks appeared, along with Arthur Townsend and Raymond Nelson and others of Patricia's entourage. There were more than fifty people mingling that afternoon in the yard.

Patricia went from one to another until she became fatigued and had to sit. The one person she had not interviewed that day was Lillian Phenwick. The greatest part of her concern had been Peter and Nancy, for this was the occasion on which she was going to announce their engagement.

Lillian made a point of seeking out Patricia and held her in conversation over trite matters for more than five minutes.

"I've seen Stuart," Patricia said, "but hasn't Gordon come to the party?"

"He will be along shortly," Lillian said, trying not to give away her apprehensive feeling that she might have been caught at something underhanded. "He and some friends had a project they were working on. He wanted to finish it. He promised to be finished by five."

Why was Patricia suspicious of Lillian's attitude? Was it that she had turned a fiery red and had tightened her lips before forcing a smile, the smile in itself being a peculiarity? Whatever the reason, she could not help but feel that Lillian was harboring guilt.

Peter and Nancy were the toast of the party. They appeared the most joyous couple of all assembled, although Olivia and Joshua came a close second. On the other hand, Prentise looked pained and Harriet seemed weak and pale. She trembled a lot. When people spoke to her, she would answer in muffled tones, gazing down at her fingers or her feet, or anywhere but into their faces. Quickly, she would dart away and try to find a place where she could be by herself. With that many people, it was difficult, and ultimately she ran into first one and then another.

Finally, Olivia, seeing Harriet's distress, invited her into the house and suggested that she go into the library to relax for a while. Excusing themselves from their husbands, the two women went inside. Windows were opened and a fresh late afternoon breeze wafted through. Still Harriet had to use her fan, which she fluttered quickly several times.

"What is it, Harriet? What *is* troubling you?" asked Olivia. "I say, you do not appear to be yourself at all. Are you having pains already? You can't be more than two or three months along."

She sighed. "I don't know. I d'clare, I'm simply at my wit's end. I want to return to Savannah so badly that I can almost feel it. I wish to have my baby down there, not here in Boston. Do you understand?"

"I understand, but Dr. Ted says that it is inadvisable for you to travel at this time."

"What does he know?" Harriet all but shouted. "He doesn't understand th' feelin's I have inside. Glory be, if he could only know how homesick I've become. How I long to see Aunt Maggie and Cousin Patrick and my own mother. She ought to be by my bedside when I have th' baby. I'm sure she'd come. I d'clare, I don't know why I evah decided not to go back with Mr. Phenwick th' last time he went to Savannah. I should have just gone and stayed there. I could have stayed with Aunt Maggie as I always have. We could have stayed together without all

108

this runnin' back and forth, and bein' away from him—not that that bothers me so much."

"Harriet," questioned Olivia, raising an eyebrow, "what do you mean by that?"

"What do I mean by *what?*" Harriet reddened slightly. "Oh, about not missin' Mr. Phenwick that much. Well, to tll you th' truth, I don't really enjoy bein' intimate with him. I'm terribly frightened and it's a painful experience for me. I want it to be over and done with as quickly as possible. Do you understand?"

"No, I can't say that I do. I love my husband very much, and our private moments together are treasured and beautiful to my heart," Olivia replied. "I can't understand why yours and Prentise's aren't."

"Oh, it isn't Mr. Phenwick's fault," she quickly inserted. "It's mine. Mr. Phenwick is every inch a gentleman, and he tries desperately to help me. But you see, it's me. Right here inside of me, it's me. I still see that terrible Elsworth Grayson comin' at me dressed like a woman. I still see other things in my mind that are hateful about men. I nevah should have married in th' first place. I'm just not right. My head, there's somethin' wrong with it. I get crazy thoughts."

Olivia hugged her arms around Harriet and tried to soothe her. As she was doing so, Nancy suddenly burst into the library.

"Oh, I d'clare, here you are. Whatevah's goin' on? Is Harriet all right?" Nancy asked.

"I'm fine, Nancy. I got to feelin' a little poorly—with th' baby, I reckon it is," Harriet replied. "You understand, don't you-all?"

"Is there anythin' I can do, honey? I mean, sugah, you just don't look yourself. I've been meanin' to comment on that evah since we returned," Nancy said. "I hate to see you so unhappy, when I feel so happy and wonderful inside because of Mr. Phenwick and me. Oh, Harriet, be happy for us!"

Harriet answered, "I'm tryin' to be. I really am tryin' to be happy for you-all. It's just me I can't be happy for.

Please, I would like very much to be myself for a little. Why don't you and Miz Phenwick leave me for a while?"

Nancy went to her friend and patted her hand gently. "Very well, why don't you go someplace where you can lie down and maybe get a little rest? I'm sure that's all you need, honey."

Olivia and Nancy saw Harriet to the room on the second floor which she had been occupying. They helped her out of her skirt and into the bed. Then Nancy got a cold cloth and placed it on Harriet's forehead.

"Now you rest, and I'll be back to look in on you in no less than fifteen or twenty minutes. I'm sure you'll feel much better then. Do you want me to have Dr. Ted come up and have a look at you?"

"No, thank you, Nancy, that won't be necessary," Harriet replied feebly. "I think if maybe I just take a little nap. I'll feel more comfortable if you can look in on me from time to time, though, just to see that I'm all right."

"I'll do that, you can be sure of that. Now you rest, do you heah," Nancy said and tiptoed from the room. Olivia closed the door behind them.

Gordon Phenwick arrived at Edward House in a fluster. His pudgy face was red from hurrying. He immediately went around to the garden where the supper party was in progress and, after the greetings to several of his cousins and others his age and slightly older, he went directly to his mother.

"Did you do it?" Lillian asked. "Did you get them?" she continued as she pulled the boy toward the wisteria arbor.

"No, Mother, I couldn't find them. They weren't where Aunt Jane Augusta last put them," Gordon replied. "I looked all over. I tried to leave everything just as I found it so no one would be suspicious."

"What do you mean you didn't find them? She must have become suspicious. That old fool, she says she's intuitive, maybe she is. Maybe she knew what we were going to do." She put her arm around Gordon, a familiarity which she seldom did. "Very well, in that case, I will have to change my tactic and see what further I can find out about the books. In the meantime, you go over and get something to eat and socialize with your brother and his friends. I don't want anyone to be suspicious about your being away. I told them you were off with friends and would be here later. You must confirm that story. We don't want to be caught in an untruth, do we?"

"No, Mother."

It was nearly dusk when Harriet awoke in the large four-poster bed. Her eyes scanned the ceiling. She cried out as stab after stab pained through her body. Helplessly, she lay in bed for ten minutes before the spasms ceased and she was able to gain enough strength to make her way to the window. She braced herself against the sill and leaned forward. Three small Ornby children were playing tag on the lawn beneath the window. She called to them begging them to get someone to help her.

Alarmed, the children went immediately to Dr. Ted and told him about Harriet's call for help. The doctor quickly left the others and with Olivia, who had overheard the conversation, behind him, he made his way to Harriet's room.

On opening the door, he discovered Harriet's unconscious body lying on the floor. With Olivia's help, he placed her back in the bed and began his examination.

Thirty minutes later, leaving Olivia with the stricken girl, Ted went down to the ballroom where the adult guests had gathered now, and quietly and discreetly pulled Prentise and Patricia aside and announced that Harriet was in grave condition.

Dr. Ted said, "I will have to operate in the bedroom." With that he went to make arrangements.

Jane Augusta, who had been sitting nearby and had heard Dr. Ted's announcement, turned suddenly pale as a vision came to her. Patricia, who had noticed Jane Augusta's pallor, stepped over to her and said,

111

"What is it? What do you see in that clairvoyant mind of yours?"

"I see that Harriet will live but she will have an illness for a long time and it will be necessary for her to return to Savannah as quickly as possible. This climate is not good for her."

"You see her having an illness?"

"It is an illness of her mind brought about by fear, and the fear will remain probably for many years. I don't like to say that, Aunt Patricia, but that's what I feel."

"Yes, I know, Patricia replied. She stared over at Prentise, who looked forlorn and lonely, dejected and as if his world were crumbling around him. "Poor Prentise."

Chapter 10

By THE LAST WEEK of August, Joshua and Olivia had left for England. Harriet had not made great improvement, remaining bedridden at Edward House. Still they left confident that Harriet was in good hands with Dr. Ted. Little was made of their departure since at the same time, Peter went with them as far as New York where he had several weeks of extensive business ahead of him.

With Peter away, Patricia took the opportunity to attempt to discover what Nancy's real feelings were toward her nephew. Although she used thorough interrogative methods, she decided to test the girl, enlisting the services of Arthur Townsend and Raymond Nelson, the writer and the artist.

Nancy spend many hours of the day with Harriet, sitting beside her bed, tending to her needs, keeping her spirits up as best she could. But Harriet was in a very depressed state. It wasn't so much because she had lost the baby as it was her state of mind in general. She had a strange reaction to Prentise, and although she loved him very much, she did not believe that she was fulfilling him as a wife should, and that disturbed her.

In the meantime, Nancy did her best to keep a lively spirit although she herself at times felt pains of some unknown physical distress. A cheerful person by nature, Nancy loved to laugh and joke, but there were times during Harriet's illness when she felt that she was sympathizing with her friend and that was perhaps the cause of the sudden little pains, particularly in her shoulder or her right thigh.

"I d'clare, sugah, you look just marvelous today," Nancy exclaimed as she entered the room that afternoon. Harriet was lying listlessly on the pillow, her hair spread out over it. She looked as if she were not particularly interested in life.

"I don't feel very good today, Nancy. If'n you know what I mean?"

"Well, I d'clare, you've simply got to shake loose whatevah's got hold of you, Harriet Pettijohn Phenwick," Nancy said, "you've just got to get back on your feet and be your old self again. Why, Mr. Prentise is not goin' to be happy to see you and lawd knows that Miz Patricia Phenwick is goin' to say if you spend all your time in her house in bed. I d'clare, sometimes I wonder whatevah ails you."

"Sometimes I wonder that too, Nancy," Harriet replied. "You know, for the last two or three days, I've had a recurrin' dream about ol' Mammy."

"Mammy? The darky who raised you most of th' time?"

"Yes," Harriet assured her, "I remember one time Mammy was talkin' to me and there was some strangeness goin' on around th' area and she made mention of th' fact that she thought voodoo was bein' practiced."

"Voodoo?" Harriet rolled her eyes toward her friend.

"That's what she called it, *voodoo*. She believed in it, you know. She told about how people would take and make a wax doll of somebody and dress it in some clothes that were made out of a piece of their clothes, and take a hank of their hair and stuff it in th' head, and stick a pin or several pins in it. Well, th' person whose likeness it was supposed to be, they could feel those pins, only they wouldn't be pins. They might be bullet shots or sword wounds or whips. That's th' way th' darkies used to get even with each other. Sometimes I think they did that on white people too."

"Lawdy, Harriet, whatevah are you goin' on about? Voodoo indeed; why, that's all superstition."

"I wonder if it is, Nancy. Sometimes I'm just not so sure. Sometimes I wonder if maybe there isn't a voodoo doll made of me somewhere that Elsworth Grayson went and had made and might still be in existence. That's why I feel like I do and that's why I lost my baby."

"Hush, hush now, Harriet. You mustn't say such things. You mustn't even think that way. Why, lawsy me, you're goin' to be healthy and all right. There's no wax doll made of you. Even if there was, there's no power in it unless you believed it."

"Maybe there isn't, but somethin's got to be makin' me feel so bad. Somethin's got to be hurtin' me. Just this morning I had terrible cramps in my stomach and I thought I was goin' to be sick, but I wasn't. I felt like I still had the baby inside of me which I don't, and I just felt terrible."

"Well now, you just put that out of your mind, once and for all. Think about some sweet thoughts, flowers or your Mr. Phenwick. He's a very nice man, Harriet. I like him right well," Nancy said. "I think you're downright lucky to have such a fine gentleman for a husband. He loves you very much."

"There's no doubt in my mind that he loves me. I only hope that I'm not a disappointment to him, Nancy. I really do." Harriet turned her head to look toward the window and then glanced back at her friend. "What's happenin' with you and Mr. Phenwick's father?"

"Mr. Phenwick is still in New York, Harriet; he's got business to tend to, but he'll be returnin' home directly. In the meantime, I'm bidin' my time."

"Do you still feel th' same way about him that you did?"

"What do you mean by that?"

"I mean, do you still think that you love him like you did when you was on th' boat?"

Nancy turned away. Her face had paled slightly. She watched her reflection in the ripply mirror. "Why, I believe I like Mr. Phenwick as well as I always have. It was different though when we were at sea. He was so, well, so close to me all of th' time. When a person is that close, you feel him, you feel th' nearness. That nearness makes you want to be near to him. With him away in New York, I sometimes do have doubts in my mind about my feelin's toward him. I mean, there is all that difference in our ages, and I suppose I do love Mr. Phenwick as I always did, but somethin' about him bein' away makes me yearn for him to be back. Yet, I find myself lookin' at other men, too, and that bothers me 'cause I always thought that if you loved a man, other men wouldn't be attractive to you."

"That isn't necessarily so, Nancy," Harriet replied. "Th' fact of th' matter is, I know many a woman who has had eyes for other men—but only eyes, I think." Harriet sighed. "I'll tell you, Nancy, I do have fear inside of me, a very deep and naggin' fear. I believe—now don't you tell this to a soul—but I do believe some sort of voodoo is bein' worked on me. Why else should I lose that baby? Why else should I feel so bad all the time? I believe a curse has been put on me, and I wish it were gone."

Nancy sat on the bed beside her friend and placed her arm around her. "Now, now, sugah, you mustn't think about such things. I d'clare if there is such a thing as voodoo, how could anyone be practicin' it on you? Why, all th' darkies are all down South. There are not many up heah in Boston and th' ones who are heah are free."

"Well, I don't know, Nancy, it's just a fear. I think th' reason I've been dreamin' about Mammy so much is that fear of voodoo. I wouldn't be surprised if I woke up some mornin' and found one of those little old wax dolls with a pin stickin' in it right heah on th' pillow next to me. Of course, if I did, I'd scream my lungs out."

"Please don't think about it any more, Harriet," Nancy said. "I want you to put those thoughts clean out of your head and plum forget about it once and for all." Nancy hugged her. But within herself she, too, had an apprehension about the workings of voodoo. She was trying to put up a brave front for her friend's sake, but it was a facade.

Raymond Nelson and Arthur Townsend arrived at Edward House looking their dapper best, all polished and shiny like the two elegant gentlemen they were. Raymond was carrying a medium-sized, brown-paper-wrapped package. The butler answered the door and showed the two young men to the library.

While waiting, Raymond unwrapped the parcel to reveal a mounted sketch that was quite unlike his usual work. The subject was the hunchbacked man he had encountered several months before in the tavern. There was something grotesque about the rendering; yet in that ugliness there was beauty. Arthur was fascinated.

The door burst open and Patricia came dancing in since she was always proud of the entrances she made. The first thing she cast eyes upon after recognizing the young men was the sketch.

"Oh, Raymond," she exclaimed. "Interesting. It has a kind of moodiness that is not in your other works. You are going to complete it as a painting, aren't you?"

"Would you hang it in your house?" asked Raymond.

"As bizarre as it is, Patricia?" echoed Arthur.

"I don't know about that, but it would be nice for a public display. Perhaps there are those who would care for that type of subject matter. When it's complete I'll gladly purchase it from you and donate it to a museum or some such place."

"You find it objectionable?" Raymond asked, his dark, almost Latin features frowning with concern.

Patricia moved toward him, gently patting him on the hand. "Don't look so upset, dear Raymond. You know I love everything you paint. It is just that your subject is —well—unusual. It is not the sort of thing I would want hanging in my house."

"Maybe after you see the finished painting you will find you like it better," Raymond remarked. "I admit when I first conceived of the idea it repulsed me a little. Why must art always be only of beautiful things? Why can't it portray life as it really is?"

"Do you mean to tell me that this unfortunate image

that you have sketched is the likeness of a living creature? Oh, dear, that is too bad. If you have accurately depicted the person as he is, I can only pray that his soul is not as tormented as the image of him appears that it must be."

"Actually he is not a very disturbed person, I should think," Raymond explained. "He has a remarkable, though somewhat peculiar, sense of humor. He never seemed to be dismal in any way. At times he even made jest of his appearance."

"My nephew Theodore would call that justification. Never mind," Patricia said with a wave of her hand. "You may leave the sketch here in the library for a while. I'll attempt to view it detachedly upon several occasions. Furthermore, I will ask my friends their opinions. I seriously doubt that I would want such a creature hanging in Edward House."

"Why did you ask us here, Patricia?" Arthur asked, his curiosity up and desirous of changing the topic.

"Because I have a little assignment for both of you," Patricia replied. "I'll not mince words, but come to the point. As you know, an announcement has been made that Nancy Cox is to marry my nephew. Although I dearly love the child, I have certain reservations about her. I would like to put a little temptation in her way to see how she reacts to it. If she is going to be the type of woman who is attracted to every man who comes waltzing by, she would not be an ideal match for my nephew, if you understand what I mean."

"That sounds reasonable," Arthur stated. "But don't I detect that you are suggesting something underhanded?"

"Underhanded? Yes," Patricia returned. "I don't mind admitting to that. There are many things I do that are slightly underhanded, sub rosa, as they say, but I *do* get results."

"What do you want us to do?" Raymond asked, taking his attention from the painting.

"I want you to make conversation with the young lady, turn on all your masculine charms and see how she reacts. In other words, I want to put temptation before her. I want you two to play it to the hilt. The fact is I want to know exactly what happens."

"But that's deceitful, Patricia," Arthur replied. "How could you expect us to do something like this to such a nice young lady as Nancy?"

"It is merely a test, Arthur. I want to find out the stuff she is really made of, to see if she can be trusted. After all, there are many years' difference between Peter and her. A young girl could easily be attracted to young men, certainly to handsome young men such as yourselves. I would like you to attempt to form a liaison with her."

"Both of us?" Arthur asked.

"At the same time?" questioned Raymond.

Patricia laughed. Sometimes the members of her entourage were naïve and innocent to the point of being humorous. "Whatever is necessary. I do assume that you will proceed with reservations and discretion. After all, I do not want to make a wayward hussy of the child, I simply want to see what her reaction is. You two being the romantic figures that you are certainly could tempt her."

"Playing the role of Satan? Is that what you would have us do?" Arthur asked, then laughed.

"If that's the way you like to put it, except it's a game. I want you to think of it as a game."

"A game? Playing with a person's emotions like that?" Raymond inquired, sitting in a chair and sprawling himself forward. "I think that's being a little cruel and certainly inconsiderate of the girl's feelings."

"I'm not asking you to fall in love with her nor to make her fall in love with you," Patricia countered. "As a matter of fact, I want you to handle it all most delicately. I merely want to know how she reacts to men other than Peter. If you set up a situation or a series of situations wherein you are alone with her, together or individually, you can report back to me what her reactions are."

"Well, as far as I'm concerned that's underhanded, Patricia," Raymond replied.

119

"Underhanded or not, I will make it financially worth-while. Just be your sweet gregarious selves. Present romantic pictures and see what her reactions are. That is all."

Separately and together, Raymond and Arthur each found moments to be alone with Nancy. Arthur entertained her with his poetry and read several of his short stories to her. She was intrigued and found him a great diversion. Raymond sketched her. When they had conversation, they spoke about art or drawing and the technique of doing oil painting, which Nancy found extremely interesting. She also found the men themselves interesting. She was physically attracted to them, yet in a very platonic way. Both men, although they were handsome and carried themselves with studied dignity, were not the epitome of what she imagined a man to be. In her mind's eye a man had a certain amount of brawn and muscle, determination to accomplish physical things. These aesthetic young men possessed none of those qualities. Certainly not as Peter did. So she played along with what was happening for nearly a week. It was all a little game. As far as Nancy was concerned, it was even more of a game.

One morning Nancy was invited into the sun-room to have breakfast with Patricia. It was usually Patricia's habit to eat alone in her room, perferably in bed. On this occasion she had breakfast in the sun-room.

"I d'clare, I didn't even know you ate breakfast, Miz Phenwick," she said as she went to the table that had been laid for them.

"I always eat breakfast. I wouldn't miss it," Patricia replied, helping herself to food and passing it to Nancy. "There is a little matter that has come to my attention."

"A little matter? Whatevah could that be?"

"A little matter of you and Mr. Nelson and Mr. Townsend."

"Mr. Nelson and Mr. Townsend? What about those

two young men? They're very nice and I find them quite interestin'."

"You find them interesting to be with. You mean physically interesting? Do they arouse you, Nancy?" Patricia asked.

"Oh, I wouldn't say that they arouse me particularly. They're fun to be with and they like to laugh and they know so many things about th' arts. Why, it just makes my head spin to hear them talk. And I do love Mr. Townsend's poetry. It's so—well—it's so romantic and beautiful."

"You find his poetry romantic?"

"Oh yes, he says such lovely things, and he has a way of turnin' a phrase that is just eloquent."

"And Mr. Townsend as a person? What do you think of him?"

"Oh, I think he's a very nice man. Why, I have nothin' but th' most respect for him in th' world."

"Has he ever attempted to get familiar with you?"

"Familiar with me? Lawsy, I don't think so. Well, we do sit close when he's readin' his poetry. I wouldn't call that bein' familiar."

"He doesn't try to touch you?"

"Not directly. Sometimes he puts his hand on my hand."

"And do you receive a reaction to that?"

"Not anything great. Sometimes it's just a friendly pat, and I do enjoy that. Oh, I do apologize for soundin' flippant, but I assure you that I am an innocent victim of a gentleman's attention. Why, even Mr. Nelson has put his hand upon me on occasion and I've gently eased it away after a few minutes. But normally. I don't think that I'm enticin' him, if that's what you're gettin' at."

"Don't apologize, Nancy, don't ever apologize. That's the only thing that angers me, when a person apologizes. It shows weakness. Very well. You, Mr. Nelson and Mr. Townsend have become friends. Through them you have gotten a better appreciation of the arts. Not that I ever expect you to be aesthetic, but I am pleased to see that you have an awareness. That is a first step in acquiring knowledge and interest. It would please me if you became interested in the arts."

"Please you, Miz Phenwick?"

"Yes, because that is the type of person I am. I really had hoped to find someone with similar likes."

"You mean that Mr. Townsend and Mr. Nelson were really pursuin' me simply to make me acquainted with the aesthetic way of life?"

"No, I shouldn't think that was the reason at all. After all, they're perfectly normal young men. They should be a kind of inspiration in more ways than one if you know what I mean."

Beginning to become uncomfortable in the situation, Nancy wanted to change the subject. "Well, I d'clare, I was just up to see Harriet. I don't think she's goin' to get much better while she's heah in Boston. She belongs back in Savannah. She keeps tellin' me about it and I realize that that is exactly where she should be because she's just not happy heah."

"Prentise is no longer here. He has had to return to Savannah himself and Harriet wasn't strong enough to make the move."

"Weak or strong, I think she should go back to Savannah as soon as she can. She's not goin' to be happy until she does."

"And what of you, Nancy? Do you want to go back to Savannah, too?"

"I might like to go there for a visit now and again, but I don't really think I want to settle back there. I'm very fond of Boston. And, of course, Mr. Peter Phenwick is here, too. And *you* are, and th' people I have become close to. Why, I was never as close to any people in th' South as I am to the people up heah."

"Thank you for saying so, Nancy. I feel very close to you in many ways," Patricia replied, and continued. "Now that you are here, if you intend to stay, I suggest that we start tutoring you out of that thick Southern drawl of yours. Although not unpleasant, it points you out as being an alien."

"Lawsy, what accent are you talkin' about? I d'clare, I don't know what it is. I don't have one that I know of. I just talk like myself."

Patricia laughed. "Yes, you talk like yourself, my dear, and it is very pleasant at most times; however, it does stick out like a wart on a finger, if you know what I mean."

"Well, I d'clare, I suppose I must do somethin' about it, but I don't know who will teach me."

"I'll teach you myself, Nancy," Patricia said, "if you will become my student. I was born in Alexandria, Virginia. When I first came to Boston, I had an accent, too —not as heavy as yours. I know it doesn't seem heavy to you, but I went to a private school here. Among the subjects I had to take was elocution."

"Elo . . . what?"

"How to speak properly. I never have regretted that, for no one guesses I'm from the South. I think that I have mastered the language problem very well. And I would like to teach you and give you full advantage of my knowledge."

"I believe I'd like that, Miz Phenwick. I believe I could learn, too. I'm said to have a pretty good ear 'cause somebody could hum a tune and I could hum it practically right after them without too many notes wrong."

Again Patricia laughed. She liked Nancy. She put her hand to hers and patted it gently. "Nancy, while Peter's away, I want you to enjoy yourself with Arthur and Raymond and anyone else who comes around. As a matter of fact, there is a favor you can do for me."

"What is it?"

"You can perhaps help both Arthur and Raymond to become more aware of their manliness. They have a tendency to be a little too aesthetic at times. Perhaps if they found that a young lady like yourself was interested, not in an intimate way necessarily, but as a friend, they

123

might make an effort to project their masculinity, develop it to a finer-honed quality."

"I d'clare, I don't know quite what you're talkin' about, Miz Phenwick, but if there is anythin' I can do for you I'll gladly do it. You know that, now," Nancy said.

"Yes, I believe you, my dear." Patricia squeezed the hand tighter. "There is one other thing I would like to speak to you about and that is Peter."

"Mr. Phenwick, what about him?"

"You know, of course, that he is much older than you are, don't you, Nancy?"

"I do, but that doesn't bother me none. He's still a very handsome man, and a delightful person to be with."

"Peter has always been my favorite nephew. I've been remarkably close to him," Patricia added quietly, her eyes staring directly into Nancy's. "I never want to see him hurt again. He has lived with much misery and he has overcome it. If I felt that there was any doubt in your mind about marrying him, I would discourage it. If you do not love him fully, I would suggest that you wait until you discover that you do. You must be fair to Peter, for he is a darling."

"I've had many thoughts contrary to others about Mr. Phenwick, Miz Phenwick, I will tell you that," Nancy related. "But I can't honestly say that I love him with all my heart and soul because I do realize he is older than me, and bein' older, well . . ."

"Think about it, Nancy. Just remember my words. If you marry Peter Phenwick, you must give him your all and be faithful to him until the end of his days."

"Be faithful? Why, it never occurred to me not to be faithful even when Mr. Nelson and Mr. Townsend were pursuin' me. I was always very cautious."

"Remain cautious, my dear, and be true to your own heart for my sake, for your sake, and for Peter's."

Chapter 11

THERE WERE A FEW WARM DAYS left in the latter part of September, days when picnics could still be enjoyed in the noonday sun. The first frost had come. Trees had begun to change color. The oranges and red were first. But it was a premature frost, and the days were comfortably warm and delightful. On a particular Saturday afternoon, which was remarkably sunny, a joyousness seemed to fill the air although in the distance, dark clouds were appearing. Nancy accepted an invitation to go on a picnic with Arthur and Raymond. They took a carriage and Arthur drove while Raymond and Nancy sat in the back. He had brought along a sketch book and Arthur had brought along his poetry to read. It was to be an idyllic situation, an afternoon of aesthetic enjoyment. Remembering Patricia's words, Nancy did not know precisely how she could bring about the desired transformation of the young men. Still she thought she might try her womanly charms on them.

They reached a picnic spot in an open field where several tall maples, elms and other trees stood. Partly shady, partly sunny, for the shade was just a bit too cool and the sun was just right. After spreading the blanket, Nancy took the food from the basket and laid it out.

"Why, I d'clare, Mr. Nelson, what are you pointin' that chicken leg at me for?"

"Am I pointing it? I didn't mean to. I shouldn't talk with my hands full," he laughed.

"That's better than speaking with your mouth full," Arthur inserted. "Raymond is notorious for doing that; sometimes you can't understand a word he is saying."

"Well, I d'clare, you gentlemen sound like a couple of ruffians when you're out like this."

"Oh, ruffians we are," Raymond explained, "not the aesthetic delicate young men we appear to be. We're more like stevedores at a time like this."

"I d'clare, stevedores, my, my, my, what a situation. I would never have taken you for a stevedore in my life. Maybe a boathand or somethin' like that, not a stevedore," Nancy said wide-eyed.

"And why wouldn't you take us for being stevedores?" Arthur questioned.

"Well, stevedores are more muscular and—well, masculine."

"And don't you think we're muscular and masculine?"

"Take off your coat, Raymond."

"Oh, I d'clare, I didn't mean to have a demonstration right here on th' spot."

Raymond removed his coat. His shirt was loose-fitting so that it did not show his physique beneath.

"Shall I remove my shirt as well?"

"Oh, I d'clare, I don't know that I could stand to see a naked chest right heah in the middle of th' country," Nancy cried, feigning innocence.

"Well, I declare that I'm going to do it," Raymond said, unfastening his shirt and pulling the tail of it from his trousers.

"Oh, lawsy, no, Mr. Nelson, I'll faint dead away at th' sight of a naked chest, I swear I will."

Arthur removed his coat. "How about me? Would you like to see me, Nancy?"

"I can see you perfectly enough just as you are, Mr. Townsend," she replied.

Arthur unbuttoned his shirt. "Wouldn't you like to see more of me?"

"I don't believe so, but if you gentlemen want to go

126

around with your shirts unbuttoned that's quite all right with me. It doesn't bother me in th' least."

"I know, why don't we play a game?"

"A game?" Arthur asked. "What kind of a game, Raymond?"

"Suppose we all three blindfold ourselves and turn around three times and begin walking toward each other. The first who reaches Nancy gets a kiss."

"Well, what if we all go in different directions? Why, I could wander all th' way to Cambridge if I was not careful where I was goin' and wouldn't even know I was goin'."

"We all have a sense of direction, and turning three times around can't confuse us that much. I think it will be fun, don't you, Nancy?"

"Well, if that's what you-all think. What will we use for blindfolds?"

"What about the white linen napkins? They'll make fine blindfolds."

The three applied the blindfolds, adjusting them so that they covered their eyes. Then, having given them sufficient time, Nancy raised hers slightly so that a crack of light came beneath. She could see the images of the other two.

"All right, now turn around three times, just be sure you make a full circle and we'll all be facing each other. One, two, three."

The three turned, then with hands outstretched as if feeling for direction, they moved toward each other. However, Nancy went to a tree, where she stood and watched as the young men came in contact with each other. They were about to kiss when Nancy began laughing loudly. The blindfolds were pulled off.

"You tricked us," Raymond said. "You weren't playing the game properly."

"I thought it was so amusin' th' way it turned out, didn't you? It was funny to see you two with your arms just about to cling to each other and your lips comin' so close. Why, it made me giggle, I was tickled that much."

127

"All right, this time," Arthur said, "we will all wear blindfolds. I will adjust yours so that there is no trickery."

The blindfolds were put in place, Nancy's being secured just a little too tight for comfort. This time she could not see beneath. Arthur turned her around three times and then told her to come and get them.

"Well, lawsy, I don't know where you're at," she said, reaching out blindly, her arms flailing in various directions. Both Raymond and Arthur could see a faint image of her coming near them and they darted out of her way.

"I d'clare, you must be able to see, and I can't. Why, if I could just get hold of you once, you'd know."

As she said that, the two men moved toward her, coming so that she put one hand on each chest. Their blouses were unbuttoned. "Oh, lawsy me," she said, letting her fingers sweep from clavicle to sternum, "I d'clare, I do feel naked flesh! I must have found one or more of you. It must be more 'cause my hands are touchin' at such a distance, it couldn't be just one." Her hand remained for a few moments gently soothing over. "Let me see who is who? On my left is—ah, Mr. Nelson, I do believe, and on my right—well, it would have to be Mr. Townsend."

"You're wrong, you don't know our chests."

"Wrong?"

Arthur grabbed her hand and held it at his bosom while Raymond put his hand to her arm and gently held it in place.

"Do you like the feel of us?" Raymond asked.

"Well, I d'clare, it's quite a manly feel, but skin is skin and chest is chest. My chest, of course, is different than yours."

"But do you like the feel of us?"

"Well, I must say there's a certain excitement to it, but it's nothin' new."

"Nothin' new?" Arthur asked. "Don't tell me we're out with a hussy."

"A hussy? Why, what a thing to say! I do d'clare,"

Nancy said, trying to pull free of the men. "I do wish you'd let me have my hands back."

"Don't you want to really explore us?"

"Oh, lawsy, no! I don't think so, not today. It's a nice samplin'. Don't you realize I'm betrothed? I'm not really inclined to—well—you know."

At that moment, a clap of thunder rolled through the sky.

"Lawsy me, what was that?"

"Thunder," Arthur said.

The blindfolds were quickly pulled from their faces. A jag of lightning slashed through the air, making a cracking sound. Almost behind it came another rumble of thunder. Nancy moved to the men, huddling close for protection against the thunder. Suddenly the clouds opened and rain fell in enormous drops all around them.

"Quickly, get under the trees! They will protect us for a while."

The three ran to beneath a tree and huddled again by the trunk. This time Nancy was pleased to feel the solid flesh beside her. It meant protection.

"Oh, lawsy me, my scarf is out there where we were playin'. I need it for my hair or it will get soppin' wet."

"I'll get it for you," Raymond said.

"Oh dear, you'll be soaked to th' skin yourself."

"Never mind that," he said, running out to where the scarf had fallen.

Another crack of lightning came and as it did, it touched Raymond and flattened him to the ground.

"Goodness gracious, what has happened to him? Th' man was hit by th' lightnin'."

"Yes, I can see that he was," Arthur said, terror in his voice.

"Whatevah will we do about it? We can't just let him stay there."

"We daren't go out until the lightning moves over."

"But lightnin' nevah hits th' same place twice, Mr. Townsend. I think you should go help your friend. I think we both should. Give me that napkin you were

129

usin' for a blindfold and I'll wrap it around my head."

The rain was coming down with great force as the two ran toward where Raymond had fallen. Arthur bent quickly to his knee to examine him. "He's unconscious. It knocked him out."

"Are you sure it's just knocked him out and not killed him? He must have been smacked pretty hard by that jolt of lightnin'."

"I feel a pulse beat. I think he's still alive. Of course he is."

"Then maybe we better drag him over to beneath th' tree."

"You yourself said lightning doesn't strike the same place twice."

"Well, of course it doesn't strike th' same place twice, but we can't leave him out heah in all this rain. He'll be soaked through to th' skin. Besides, if we get him over on his back and prop him up against th' tree, he'll come out of it."

Together, Nancy and Arthur were able to drag Raymond to the tree; but no matter what they did, applying a wet cloth to his brow, rubbing his hands, he did not revive. The storm was short-lived and the rain quickly moved over beyond where they were. They could see it going over the fields and beyond in a northerly direction.

"Now what do we do?" Nancy asked. "Should we put him in th' carriage and drive back to town?"

"I'm not all that strong, Nancy," Arthur complained. "Can you drive the carriage?"

"Well, I don't think I can, I'm not too good with horses."

"In that case, I'll take the carriage and go back into town and find Dr. Ted or someone else to help me. You stay here with Raymond and see if you can bring him around. It shouldn't take me more than fifteen or twenty minutes. By then he probably will have regained consciousness anyway."

"Very well, if'n you say so, Mr. Townsend," Nancy replied, "but do hurry. I don't like bein' out heah by myself, especially with Mr. Nelson passed out this way."

"It's all right, Nancy. I'll be back as quickly as possible," Arthur declared, getting into the carriage and driving for town. He only briefly waved back and then the carriage was out of sight down the road.

Nancy sat for nearly five minutes staring at Raymond Nelson. She thought he was an attractive man, she always had. His dark coloring, almost swarthy appearance, gave him a Latin romantic look. She had not seen many Latins, but she had seen pictures and that was enough to make her decide that he was, indeed, a handsome man and probably a very romantic man at that. She wiped the wet napkin over his brow several times and as she did, she pushed the tousled hair back from his face. It was a very pretty face, she thought, and she liked the touch of it. Most of all she liked the fact that he was unconscious and that she could explore with her fingers the feel of the texture of his skin and the contour of his bone structure. Her hands slipped down to his throat and over a rather prominent Adam's apple.

Although she could tell he was breathing, she put her ear to his heart and listened. There was definitely a regular heartbeat. Finally, she let her hand play down to where the heart was, slipping beneath his shirt and touching it softly to be sure that what she heard was actually there. She liked the feel of his young smooth skin with only traces of hair sprouting about. Then she gently pushed the blouse aside, first to the left, then to the right, and gazed at the torso that he had been eager to exhibit only a short while before. Not a muscular torso, but handsome.

She pushed the blouse to his shoulders so that in effect his entire upper torso was exposed. Her glance rolled over it, examining as if she were admiring a forbidden object. Then in the upper left-hand part of his chest above the pectoral muscle, she saw a scar in the shape of an X, the same lines, bonelike in appearance. A sudden shriek of panic jolted through her as she recognized that symbol from the past. "Lawsy me," she exclaimed to herself, "it's a voodoo sign. Th' same one that was on that dreadful note I received on my dresser and th' same as th' crossbones that were on my bed on th' ship. This lovely man, can he possibly be a disciple of Satan?"

She further explored his body, looking for other marks. There was a mole, four freckles—no further scars on the upper torso. Looking about to see that she was not being observed, she gently unfastened his trousers and lowered them to the base of his torso. She found nothing further as far as scars or marks were concerned.

A sudden thought came over her. She rose and went to a leather bag which the artist carried and in which he kept his sketching supplies: pencils, charcoal. Hurriedly, she fumbled through it until her hand found a scarf. A scarf she recognized as being one of her own. It was wrapped in a wad and she could tell that there was something within it. Pulling it out of the bag, she cautiously unwrapped it. Again, a shriek of terror went through her. What she found was a wax effigy of herself. The likeness was not good, but the hair was hers. The dress material that was crudely wrapped around and tied with a string was that of one of her better party dresses. Perhaps part of the hem had been removed to make it. The doll was no more than four inches tall. There was no doubt in her mind—it was meant to be a likeness of herself. She examined her own hair. Had someone taken tresses of it, strands from her hairbrush, and matted them to make a wiglike creation for the image? A cold, terrified feeling went through her as she quickly rewrapped the doll and started to return it to the leather bag. On second thought, she pulled it out again and unwrapped it. Lifting the skirt, she discovered two pins plunged into the thighs of the wax doll. Jerking the pins free, she felt a pain of response in her own thighs, yet it was a sensation of release.

Hurriedly, she rewrapped the object in the scarf and returned it to Raymond's leather bag. Turning, she stared at the man who was still unconscious under the tree. Could that beautiful person be an agent of Satan?

132

Was this artist friend of Patricia Phenwick's really a devil worshiper, a practitioner of voodoo?

Slowly she rose from her crouched position beside the leather bag and moved back to where Raymond was propped against the tree. Was this man some kind of a warlock? A man, as Mammy had said years before, who had made a pact with the devil to do the devil's work to cause evil to happen to others? Leaning against the tree, she only occasionally glanced down at the man, fear thumping through her.

A few moments later—or was it longer than that?—she had lost all concept of time because her mind was disturbed by what she had discovered—she saw the carriage on the horizon. Immediately, she went back to the bag and took the scarf-wrapped effigy from it. Removing the dress material, she ripped it into three pieces, scattering them into the winds. Next came the hair, which she tossed away. Then she broke the pieces of wax which had a terrible odor as if it had been mixed with dung. Scratching holes in the ground with her bare fingers, she buried each part separately so that they were not in any way connected. She covered them with the soil and tapped them down hard with her shoe to be certain the pieces were solidly buried. She wished on second thought that she had done the same with the costume and the hair, but they had blown with the wind going in separate directions.

What had she done with the pins? Thrown them away? Where? She felt she had to bury them, too, completely to destroy the creation of Satan that had been made in her likeness.

Moments later, the carriage arrived. Stuart and Gordon Phenwick were with Arthur. All three leaped from the carriage and ran to where Nancy was standing, still stomping her feet on the earth. Because of the distraught expression he saw on her face, Arthur put his hands to Nancy's shoulders while the two brothers went to examine Raymond.

"What's the matter, Nancy? Are you all right?" questioned Arthur.

"I do believe I am," she replied, her voice quivering with a mixture of fear and rage. "I've just been standin' heah in th' sun tryin' to get warm."

"Stomping your feet?"

"They got real cold. I haven't got time to talk about me," she said, "I've got to get over there and see that Mr. Nelson gets to th' doctor. I can't revive him no way."

Arthur left the girl and went to the spot where his friend Raymond Nelson was lying. Immediately, he could not help but observe that his friend's clothing was askew, particularly that his trousers were unfastened. Upon discovering this he glanced back at Nancy. The thoughts that came to his mind were suspicious, at least. Had she molested the unconscious man? What difference did that make? The important thing was to get him into the carriage and back to town.

"Looks like he was burned," Stuart said as he knelt beside Raymond. "I believe the three of us can get him into the carriage and back so Uncle Ted can have a look at him."

"You're right," Arthur said, again looking back at Nancy.

The three with some effort managed to get Raymond into the carriage and propped against the side. Arthur got in beside him so that he was in the middle and Nancy got in on the far side. She was still trembling and staring remotely out into the horizon as Stuart and Gordon got into the driver's seat. Within moments they were riding down the road, Stuart pushing the horses as fast as he dared for it was bumpy and the jolting could be uncomfortable.

Arthur had his arm around his friend trying to keep his head from banging against the side of the carriage. He had managed to button his shirt and trousers. His coat was put over the front of him to keep him warm.

Nancy sat strangely silent in her corner, barely touching against Arthur as the carriage moved. But there were moments when the jolting caused them to come in contact. Finally, Arthur turned to Nancy. His suspicions had not diminished.

Arriving in town, Stuart directed the carriage immediately to Dr. Ted's office. Again, the three, with the help of an assistant of Dr. Ted's were able to get Raymond into the office, where he was placed on an examination table and the kind doctor began his work.

Nancy sat in an outer room, trembling now. She was wet, her hair stringing in her face. Most of all she wore a distraught expression, one that Arthur could not decipher. What had frightened her so? The entire experience of the lightning? Or had something occurred when he had gone to get help? Nancy tried for a smile, but she was weak with fear. Her body quivered and she seemed to have a chill. The only thing she could see in her mind's eye was that voodoo symbol that she had seen on Raymond's upper chest. She wondered since Raymond and Arthur were such close friends, if Arthur, too, might not be in cahoots with Satan. A greater fear came over her as she sat in the same room with that man.

Chapter 12

RECUPERATING AND RELISHING the attention that he was getting, Raymond Nelson remained in bed for nearly a week. Curiously, Nancy went to visit him several times, and avoided mentioning the picnic as much as possible. Few references were made to it and the fun that they had had prior to the time Raymond was struck by lightning. She carefully maintained a pleasant attitude, never once indicating that she had observed the scar on the man's chest. She never let on that any sort of impropriety might have occurred.

On the other hand, she encountered Arthur Townsend on several occasions that week. At each meeting a twinkling insinuation came to his eyes whenever Raymond's name was mentioned. That annoyed Nancy, but she refused to make an issue of the matter. Instead she maintained a congenial attitude and pretended, at least as far as Arthur was concerned, that the incident had not occurred and that Raymond's shirt was opened merely because that was the way it had been when he had fallen. She did not attempt to justify the fact that his trousers were unbuttoned.

Arthur tried on several occasions to get Nancy alone on the excuse of wanting to take a walk or to take a ride. She was not in the mood to fraternize with the man, not while he still thought those things about her reputation. Surely that was what was motivating him.

Harriet, too, was bedridden most of that week. Despondent. Old fears returned to her along with unfortunate pictures from the past. Somehow, in her tormented mind, she was convinced that the loss of her baby was a kind of retribution for having been accosted by black Tom Cleghorn and bearing his child when she was only twelve years old herself. At times, she even questioned her love for Prentise, feeling guilty because their child had been prematurely born dead, guilt in that she had caused her husband grief and some sort of disgrace by not being able to give him a child. She spent many hours in tears remorsefully lamenting her inadequacies.

Nancy called on Harriet as often as she could, spending much time reading to her, talking, telling of her aspirations. She also explained her confusion as far as her love for Peter was concerned. Had too many people put doubts in her mind about the difference in years? The thought that she would be married to him possibly only a short while before he made a transition disturbed her. Still she argued within herself that if she were to have children by him she would be contributing to the Phenwick family and basically to her own happiness. She even rationalized that if Peter were to go before too many years, she would certainly be young enough to marry again and wealthy enough to have whatever type of husband she liked. At no time did she want to feel that she was simply marrying Mr. Phenwick for his money or his name, but for the fact that she was very much in love with him.

Nancy told Harriet of the picnic, but declined to give details other than to mention that Raymond Nelson had been struck by lightning.

Touched with the feel of autumn, more and more leaves were turning color. On leaving Edward House one Thursday afternoon, a slight chill in the wind, Nancy decided to make further acquaintance with the one woman in the Phenwick family who might shed light on the strange markings that she had seen on Raymond's chest.

Jane Augusta Ornby-Clark lived in a large, roomy house which could hardly be called a mansion. Many of the rooms were already closed off for the winter. They were rarely used anymore. She kept only the downstairs rooms heated and a bedroom for sleeping. The upstairs rooms were locked, the furniture covered, and would not be opened and aired again until spring was well into season.

"Why, Miss Cox," Jane Augusta exclaimed, "what a pleasant surprise seeing you! You're just in time for tea."

"I didn't come for tea, Miz Clark," Nancy said. "I actually came to visit for a spell, if'n you don't mind. I have a few things I would like to discuss with you, if it's all th' same."

"My dear, we can discuss them over tea," kindly Jane Augusta said. "Won't you come in? Take off your cloak, and we will sit in the warm parlor. I've had a fire laid since early morning. The nippiness in the air has put a little chill in my bones."

"Yes, I d'clare, autumn is certainly comin' on fast, isn't it? Why th' trees are so lovely and beautiful, all those reds. The yellows will be comin' after, I suppose."

"Yes. I like the autumn," Jane Augusta said as she led Nancy into her tidy parlor. "It's one of my favorite times of the year except that it always is a prelude to winter. I'm not so fond of that season anymore. There are times I can recall when the winter months used to titillate my fancy, and I enjoyed sledding. Oh, but never mind, we all grow older and the joints get a little creaky with aches and what not. Are you sure I can't fix you some tea?"

"Well, I do think that's right neighborly of you. I mean, I am a little cold from bein' outside."

"Then you sit there right by the fire. I'll only be a moment."

Jane Augusta returned from the kitchen with a tray and tea things, a plate of biscuits and some sweet ginger. "I do keep servants," she said, "but not full time anymore. I don't need them living in. They come and work and go about their own business. My brother seems to think I should have at least a maid with me, but I don't know. There's something about being in a house alone with one's memories that makes it a little irritating to have someone constantly around. I'm not helpless, I can do my own cooking and take care of myself."

"You certainly can, Miz Clark," Nancy said, "and it is a lovely house you have here. I think it is perfectly quaint."

"Why, thank you, Nancy Cox," Jane Augusta replied. "You know, I would very much like to call you Nancy, if I may. I think Mrs. Clark and Miss Cox sounds too formal. I don't like to think of so much formality among my own family."

"There are several things I would like to talk to you about, and I don't really relish talkin' to a stranger about them. If'n I thought of you as *Aunt* Jane Augusta, it would be much easier for me," Nancy stammered. "I'm not makin' a great deal of sense by sayin' that but that's how I feel."

"You're making quite good sense, my dear," Jane Augusta said as she handed the girl a cup of tea and passed the plate of biscuits.

"Thank you kindly, Aunt Jane Augusta," Nancy remarked taking the tea and one of the biscuits.

"What do you wish to discuss with me?" asked Jane Augusta, pouring a cup of tea for herself.

"Well, I really don't know how to begin."

"Is it about Peter? I suspect it might be. You're concerned because Peter is much older than you, and you're wondering about your marriage to him, aren't you?"

"That isn't exactly what I wanted to talk about. But as long as it came up first, I will mention that I do have thoughts in that direction," Nancy replied. "I have uncertainty, if'n you know what I mean."

"You're still just a girl and Peter is a middle-aged man. I will tell you this, my dear, despite the fact that Peter is my cousin. I think he is one of the finest men in the whole world. He's always been good to me, especially when I lost Eustace. He was so understanding, gentle. He called several times to see what he could do for me. He was closer to me than my own brothers—and you know how close my brothers are to me."

"Oh, I d'clare, I know he's a righteous gentleman,"

140

Nancy replied. "He is kindness itself. He is so very gentlemanly. I do admire him."

"Then what is the problem?"

"Well, I just have a question in my mind, that's all. It really shouldn't be there, I reckon, because I find him much more interestin' than any other man I've met in Boston or in Savannah for that matter. He's—well—he just does somethin' to me inside. Why, I feel all excited when I'm near him."

Jane Augusta laughed. "And the other young men don't fill you with that excitement, Nancy?"

"Well, I tell you, Aunt Jane Augusta, sometimes they do and sometimes they don't. It just depends on how I set my mind. I mean, I do find other men attractive, but only from a casual point of view. I simply enjoy lookin' at them. Then I think to myself what would it be like bein' married to a man like that, and I have second thoughts and third thoughts and sometimes even fourth thoughts. I realize I would much prefer bein' with Mr. Phenwick than with any of those others. Why, do you know that Mr. Townsend and Mr. Nelson are always pursuin' me? I don't think they're all that interested. It's kind of a game they're playin' like maybe Miz Patricia Phenwick put them up to somethin'. Do you know what I mean?"

Again, Jane Augusta laughed, chuckling as she sipped her tea.

"You are on to Aunt Patricia, aren't you? Well, that is her way. She likes to maneuver people, and if in maneuvering she manages to make little arrangements, that's fine, too."

"Well, I d'clare, it does seem peculiar," Nancy said, then drank again from her teacup, casting a sharp look at the fireplace and the flame that was dancing lightly over the log.

"Now then, what is the real reason you came to see me, Nancy?" asked Jane Augusta perceptively.

"Th' real reason, why I d'clare, it's difficult for me to get to it directly. It's kind of peculiar and—well—I suppose I might as well come right out and tell you. You see,

I heard that you were—I think th' word is 'clairvoyant' or somethin' like that . . ."

"I do have a few moments of clairvoyancy," Jane Augusta admitted, gently setting her cup on the table, folding her hands and staring directly into Nancy's face. "Why is this important to you, my child?"

"Well, because of certain things that have happened," Nancy replied. She then went into an animated narration of finding the crossed bones on her bed on the ship and the note she had received with the same symbol on it, as well as the scar she had discovered on Raymond Nelson.

"I would say that these were all mysterious circumstances, Nancy," Jane Augusta remarked, raising an eyebrow and wearing a curious expression, "perplexing, at best."

" 'Perplexing' is not the word for it, Aunt Jane Augusta, it's down right scary," Nancy replied. "I understand there are some books with somethin' about matters of th' occult, and realize they are in your possession. Perhaps there might be somethin' in them that might tell about this."

"What makes you think that what you related to me would have anything to do with the occult, Nancy?" asked the older lady.

"It's kind of a hunch I have," Nancy replied. "It seems to me there's somethin' mysterious about this and a little supernatural, if'n you know what I mean."

"Supernatural?" Jane Augusta questioned. "The bones on the cabin bed were probably placed there as a prank. The note also may have been a prank. I suspect there was nothing supernatural about it. As for the scar—well—many young men have scars and tattoos upon their person that may have come from some childhood ritual."

"Well, I know for a fact bones have to do with voodoo, Aunt Jane Augusta," Nancy commented. "I remember th' black woman who practically raised Harriet—we all called her Mammy—used to tell us about voodoo among th' nigras. It did disturb us because she had a way of widenin' her eyes and makin' them almost pop outa her head when she'd tell us. She'd say, 'You-all better watch

142

out or dat dere ol' boogyman'll gitya.' Then she'd tell about these ladies down in th' swamps who would toss bones. Then they'd read th' design of the scattered bones. I remember I asked her more than once what that was called and she said, 'Honeychild, dat dere's voodoo.'"

"Voodoo? I don't know if Rosea Hackleby ever wrote at length about that subject," Jane Augusta remarked. "Fortunately, I have had her books edited for publication and copies made. The copies are at the printer. I still have the originals put away." She sat back in the chair and put her old hands together. A faraway expression came to change her face. "May I tell you something, Nancy?"

"Why, certainly, Aunt Jane Augusta. "Whatevah you would like to."

"I never speak much of him—not anymore—my late husband Eustace Clark. He was a seagoing man and an adventurer who was killed during a whaling accident. However, Eustace had had several occasions in his youth to make trips to Africa. Sometimes from various different ports, he brought back many trinkets, as he called them. He once claimed to have witnessed a voodoo ceremony. Later, while in the West Indies, he encountered another similar ceremony. In each case they were led by black people, usually ladies. There was always the killing of a chicken or some other animal and the blood used in weird rites, smeared and consumed. In any case, he was given a little wax doll as a memento, at least he thought it was, little realizing that the wooden pin stuck through it was symbolic. He was killed, accidentally harpooned in the same anatomical place where the effigy was stuck with the wooden pin."

"That's what I was thinkin', 'cause you see, I found this wax doll that looked like me with a dress made out of some material from my good yellow dress. And it had some hair that was just the same color as mine, and there were pins in th' thighs. Strangely I keep gettin' pains right where th' pins were."

Jane Augusta sighed, "My child, you did right to destroy

143

that little doll. But you must know one thing. The doll itself has no influence over you, it is only your belief in evil that will harm you. I am basically a good Christian lady, and I believe the only way to protect oneself from such evil is to believe in the love of Jesus Christ and the salvation promised by Him."

"I've always considered myself a good Christian. I know many of th' stories of Jesus and I can quote freely many verses. Why, my daddy used to have us memorize and recite Bible stories. That's how we were amused when we were little children. Somehow we got away from that. But I still believe that I'm a Christian. I regularly pray, too."

"Prayer, yes," Jane Augusta sighed. "Still I am torn between superstition and actuality. I wonder sometimes how much is superstition in the Bible—not that I mean to question it, but occasionally the thought strikes me."

"Why, Aunt Jane Augusta, how could anyone doubt what was in th' Bible bein' absolute truth?"

"Oh, I believe it as the absolute truth. I just have my suspicions at times, that's all," Jane Augusta replied. "My advice, Nancy, is to spend much time in prayer and purge yourself from all evils. I'm also of the opinion that if this Mr. Raymond Nelson had made the doll of you, it was for you to see; meaning that voodoo works if the individual of whom the doll is a likeness becomes aware that the doll exists."

"You mean he wanted me to find it?" Nancy asked.

"Perhaps he wanted you to find it, perhaps he would have revealed it to you in another way."

"But you know, I've been thinkin'. There's one thing peculiar about it. Mr. Nelson is an artist and I've seen some of his drawin's," Nancy said, "and they're very fine pieces of work. That doll was very crudely made. In fact, it looked like somethin' a child might have done."

"Making you suspicious that Mr. Nelson perhaps didn't create it after all. Is that the case, Nancy?"

"That's what I been thinkin'. I reckon I'm not sure what I do believe at this point. I'm awful glad that we had this little chat, Aunt Jane Augusta, I'm awful pleased because when I was talkin' about it, somethin' sorta snapped in my mind and I was beginnin' to see a little light."

"It's possible that Mr. Nelson had no idea that the wax effigy was in his bag. Someone may have put it there unbeknown to him," Jane Augusta suggested. "In that case, we're dealing with a third party."

"Arthur Townsend? Oh, I shouldn't think it was Mr. Townsend either. However, one can never tell, can one?"

On the way home, Nancy felt a dizzy sensation come over her. Twice she nearly lost her footing and her balance. A pain stabbed at her shoulder. An image of the wax doll she had found in Raymond Nelson's leather bag at the picnic flashed into her mind: "No, I won't believe in that old superstition. I won't believe in voodoo."

Always having been a daring person, Nancy did her best to maintain her composure as she determined to get to the bottom of the matter. The first step was to discover all she could about both Raymond Nelson and Arthur Townsend. Where better to begin than by interviewing Patricia Phenwick?

Patricia had plans to attend a concert that evening. She invited Nancy into her private rooms while she lounged by the window watching the twilight hour come. It was progressively coming earlier and earlier with the advent of autumn. Soggy compresses made of wet camomile tea leaves were on her brow and beneath her eyes. She believed these a beauty aid that helped to rejuvenate her skin.

Light small talk was indulged in for several minutes until Patricia finally said, "Nancy, I don't have all evening for chatting. I do wish you would get to the point of coming here."

"Well, I d'clare, I have been dallyin' around with chatter, haven't I? I'm sorry about that, Miz Phenwick," Nancy returned. "It's just a way I have when I'm a little excited and got other things on my mind which are really more important, but I'm a little hesitant to get to the point."

145

"Get to the point, then, Nancy," Patricia said, sounding a bit impatient. "What is it?"

"I'm curious about Mr. Nelson and Mr. Townsend. I mean about their backgrounds, where they come from and the sort of people they really are."

"Is that it? You fancy my two young artistic friends, do you?" Patricia commented with a slight chuckle. "I'll tell you about them. Raymond Nelson—although his father was of British extraction, his mother was a member of the French royalty, distantly related to almost anyone of importance in Louis's court. His father was born in this country, a merchant who is highly successful in his work. Raymond discovered at an early age that he was an artist and had artistic temperament. He wanted to pursue that line of interest. He was encouraged greatly by his mother, while his father was not as appreciative of his talents. When he was old enough, he went to Paris and studied with several fine painters. He returned to Boston after about three years at his father's request. Never married, Raymond is the sort who gets unbearably cumbersome with romantic notions. For several days running he believes he is madly in love. You see, he was raised by priests in a monastery in his early years. One time he considered taking vows in a holy order. However, Raymond is not a person who could live a monastic type of life. He, like myself, needs artistic people. Arthur, on the other hand, is a bit more inverse. His parents have descended from several generations of Bostonians. Although he does not come from the wealth that Raymond does, Arthur is financially able to take care of himself. His writing is improving every day, and I have taken him on as a student in a sense, or at least I did at one time. We rarely have lessons anymore. He reads his poetry to me, and I read mine to him."

"I suppose Mr. Townsend has nevah been married either."

"Quite right. Although he does get a few romantic notions from time to time I suspect he will remain a bachelor most of his life, perhaps choosing to marry in later years when he feels the need of companionship more so than he does now. He and Raymond are quite close, spending much time together."

Nancy explained about the voodoo doll she had found in Raymond Nelson's leather bag.

"I imagine that that was not of Raymond's doing. He was probably ignorant of that situation," Patricia said. "However, next time I see him, I will bring up the matter. What I am curious about, Nancy, is your reaction to both Arthur Townsend and Raymond Nelson."

"Why, my reaction?"

"Yes, your reaction to them as men," Patricia said, now removing the compresses from her face and sitting in an upright position. "Do you find them romantically attractive?"

"I thought at one time that I might. I reckon maybe it is true. That day at th' picnic, I began thinkin' about it, lookin' at them and seein' how boyishly playful they were," Nancy remarked. "I suddenly decided that they were just a couple of men who were grown up, but who were still little boys at heart; and their whole lives would be filled with game playin', just fritterin' away time in idle kind of whatevah they do. I realize somethin' else, Miz Phenwick, and that is that as attractive as they might be, I don't believe they would make very good husbands. Furthermore, I appreciated how much I was in love with Mr. Peter Phenwick."

"Arthur and Raymond were responsible for you realizing you are in love with my Peter?" asked Patricia.

"Yes, I believe they were. I have to admit that I definitely do feel a deep sense of love for Mr. Phenwick. It wasn't that way at first, I confess. I reckon I had to compare him with others, and in so doin', I discovered that nobody else could hold a candle to Mr. Phenwick in so many ways, gentlemanly ways."

"But you are young, Nancy. Don't you care for those playful games with the young men?"

"I find them amusin' at times," Nancy replied, "but basically, I like people who are serious and enjoy life with more depth and quality—like Mr. Phenwick does. Oh, I do have fun with Mr. Phenwick, I mean, we enjoy ourselves. He sometimes tells very funny stories. I do believe I love him very much, Miz Phenwick. I do believe that *now*."

It was announced that Arthur Townsend had arrived, and Patricia allowed him three minutes to visit.

"What is it, Arthur, what brings you this time of day?"

"I just came with news about Raymond. Dr. Ornby says he can be up and about tomorrow."

"That's good news, Arthur. Then you two can go about having another picnic or two before autumn sets in fully, can't you?"

"I suppose we can, that is, if Nancy would care to join us again."

"Well, I have to take that into consideration, Mr. Townsend. I believe I'm not goin' to want to be goin' on too many more picnics, not unless Mr. Phenwick happens to go along—if you understand what I mean."

"I hate to interrupt this little conversation, my dears," Patricia said, "but I must prepare myself for this evening. At my age, it takes a great deal of preparation. So I must ask you to excuse me now."

"Shall I walk you someplace, Miss Nancy?" Arthur asked.

"I would like to go down to th' apothecary and get some powders for a little ache I've been havin', if'n you don't mind walkin' with me, Mr. Townsend."

"It will be my pleasure, Miss Nancy," Arthur replied.

"Good day then, Miz Phenwick. We'll have another talk later, won't we?"

"Precisely, Nancy, precisely. Run along and enjoy yourselves." Patricia watched them leave, thought a moment, shook her head and went about preparing for the evening.

Chapter 13

LAMPLIGHTING TIME. A breeze had come up from the harbor with a distinct chill in it. The old lamplighter who moved along the street shielded his flame and twice had to relight it.

Nancy pulled her cloak about her, but the biting wind was irritating and cold enough to make her uncomfortable. Arthur suggested that they take a hansom cab.

"But it's only a few blocks. I d'clare, I think I can stand th' cold till we get there," Nancy said.

"I think it would be wiser to take a cab. After all, there is no sense in getting your face blistered with the cold."

"I don't believe th' weather is that cold, Mr. Townsend. However, if you insist."

It was fortunate that they had taken a cab because the nearby apothecary was closed. Arthur suggested they drive down by the wharves to one which he knew was open until at least nine o'clock at night.

They settled back in the coach for a somewhat jerky but pleasant ride. Nancy bundled herself, pulling her cloak tightly around her, wishing she had brought along a muff and warmer gloves. Early conversation was basically small talk, chatter about inconsequential matters, directed by Arthur to a particular point he wanted to make.

"You know, I have a confession to make to you, Nancy," Arthur said.

"Why, what is that, Mr. Townsend?"

"I know that while we were on the picnic, when I went to get help for Raymond after he had been struck by lightning," Arthur explained, "you became familiar with his person."

"I beg your pardon."

"There was no mistaking that his clothes were askew, that his blouse was undone."

"Why, Mr. Townsend, don't you recall Mr. Nelson unbuttoned his shirt himself?" Nancy quickly asked.

"That well may be, but I don't recall that he unbuttoned his trousers as well."

"Well, I d'clare! Whatevah are you suggestin', Mr. Townsend?" Nancy asked, trying to sound indignant.

"To be perfectly frank, it is my opinion that you had romantic motives for so doing what you did."

"Romantic motives? You mean with Mr. Nelson?" Nancy questioned incredulously. "Why, lawsy me, I don't know whatevah you're sayin'."

"I've observed you, Nancy. You know quite well what I'm saying. You know what men are all about."

Nancy swelled her bosom and made a sound that even greater showed her indignation. "Why, I assure you, Mr. Townsend, I don't know what precisely you're talkin' about. Most emphatically I have never been intimate with a man evah in my life, much less have I seen one unclad. I'm a lady, prim and proper, that's what I am. The very idea of your suggestin' such a thing makes me want to order this hansom cab stopped and get right out."

"Forgive me, Nancy, I didn't mean to offend you," Arthur said still playfully. "It was just a supposition I had because of the circumstances."

They pulled up to the apothecary. "Well, I wish you would keep your suppositions as clean as possible, Mr. Townsend. I'm a lady and I don't like such insinuatin' remarks about me."

Nancy quickly got what she wanted at the apothecary. Arthur accompanied her. When they returned outside, the cab was gone. The wind came up with a sudden gust.

"Lawsy me, but it is cold all of a sudden! I didn't

expect it to be icy like this so soon in th' year," Nancy complained. "I'll be chilled clean to th' bone. I do wish it wasn't so far away. There was heat in that hansom cab. Why evah did I let you persuade me to come this far to go to th' apothecary?"

"Well, if you've never seen a man unclad," Arthur began, "perhaps you'd like to come up to Raymond's studio. It's only two doors down and we can light a fire and get comfortable."

Nancy laughed skeptically, "Oh, Mr. Townsend, I don't fall for that sort of line, I hope you realize. Besides, I do believe your suggestion is absolutely perverse. Th' idea that I would want to see a man without any clothes on is a gross indignation."

"I wasn't referring to my own self, Nancy," Arthur assured her. "Raymond has painted several nudes. I think that you might enjoy seeing them."

"Oh, paintin's! That's a different matter. I suppose I wouldn't mind seein' just one or two so I can get out of th' cold for a few minutes, Mr. Townsend," Nancy said coyly. "How far away did you say this place was?"

"Two doors. Come along."

"Well, all right, but I can't stay no more than fifteen minutes 'cause I've got to get back."

They hurried up the street until they reached the entrance to the second-floor studio. As they arrived, they encountered the sleazy ominous personage of Milford Wartstone, the hunchback, who was looking for Raymond Nelson, saying that he had an arrangement with the artist.

"You have an arrangement with Mr. Nelson?" asked Nancy, her eyes unable to move from the almost hypnotic eyes of the ugly man in front of them. An evil glance exuded from them. She felt a slight shiver of fear from being in his presence.

"I have an appointment with Mr. Nelson. He promised to pay me tonight. I've been waiting for it."

"Mr. Nelson has been ill," Arthur related. "He's been at the doctor's house."

"I don't care where he's been," Milford Wartstone snarled. "I want my money, and I want it directly or I shall take other measures."

"I don't know what you mean by 'other measures,' Mr. Wartstone."

"I will take that up with Mr. Nelson. He'll know what I mean. I'll take my leave now." With that, he wrapped his black cloak around him, pulling his short-crowned hat lower down on his face, and lurched off with an awkward walk.

"Merciful heavens, I don't know when I have seen such a disagreeable man in my life," Nancy exclaimed. "Why, he was perfectly hideous. I can't imagine what possible business he could have with Mr. Nelson. I swear it is a puzzle."

Arthur shrugged. He was not sure what sort of answer he should give so he did not give one. Instead he turned to the downstairs door which he opened with the key he possessed and allowed Nancy to enter.

"The stairs are dark, Nancy, but if you hang onto the railing, you'll find your way. There are actually twelve steps."

At the top of the stairs, Arthur pushed ahead of Nancy and went into the main part of the studio, where he quickly found a candle and matches. The candle lit, he lighted several others. He beckoned for her to enter. The room was quite large, considering the size of the building. A wide fireplace gaped at one wall where logs were laid. Arthur quickly ignited the wood. Then he lit several oil lamps so that the room was bright.

"There's water in the teakettle. I'll make us a cup of hot tea. That'll warm the cockles of your heart," Arthur said.

"Warm th' cockles of my *what?* I don't believe I've evah heard that expression before," Nancy exclaimed, looking around. "My word, I've nevah seen so many paintin's in all my life. Do you mean to tell me Mr. Nelson painted all these himself? Why, some of them are absolutely lovely. No wonder Miz Phenwick has taken

152

him on as a protégé. Why, he's a very talented man, isn't he?"

"You've seen his paintings at Edward House, haven't you?"

"I've seen those but I thought it was just a rare occasion when he came up with a fine masterpiece. Lawsy me, these are downright beautiful."

"Wait until you see some of the others," Arthur assured her as he guided her around the room. "I've always been proud of Raymond's paintings. He has great talent. I'm pleased that Patricia Phenwick has found it in her good nature to patronize him as she does."

"Well, I d'clare, why wouldn't she? These are absolutely beautiful. Why, that landscape there, I just love it. I can even hear those cows mooin'."

Arthur laughed lightly and went to a cabinet, opened the door and slid out three large canvases.

"I trust that you won't be shocked at what you see."

"Well, Mr. Townsend, you're not goin' to show me somethin' that is lewd and insidious because I swear my eyes are unsullied and I would not care to see anythin' that is offensive."

"I don't think you will be offended by this," Arthur said. "I think this is some of Raymond's finest work. An artist usually expresses himself best with the subjects he likes most."

Arthur brought forth the first canvas, which was a semiprofile of an unclad lady.

"Lawsy me, she hasn't got a stitch of clothes on, has she?" Nancy exclaimed. "It is beautiful though, once I stop blushin' a bit."

"It's called *Venus Rising,*" Arthur informed her. "It's one of his better nudes. The model was a tavern girl. I think he paid her a very small amount to have her come up and pose for him."

"You say, come up and pose for him. It sort of has a naughty undertone, doesn't it?"

"Depends on where your mind is, Nancy," Arthur re-

153

plied, scooting the second canvas out. "This was a picture of a Pan, a teen-aged boy with goat legs."

"Mercy me, I swear he looks quite attractive wearin' those furry pants."

"Furry pants, Miss Nancy? Those are his legs. He is part man and part animal."

"He looks more like a boy to me. What kind of an animal could it possibly be?" Nancy asked. "He has a very pretty face, but a little devilish, don't you think? And look at those horns."

"He's playing his pipes. It's called *The Pipes of Pan*. It's from Greek mythology."

"Oh yes, I do recall that, I do believe," Nancy said, her fingers crossed because she had not had much of a classical education up to that point.

Arthur finally exposed the last of the three paintings. It was a self-portrait of Raymond Nelson, entirely unclad, but in such a position that his modesty was shielded. The artist had taken license and given himself a more bountiful body than he actually possessed. Still it was romantically handsome and quite exciting to behold. Nancy stood back.

"Why, I thought when you said it was goin' to be without clothes, that you would see everythin'," Nancy exclaimed. "But I see it's quite proper—I mean everythin' isn't exposed. I do find it quite attractive. Very attractive as a matter of fact. Although I would hardly think that was Mr. Nelson from what I saw of him and from what I see there."

"Perhaps he was a little healthier when he painted this."

"How long ago did he paint it?" Nancy asked, stepping closer to the canvas.

"Early last summer," Arthur replied.

"I d'clare, well, he couldn't have fallen off that much in weight in such a short time."

Again Arthur laughed and watched as Nancy went up close to the painting. Her interest was at Raymond's bare shoulder. She scrutinized closely to see if she saw the scar she had seen on the man's body. The voodoo mark had not been included.

"You certainly are curious, my dear," Arthur said, going nearer to her.

"I was just lookin' for somethin' in particular, but I don't seem to see it."

"Perhaps if his leg were in another position," Arthur suggested.

"Mercy me, that was *not* what I was referrin' to at all. I was lookin' for somethin' up on his shoulder, at the top of his chest. Good gracious, what a notion, Mr. Townsend, what a notion!" exclaimed Nancy, still searching the upper part of the painting.

Arthur came closer behind her, gently placing his hands on her shoulders. "Perhaps one day you would like to pose for Raymond."

"Pose for Mr. Nelson? Why, I suppose I'd let him paint my portrait."

"I was thinking of having him paint all of you," Arthur continued.

"You mean in th' altogether, is that what you mean, Mr. Townsend?" Nancy blurted out, turning to stare at the man's face with a shocked expression. "Well, I d'clare, what sort of woman do you think I am?"

"I think you are a very lovely creature. Anatomically you are perfectly formed. You would make his picture of Venus look plain and ordinary."

"Why, Mr. Townsend, you do have a way with words, don't you? However, I must confess, my modesty would nevah permit me to be painted without clothes on. That's all I got to say about that. As a matter of fact, I find lookin' at pictures of naked people a bit—well—not necessarily offensive but a little . . ."

"Stimulating?"

"I don't think that would be th' proper word either. But I do find them fascinatin', I will admit that, Mr. Townsend. I do want to thank you for showin' them to me. Now I believe it's time to be gettin' on home," she said.

155

"We just got here and I have water on for tea. It should be ready in a moment."

"I've had enough tea for today, Mr. Townsend. I think it best that I leave."

"If I asked you to stay in a very kind way, would you?" Arthur asked. "If I promise that I will behave myself as a gentleman at all times while you are here, will that persuade you?"

"Do you make promises to keep or promises to break, Mr. Townsend?"

"I always keep my promises."

"In that case, I'll stay long enough for a cup of tea."

At that time, footsteps were heard coming up the stairs, trudging with a slowness that indicated the climber was somewhat physically exhausted. Moments later, Raymond appeared.

"Hello, what have we here?"

"Raymond, I wasn't expecting to see you here."

"Hmmph, that goes for me, too. I wasn't expecting to see you nor was I expecting to see lovely Nancy."

"I came up here to see your paintings, Mr. Nelson. It was Mr. Townsend's suggestion since we were in th' neighborhood," Nancy stammered, feeling that she had turned a light red. "I was just preparin' to leave when Mr. Townsend said that he had some tea things on and that I should wait for a cup of tea. Now th' three of us can have tea, isn't that a marvelous idea?"

"I've just come from Dr. Ornby's. He said I could come home today. I'm delighted since I was getting tired of being confined to bed. Besides, I had an appointment this evening."

"An appointment?"

"Yes, a man was to meet me here around this time. He hasn't by any chance come yet, has he?"

"Is the man a hunchback?" asked Arthur.

"As a matter of fact, he is. Then he has been here?"

"He was at the door when we came. He said that he would contact you later," Arthur replied.

"It wasn't of great importance," Raymond said, assess-

156

ing the paintings that had been brought out. "I see you have shown Nancy my special collection. Do you recognize me, Nancy?"

"Well, I don't really recognize you other than in th' face," Nancy said uneasily, "but there's no mistakin' th' face. It is a very good likeness."

"I admit I did exaggerate a bit on the physique, but an artist has that prerogative, hasn't he?"

"I was noticin' that somethin' was missin' in th' painting," Nancy commented.

"Something that is missing?"

"Yes, that cross mark on your upper chest, near your shoulder—th' scar."

"The scar?" Arthur asked. "I didn't realize you had such a blemish on your person, Raymond."

Raymond self-consciously rubbed his shoulder. "As a matter of fact, I do have one."

Arthur said, "Well, let me see it, she's seen your naked portrait. Let me see the scar, I'm curious about it."

Hesitantly, Raymond removed his coat and vest, then unbuttoned his blouse so that the x-shaped scar could be seen.

"Good heavens, why did you have that done?"

"I didn't have it done," Raymond confessed. "It happened by accident."

"A scar like that doesn't just happen, Raymond," Arthur said. "I wonder why I've never noticed it before."

"It's a fairly recent scar. Frankly, I don't know where it came from," Raymond confided. "You see, I had been doing a little drinking—quite a little—on off days, particularly after I spent a hard day at the easel. After having more rum one night than I should have, I awakened the following morning to find I had a wound cut in my shoulder. I dressed it myself, uncertain how it had come about. I've only taken the bandage off recently. I hadn't realized anyone had seen my scar."

"That would explain why it wasn't on th' portrait."

"Even if I had had such a blemish when I painted that

157

portrait," Raymond replied, "I would never have put it in the painting."

"Mr. Nelson, there's somethin' I been meanin' to ask you, but I didn't want to trouble you while you were still in bed."

"What is it, Nancy?"

"Th' day of th' picnic, I happened to go to your leather bag to look for somethin' to help you—like a rag or a cloth to wet and mop your brow. As I was lookin', I found a scarf and wrapped in th' scarf there was a wax doll. I think it was a voodoo doll."

"You found a wax doll in my leather bag?" Raymond asked. "A voodoo doll?"

"Well, I believe that's what it was, at least that's how it looked to me."

"I certainly don't have any knowledge of it. After all, I don't know anything at all about voodoo or witchcraft for that matter," Raymond replied.

"Nor do I," Arthur said. "I know nothing of the subject of witchcraft other than that it has to do with certain sexual encounters as part of the ritual. I don't know what that has to do with anything."

"Sexual encounters?"

"Yes, I understand they play a great part in the rites," Arthur said. "They also help in warding off the effects of curses," he contrived.

"Well, I d'clare, I don't see how that could possibly be, 'cause I don't know about such things. I mean either witchcraft or th' other kind of encounters you mentioned. As a matter of fact, I think it's time that I go."

"Why, whatever for, Nancy? The tea is just ready."

"That well may be, but I'm not ready for it or such further conversation if you don't mind. If you will please excuse me."

"Mayn't I drive you?" Arthur asked.

"No, that won't be necessary, I'm certain I can find my way. Goodnight, gentlemen, and thank you kindly for letting me see your paintin's. I'm most impressed. As for me ever posin' for one, I think that's out of th' question unless, of course, I'm properly dressed. Goodnight, gentlemen." With that she hurriedly left the studio, tripping lightly down the stairs as she held her skirt, reached the street and hailed a cab.

Arthur followed closely behind her to see that she was safely into the carriage. He only waved as she departed.

Chapter 14

RAYMOND NELSON, while well recovered from the incident that occurred at the picnic, was still weak and did not intend to get back into the social swing of things at least for a few more days, isolating himself in his studio and spending long hours with his sketch book.

Two evenings after Nancy had been to the studio, Raymond received a call from Milford Wartstone.

He had gone to the downstairs door and when he had seen the hulking figure with the hideous shape, he was hesitant to invite him in.

"I think it would not be wise to refuse me entrance, Mr. Nelson," Mr. Wartstone said, pushing past the artist and tramping up the stairs in his usual jolting manner.

Raymond hurried up the stairs after him. "Now see here, what do you want?"

"I want my money," Wartstone said. "We made a deal. You promised to pay me for posing for you. I have not been paid as yet."

"The fact of the matter is I have been quite ill for the last week or so. I have not been able to get an income nor have I been to see my parents."

"That is not my fault, Mr. Nelson," Wartstone sneered at him. "Our agreement was that you would pay me for the time. Well, my time has come and gone and the time for your payment has come and gone."

"Give me until the end of the week, Mr. Wartstone."

"Until the end of the week? If I were to wait till the

end of the week for everyone who owes me, I would be poverty-stricken. I survive by doing odd jobs for people. That is my only means of livelihood and I admit I have done well, accumulating quite a treasure for myself. I have done so because I am meticulous about collecting my debts."

"I swear I do not have the money, Mr. Wartstone," Raymond pleaded. "Can't you see that I am telling you the truth?"

Milford Wartstone sneered as he paced about the room with that swagger of his. "The truth, ha, what do you know of the truth? Have you heard of voodoo, Mr. Nelson?"

"Have I heard of what?" Raymond asked, shock in his voice.

"Yes, I thought as much. But you know a little about it. I will tell you this," Wartstone commented, "you are already a marked man, and if you do not pay me the money in full now with interest, I will see to it that you never paint another picture again."

"Do you mean to say that you actually practice voodoo, Mr. Wartstone?" Raymond asked incredulously.

Wartstone laughed with a menacing sound. "I have been known to dabble in the black arts, but not without reason. Oh, I do not create the actual works myself, I have a friend who does that for me; but I hire out to other people who want curses put on persons who are in the way. If I find that you are in the way of my living, Mr. Nelson, and I don't receive the monies promised me, I will see that a voodoo doll is made of you. It will take its effect, possibly paralyzing your hand, the one with which you hold your paintbrush. I will give you to the end of the week, Mr. Nelson, but no longer. Now I want four times what I was originally promised. You come from a wealthy family. They will supply you with cash. I advise you to go to your father immediately to acquire it."

"Four times the original amount agreed on?"

"Four times the originally agreed price to begin with, Mr. Nelson. You have angered me, caused me to seek vengeance. I shall call on you at the end of the week. If you do not have the money, be prepared to suffer the consequences."

"But if I can't?"

Wartstone reached the door. "Ah, but you can, Mr. Nelson, you will see to that, I am sure." With that he pivoted about and went down the stairs, making a terrible racket as his misshapen feet on unsteady legs clomped their way.

Nancy had not felt particularly well the last few days. She was invited to dine with Patricia Phenwick on that Friday evening. She was weak and was not her usual buoyant self; still she put in an appearance in the dining room where Harriet and Prentise, Lillian and Gus, Stuart and Gordon were guests. It was one of those obligatory occasions as far as Patricia was concerned when she had to entertain members of her family. Since nothing else of consequence was happening that night, it was as good a time as any to take care of family matters.

No more had Nancy reached the dining room than she suddenly felt a strange pain in her legs. She managed to get to a chair—not the one normally assigned to her—as Harriet ran to her assistance.

"I d'clare, sugah, what on earth is th' matter with you? You look all pale."

"It's my legs, they hurt. I can't imagine what th' pain is. It's frightful," Nancy exclaimed.

"Are you certain you are all right, Nancy?" asked Pren.

"At this moment, I'm not certain of anythin', Mr. Phenwick," Nancy replied. "Lawsy, I've nevah had such pains in my legs in my life."

"Are they cramps?"

"No, I don't know what they are."

"Nancy, perhaps you had better go lie down for a while," Patricia suggested, concerned over the girl's condition.

163

"Perhaps you're right. I don't mean to miss dinner this way, but I do feel terribly strange."

"Prentise, perhaps you better go for Dr. Ted and bring him here at once," Patricia instructed.

"Are you able to move, Nancy?" Lillian asked, going to her. "Can I give you a hand? I think you can just go in the sitting room and relax. I'll be glad to sit with you."

"I'll go get Ted," Gus commented. "You stay here, Prentise, with the young ladies. I'll be just as pleased to get a bit of fresh air."

"Be careful that you go directly to Ted's house, Augustus," Lillian warned. "I don't want you dallying along the way. After all, the poor child might be quite sick."

"I d'clare, I can't move. My legs just won't move, they feel like they're goin' to collapse under me."

When Dr. Ted arrived, he examined Nancy in the parlor, and determined that indeed a kind of paralysis had set in in her legs. The others, while Nancy was given a tray, concluded their dinner, then went in to sit and discuss whatever had happened to the girl.

"I for one suggest," Lillian said, "that she be brought to our house. We have plenty of room, and I can keep a steady watch on her. I'll see the servants do the same when I'm busy."

"I don't deem it wise to move her," Ted suggested. "I don't know what condition she has. It may be dangerous, first, for her to be moved; second, for her to go out in the cold. I suggest she stay here at Aunt Patricia's house and remain where it is warm."

"By all means, Ted, I'm certain you're right," Patricia exclaimed. "If Lillian feels herself a Good Samaritan, she may come and watch over our precious Nancy from time to time."

"By all means, Aunt Patricia," Lillian replied. "I'll be more than happy to do it. I feel it my Christian duty."

Without further ado, Patricia went about making the arrangements for a downstairs room to be prepared for Nancy, warm and comfortable, accessible to her and to the servants.

While Nancy preferred the company of Harriet and Patricia, Raymond Nelson and Arthur Townsend, those persons were not always available. More and more as the autumn turned to winter, she found herself being cared for by stoic Lillian Phenwick with her tight-mouthed expression of piety. Patricia did not have the time to spend sitting at the bedside with an invalid and Harriet, while she often found time to be with her best friend, was not herself that well.

Dr. Ted could not come up with an adequate diagnosis of Nancy's case. It was extraordinarily contrary to what known facts they had about paralysis. He called in several different colleagues from the universities in Boston where the medical schools were advancing many new treatments. Recommended were hot towels about her legs several times a day. The servants, at first, took care of this matter. When Lillian began coming on a regular basis, she took over the handling of the towels and even the feeding of Nancy, whose hands had also become slightly crippled.

"Ah, I d'clare, I don't know what's happened to me, Miz Phenwick," Nancy said as Lillian prepared the towels one day, putting them around her legs. "I d'clare, that's awful hot, couldn't they be just a little cooler, ma'am?"

"Dr. Ted said they were to be hot and hot they are. If you ever want to walk again, you'll have to take his advice. After all, he is the physician," Lillian said. "This is God's way of punishing."

"Punishin' me for what? I've done nothin' wrong," Nancy said.

"Poppycock, we've all sinned, every last one of us. We were born of sin and we will die of sin," Lillian scowled. "That's the problem, you've not sought salvation, Nancy. Your soul is crying out to be saved. Until you reach the point in your consciousness where you allow yourself to be saved, redeemed for your sins, and beg forgiveness of precious Jesus, you will be a cripple."

"I don't believe that, Miz Phenwick. With all due respects, I have to say I don't believe that. Somethin' about what you say just rubs me th' wrong way. I've heard that kind of preachin' done before—oh, that's so hot—I must confess, I nevah could cotton much to it. It was too . . . I don't know what you would call it, too primitive for me."

"Oh, wretched child of Satan! If only you could get on your knees and beg Jesus to purge your soul of all its sins, the iniquity," Lillian all but shrieked. "Your legs are burning because it's the devil's fire within you that's causing it. The towels were perfectly comfortable to my hands."

"Then I swear your hands must be made of asbestos, Miz Phenwick," Nancy groaned. "They're sure burnin' th' livin' daylights outa me."

"I will pray for you, Nancy," Lillian intoned, getting on her knees beside the bed where the girl squirmed beneath the hot compresses. Her prayer was fanatical. She ranted and raved in a loud beseeching voice for God Almighty to purify the girl, certain that she would not be healed of her physical ailment until she had purged herself of all sin and committed herself to Jesus Christ for the rest of her days.

When she was not praying or applying hot compresses to Nancy's legs, Lillian read aloud from the Bible, inserting her own translations as she did.

Emotionally distraught and physically weak, Nancy was vulnerable to the woman's raving. Often she felt that perhaps this strange woman was right in her beliefs, yet she could not accept the words in her reasoning mind.

Raymond Nelson and Arthur Townsend singly and together visited Nancy. If Lillian was present, she arranged to be elsewhere when the young men arrived.

"Are you doing well, Nancy?" Arthur asked.

"I reckon I'm doin' as well as expected," Nancy replied, "I feel so perfectly helpless in this bed. I do wish I could walk."

"Nancy, you said something about finding a voodoo

166

doll in my leather case," Raymond mentioned. "Of whom was that doll made?"

"Why, I believe it was a likeness of me. It seemed to have my hair and a dress made from material from one of my good dresses."

"You're certain it was a lady doll?"

"I'm certain of that. I'm almost convinced it was me or supposed to be me. I destroyed it instantly, tearin' th' pins out and th' clothes off of it and breakin' th' wax into pieces and buryin' it in th' ground."

"I had an encounter with a man who claimed that he was a go-between of a voodoo lady and persons who wanted such dolls made for their enemies. In fact, he threatened to have one made of me if I didn't give him a certain amount of money."

"Good heavens, Raymond, you didn't tell me about this," Arthur exclaimed. "Why didn't you say something?"

"It's over and done with now."

"Where was this man?" Arthur asked.

"I haven't seen him in quite a while. He disappeared after he got his money. He claimed that he traveled around from place to place, not staying long in each city, but that he would return to Boston one day and at that time he might come seeking more."

"That may be just a ploy. He may still be in Boston."

"True."

"You don't believe that he, I mean, that he's responsible for Nancy, do you?" Arthur asked.

"I don't know," Raymond replied. "Nancy, do you believe in voodoo?"

"Yes, as a matter of fact, I do, I think, because of what Mammy used to say about it. I reckon it may be true," she said reflectively. "I've seen it happen to people down in Savannah where I come from. Maybe I should just go back there to see if'n I could find a voodoo lady who could take th' curse off of me, if that's what it is."

Arthur said, "Perhaps we should see if we can find

167

this person who threatened you with voodoo, Raymond, and see if he is the one who is responsible for Nancy's illness."

"I told you, he's gone."

"Well then, let's go out and look for him."

After each of their visits when Arthur and Raymond were gone, Lillian would always appear as if she had emerged from the wall where she had been overhearing their conversation.

"Nancy, it appears to me that you should take one of those young gentlemen seriously. I think they're both smitten by you, and probably could be very much in love with you. Raymond Nelson particularly would make an ideal husband. He comes from great wealth, his family successful, his mother from royalty, his father an affluent merchant. Why, he would be an ideal mate for you."

"But I d'clare, Miz Phenwick, I would not be an ideal mate for anyone in my present condition. I'm nothin' heah but a lumpa flesh that seems to be rottin' on th' vine."

"You'll be well shortly. I'm sure if you were to fall in love with one of these two men that you would begin getting well in no time."

"Th' fact of th' matter is, I'm already in love with Mr. Peter Phenwick—as you well know. Even though he's been gone all these months on business."

"Peter is always gone for many months at a time, that's his way," Lillian sneered contemptuously. "Besides, Peter is far too old a man for you. Being married to an older man like that would be a terrible existence for a young girl like you. Him being away on business through the winter was one of the problems my mother-in-law used to have, spending those long dreary winters by herself, raising the children. After the children were grown, she was alone and deserted by Peter. Oh, he's a fine man, everyone admires him greatly, but do you realize how alone you would be married to him?"

"He swears to me that this is goin' to be th' last time he

has to be away for such a long period because he's finishin' up th' business he has in New York and leavin' th' office in th' hands of someone else."

"Do you really believe that, silly child? Peter Phenwick is a womanizer. He goes after—well—all sorts of tramps. I know what kind of man he is. His Helen knew, that's why she grieved till her death."

"I don't believe that about Mr. Phenwick. I don't believe it at all!"

"I think it is high time that you did, child. If you think you have a sinful life now, wait until you marry a sinful man and find how terrible your life becomes."

"I'm afraid Mr. Phenwick won't want me if'n I'm to be a cripple th' rest of my life," Nancy said softly. "Perhaps I better return to Savannah and be with my own people where it's warm and I can stay bedridden there with my family."

"You have a defeatest attitude, Nancy, because you do not have the love of Jesus Christ in your heart. You are a sinner and therefore doomed to eternal Hell! Oh, if you could only repent and save yourself, child," Lillian preached. "If you could only have faith, then you could pick up your bed and walk. Your faith in Jesus Christ will make you whole."

"How does one find a faith if they don't have it, Miz Phenwick?" Nancy asked.

"One purges oneself of sin and believes that Jesus Christ died for their sins, that He has paid the price with His precious life for you. All you have to do is love Him. Give your life to Him, and be clean in body, mind and soul!"

"I always thought I was clean in body, mind and soul, Miz Phenwick. I don't know where you get th' notion that I'm such a sinner."

"Because we were all born of sin, born of Satan; and only through the redemptive love of Christ can we be made whole again and be saved. Seek eternal life, love Jesus and it will be given to you."

Nancy admittedly was confused about Lillian's ranting and raving about religion. She often thought of the words when the pain was devastating. Her emotions were rife with fear, she began having second thoughts and wondered if perhaps the zealous woman was not right in that which she said.

Harriet, although she loathed the cruel winter in Boston, had become stronger over the months and at last was spending at least half a day in the company of Nancy, relieving Lillian of her task. Lillian reluctantly gave up her position for she sincerely believed that she was making headway with Nancy's salvation.

"I d'clare, Nancy, you do look one hundred per cent better with all this good food and long hours of rest," Harriet announced.

"I hardly touch my food, Harriet," Nancy replied. "And all these hours of rest are gettin' on my nerves. I itch and scratch from lyin' heah so long. The doctor says there's nothin' I can do."

"Nancy, Prentise has promised that we will return to Savannah with th' first thaw. Why don't you come with us?"

"But Mr. Phenwick, Mr. Peter Phenwick . . ."

"Oh, my precious Nancy, don't you realize that th' way you are now, no man like Mr. Phenwick is gonna want you. Don't you suppose he's got word what your physical condition is and he's staying away because of it?"

"That cannot be true. I won't believe that in my heart of hearts. I just won't believe that because I do love Mr. Phenwick so very much." Nancy was on the verge of tears. "Th' only thing that has kept me alive these days when th' pain was so excruciatin' was my hope and belief that Mr. Phenwick would return and somehow that his returnin' would make me well again. Just knowin' he was comin' back would strengthen my legs and my hands would get strong again, too. Harriet, I want you to help me. I want you to support me and see if I can walk."

"But Dr. Ted said you are not supposed to get out of bed, Nancy. You're a very sick girl."

"How does he know I'm a very sick girl, he doesn't even know what's wrong with me. Nobody knows what's wrong with me. Maybe I've just been talked into bein' paralyzed and I can walk after all. Help me, Harriet," Nancy pleaded.

Harriet agreed and tried to help Nancy maneuver her way from the bed. The results were disastrous and one of the servants had to be called to help Harriet put Nancy back into bed.

In the days to come, each time Harriet arrived to be with Nancy, the latter begged her to try again to assist her. Each attempt, while unsuccessful, proved to Nancy that she was getting a little more strength in her legs. No longer did she have to have one of the servants help her back into bed for she was able to crawl back. If she could crawl, she believed, there was still life in her legs and they were not totally useless.

Once she was tucked back in bed exhausted but happy with her accomplishment, she would talk to Harriet about Prentise or about Peter and any number of things. Or when they would not talk, Harriet would read from romantic novels written for ladies that helped to stimulate Nancy's desires more and more for Peter Phenwick. If only he would return, come back to her, she was certain she would get well again. Yet, how long had it been since the man had been away from her? Had he forgotten about her? There were his letters. In them he declared his love for her over and over again, apologizing for having to be away for so long and promising it would be the last winter she would ever be alone. She only mentioned in letters to him that she was not well, not wanting to disturb the man or force him to return home when he had business to which he had to attend.

At night when she was alone, by dim lamplight she would read and reread, going over the letters, reaffirming her love for him, putting all of her hopes for the future in his love for her. She prayed—not the hysterical prayer that Lillian did—but a quiet confident believing

171

that the Divine Creator of the universe would somehow heal her and fulfill her love for Peter Phenwick. That was her only prayer. That was all she wanted: to be well and to be married to the man she loved.

Chapter 15

Jane Augusta Ornby-Clark awakened on that March morning to discover the sun shining brightly in her window. She had had a strange dream, disturbing, yet she did not recall precisely what it was about. She only remembered waking with a peculiar sensation.

After arising and dressing, she hurried about her dainty breakfast as she kept getting strange thoughts about the second floor of the house. Had she dreamed about it? As she concentrated upon what had occurred in her dream the night before, it seemed she recalled things about Rosea Hackleby. With that in mind, she began letting a series of thoughts develop. One clinging to another made her decide to go the second-floor room in which Rosea's books were well put away.

The room was icy cold, having been closed off all winter. Fortunately, Jane Augusta had worn several overcoats and a shawl, not to mention her mittens. The mittens were cumbersome for finding that for which she was looking. She came upon the box in the chest, placed delicately below two cartons of old clothing. These she removed and opened the box. The books were just as she had left them in the fall after Olivia and Arthur Townsend had made copies of them and the edited copy was taken to England with Olivia Phenwick. Everything was intact. Why had she been so concerned about it?

She opened the third of the books as if she were being directed by some unseen force. Taking the book and parting the pages at random, she found that she opened to a section on witchcraft. Thumbing through several pages, she found two rather short paragraphs titled "Voodoo." Quickly, she scanned them, finding no particularly fascinating facts other than that old Rosea had believed in voodoo and had seen its workings, especially disastrous when victims were told that wax effigies had been made of them and that the wax effigy had been stuck with pins. Rosea was of the opinion that such phenomena occurred simply because it was a matter of psychological suggestion and the victim was affected because he believed he would be.

That was all there was about voodoo with the exception of a brief description of voodoo rites of which Rosea had heard from some source and which had little verification. Jane Augusta put the books back in place and covered them in the same way they had been covered before. For some reason she was apprehensive that they needed to be protected, even after the printed manuscripts were released.

She was about to leave the room when she turned to notice a sewing basket which she had not used in a long while, having acquired a new one in the meantime which was larger and more adequate to her needs. In the sewing basket was a doll used for holding pins and leaning against the doll was another, this one stuck with two pins in the lower part of the body.

Jane Augusta immediately examined the alien doll, and discovered that it was made of wax, now quite hard and brittle from the extreme cold that was in the room. The effigy was crudely made and had a foul odor to it. The face was not recognizable as belonging to anyone she knew, but the hair was black and the eyes made of two clove buttons were brown. The dress that was crudely wrapped around the doll was made of a material that Jane Augusta recognized as belonging to a dress that Nancy used to wear.

The pins were jabbed into both legs, sticking out the front at the thighs so that the skirt was lifted to reveal the exact location. Disgusted and somewhat apprehensive of the bit of wax, Jane Augusta found an old scarf and tied it together in such a way that it could be a carrying sack for the doll.

A short while later, Jane Augusta appeared at the offices of her brother, Dr. Theodore Ornby. She was informed that he was busy. Thus, she had to wait for nearly ten minutes. Although there were other patients in line ahead of her, Jane Augusta insisted on seeing her brother as soon as he was finished with the first patient.

"What is it, Sister?" asked Dr. Ted, always understanding and particularly kind to his sister.

Jane Augusta unwrapped the wax effigy she had brought and laid it on his desk. "You see this? I found it upstairs in the room where I store most of my summer things. It was in an old sewing basket."

"What the devil is it?" asked Dr. Ted, examining it with curiosity.

"I think it's a voodoo doll."

"A what?"

"A voodoo doll, Ted. Can't you see? Smell the vile odor. I think it is made in the likeness of Nancy."

"Good heavens, who do you suppose did this?"

"I don't know, but whoever did apparently at one time or another has had access to my house. Why would it be put in a room I had announced earlier would be locked up during the winter months to conserve heat?"

"It's a good question, my dear. I don't know," Ted replied. "What do you suggest we do about it?"

"I suggest first and foremost that you remove the pins from it, Ted," Jane Augusta said. "Use one of your surgical instruments and pull them out."

"Why not just use my hands?" Dr. Ted asked.

"Because I think it important for you to do it the way I say."

Dr. Ted, who had always believed in his sister's intuitive ability, took her word and followed her suggestion.

"I wanted you to see this first and remove the pins before I go to Edward House," Jane Augusta said. "Then the next time you see Nancy convince her that you have performed this operation. I sincerely believe that the young lady's problem is in her mind and that she honestly believes a doll has been made in her likeness. Now she may not consciously believe that, but unconsciously, because she found one such doll, she may believe there is another, which there is. Let's pray to God that this is the last that there is. If she can be convinced, and I will take the doll now with the pins to show her, then perhaps she will begin to recover."

"My dear Jane Augusta, I do not see how you can believe in such superstition," her brother said, putting his arm around her shoulders, "but I know you do. You have Aunt Rosea's books, you've no doubt thoroughly digested them. If anyone knows anything about such things, it would be you. Very well, I will do what you wish."

Raymond Nelson took the oil portrait that he had done of Milford Wartstone to Edward House. He was accompanied by Arthur Townsend, his usual companion. When they were finally led into the presence of Patricia Phenwick, she was startled at the ugliness of the painting, yet intrigued by it.

"Why have you created such a monstrous thing?" Patricia asked. "You have executed a creature of diabolical proportions."

"Perhaps I have, Patricia," Raymond replied, "I have done so from a model. This is quite an adequate likeness of the man, isn't it, Arthur?"

"I can only say yes," Arthur replied, "although I've but seen the man once. He was hideous."

"I can't understand why you would want to use such a monstrosity as a subject for your work, Raymond."

"Curiosity more than anything else," Raymond replied. "I think an artist must explore many different types of subjects, not only the beautiful but the unbeautiful as well."

"You've certainly picked a classic example of the latter," Patricia replied.

While Patricia was appraising the picture, the butler announced that her niece, Jane Augusta Ornby-Clark, had arrived and was waiting downstairs to see her. It seemed to be an urgent matter. Patricia instructed the butler to show her into her private suite. Then she returned to observing the portrait.

"I do find it interesting in a bizarre way."

"I hoped you would. It cost me a great deal of money," Raymond commented. "As a matter of fact, more than I usually pay a model. In a sense, I think he has blackmailed me."

"An extortionist for a model? I can see where his face has a felonious character to it. Well, how much do you want for it?"

"How much do you think it is worth?" Raymond asked.

"To me it is worth nothing. However, I know a place where it could hang perfectly—not at Edward House, of course," Patricia said, "but in a building. I will offer you five hundred dollars for it, which is exorbitant except that the workmanship is quite marvelous. You've improved, in fact, your style has progressed. For that reason I will pay the price."

"Bless you, Patricia," Raymond said, going to her, taking her hand and kissing it lavishly. "It will well pay the man's fee and still give me a little to live on."

"What would you do without me to support you?" Patricia asked, grandly going back to her favorite chair and taking a regal pose.

"I would probably have to go to my father for funds, and listen to his tirade about the economy. What a spendthrift he thinks I have become."

"Well, haven't you?" Patricia asked, flippantly.

"I do hope so," Arthur inserted. "A gentleman of quality needs to have the affluent consciousness to fritter away money if he pleases, don't you think?"

"By all means," Patricia replied. "Is your consciousness that way, too, Arthur?"

"Not yet, but I'm working on it."

At that moment, Jane Augusta arrived. She greeted Patricia with a kiss and cast suspicious glances at the two young men. "Aunt Patricia, I'm so glad that you could see me."

"My dear Jane Augusta, you're looking perfectly flushed and not quite yourself. I sense a certain anxiety in you. Is there something wrong?"

Jane looked from Raymond to Arthur and then back to her aunt.

"These gentlemen, whom you know, of course, can be completely trusted. They are in my confidence."

"Then I shall come to the point immediately," Jane Augusta replied. "I am disturbed and upset over finding this." She opened the scarf in which the doll was carried.

"Good heavens, what on earth is it?"

"It's a voodoo doll made in the likeness of Nancy Cox."

"A voodoo doll?" Patricia questioned. "One similar to that found in Raymond's leather bag on the picnic last fall?"

"It could well be," Jane Augusta said, "since nobody knows precisely what that doll looked like except Nancy, but I would guess that it is similar."

"Good God, I've never seen anything so terrible, nor smelled such a foul odor," Arthur commented.

All eyes seemed to turn to Raymond Nelson. "I swear I know nothing about how that first doll possibly got into my bag. I don't recall having seen it there that morning of the picnic. It may have been, of course, because I just picked up my bag without looking through the things. Someone else must have placed it inside." Then an image of Milford Wartstone came to his mind. "Come to think of it, the evening before the picnic, I had a visitor, the subject of that portrait. Perhaps he . . ."

"Good heavens, don't tell me this grotesque individual you painted is a dealer in witchcraft and voodoo relics," said Patricia, looking with disgust at the painting.

"Yes, I must admit that he is. He came to me at another time, demanding money."

"Demanding money for what?"

178

"For not paying him on time," Raymond confessed. "When I told him that I didn't have the money, he threatened to have a voodoo doll made of me. Since he had showed his hand, suddenly his price quadrupled. I confess I was in terrible fear of the man."

"I see. But could this man," Patricia asked, "have gained access to your house, Jane Augusta?"

"Not that I know of; I've never seen a creature such as this ever in my life," Jane Augusta replied, as a shiver of disgust went through her. "I've never seen the man. Certainly, if he'd gotten in, it was at a time when I was away from the house."

"Who has access to your upstairs rooms?" asked Patricia.

Jane Augusta replied, "Why, the servants do, of course. But I keep the keys in my possession most of the time. When they are not in my possession, they are safely put away."

"No one else knows of your storage room?"

"I suppose certain members of the family do, the ones I've talked to, had words with—I don't know who for certain." Jane Augusta sounded confused. "I didn't come here to be put on the defensive."

"I'm sorry, Jane Augusta, I didn't mean to make you feel uncomfortable," Patricia remarked, "but we really must get to the bottom of this, mustn't we?"

"I have no idea how we are going to discover who was in my storage room unless it was one of the servants. I trust them all implicitly," Jane replied. "As a matter of fact, none of them has taken anything there without my knowledge of it. I was with them at all times."

"Where do you keep your keys, Jane Augusta?"

"I keep them in my dresser drawer, in the very back under a roll of stockings."

"I see," the old lady said, putting her finger to her lips as she thought. "Now then, who else has seen this besides us?"

"Only my brother, Ted."

"And his opinion?"

179

"Frankly, Ted can find nothing physically wrong with Nancy Cox except extreme weakness. There's no reason why her legs should be paralyzed whatsoever, except indeed if voodoo is being practiced on her."

"Good heavens, is that sort of thing really possible?" Arthur Townsend asked.

"Apparently it is, Arthur," Patricia replied. "I've heard one or two stories about it in my time. I remember a singular incident involving a precious stone that was called the Raja Eye that was indirectly given to my daughter Susannah and caused her to have a tremendous physical reaction. Since then I have not negated any possibly supernatural phenomenon without investigating it thoroughly. That, of course, is what we are dealing with here if, indeed, this is indication of the practice of voodoo."

With Arthur and Raymond trailing behind, Patricia locked her arm in Jane Augusta's and told her to carry the doll in the scarf to Nancy's room. The procession made quick time. When they arrived, Lillian was just removing hot compresses from the girl's legs.

Bypassing her niece-in-law, Patricia went directly to Nancy's bed and asked her to prop herself up on pillows that she might show her something.

"Why, I d'clare, what is it, Miz Phenwick?" Nancy asked. "I've just gone through such excruciatin' pain with th' hot compresses, which I think do absolutely no good. I reckon there's no cure for those legs of mine. They're just plain numb now."

"Nancy, I want you to look at this," Patricia said, reaching for the scarf Jane Augusta was carrying and placing it on the bed beside Nancy to open.

"Merciful heavens," Nancy shrieked, "it's like th' doll I found in . . ." She shot a quick glance at Raymond. ". . . in Mr. Nelson's leather bag at th' picnic that time. Why, it's identical! Heah I took and tore it up and buried th' pieces. How did it get put together again?"

"I believe this is another one, Nancy. The doll you demolished is still destroyed and buried. This is another."

Jane Augusta stepped forward. "My brother, Dr. Ted,

has removed the pins that were in the legs. He wanted me to show you the pins and the holes where they had been."

Lillian Phenwick moved closer to the bed, still holding the hot towels as she observed what was going on. "It's the work of Satan!" she screamed. "You are all black with the work of Satan!"

"Lillian, control yourself!"

"I will *not* control myself. It is my duty to proclaim the name of Jesus Christ and tell you that as long as vile things like that are kept in this house, as long as sin goes on—and there is sin going on in this house—the work of Satan will continue here! That girl, that Nancy Cox, is a target of the devil and you have chosen her to become a Phenwick woman. A likely choice she is to bring sin and damnation on the family of Phenwick! Oh, God, forgive us, forgive us all! Pray for her soul!"

"For pity sake, get that woman out of here," Patricia ordered, turning to Arthur and Raymond.

"You'll not throw me out! I will say my piece," Lillian shrieked.

Arthur and Raymond each took hold of an arm and propelled Lillian from the room.

"I *will* be heard! God Almighty has sent me here to purge this house of sin! That girl, *that* girl must be saved! Salvation is her only hope!"

Lillian could still be heard screaming as she was led down the hall. Patricia turned to Jane Augusta, who had always been her favorite niece. "What do you make of all this?"

"I have known Lillian for as long as she has been married to Augustus, longer. She's always been a bit fanatical when it comes to religion," Jane Augusta replied. "I didn't realize she was as fanatical as this. I would suggest that she no longer be around Nancy. As long as Nancy is not well, Lillian should be forbidden in the house."

"Every day Miz Phenwick has given me a lecture like that," Nancy said. "She's always talkin' about what a

181

sinner I am. Glory be, I don't know that I've been such a wretched sinner all my life as she claims I have. I don't understand what she means that I should confess my sins to Jesus and all that sorta nonsense. It makes me feel like a perfect fool at times because I don't understand what she's gettin' at."

"Lillian has been doing *this* to you? So that's her purpose for being such a Good Samaritan, she wants to save your soul, Nancy," Patricia commented. "Well, we're going to have to find a new nurse because I'm not going to put up with anymore of this nonsense in this house."

"That will be one of th' kindest things you have done for me," Nancy replied. "I d'clare, sometimes she frightens th' livin' daylights outa me to th' point where I just want to scream and scream. She knows she's got me trapped here in this bed and there's no way of me escaping."

"Why haven't you told me about this, Nancy?" Patricia asked.

"I didn't want to burden you with it. I thought it was my problem. After all, Miz Phenwick has been kindness itself other times. Why, she reads to me from th' Bible. I know more about th' Bible than I evah knew in my whole life. She even helps me memorize verses. I've learned an awful lot from her, but there are times when she gets just plain crazy-like, that's all I can say. I confess, she frightens me."

"I will have a talk with Lillian. Now then, I think we better get more to the point," Patricia said. "What can we do? We've discovered this second doll. We don't know if there are others, but I think we should assume that there are not any others."

"Why can we assume that? I mean, how? It seems to me there might be hundreds of them."

"I rather doubt that, Nancy," Patricia said. "From what little I know about this thing called voodoo it's only necessary to make one doll or perhaps two. Whoever made it must have been aware that you had destroyed the first one, hence the second was created."

"But isn't it strange," Jane Augusta asked, "that Nancy was not made aware of the second doll?"

"I should suppose that's because of the first doll. The situation was planted well into her mind and the fear was there whether or not she was consciously aware of it."

"You mean, I have done all this to myself just by bein' afraid because I saw that doll?" Nancy asked.

"It's not as simple as that," Patricia replied. "I do not understand the complexities of it, but I am certain that one day we will get to the bottom of this. Once we can discover who is behind it, then we can rectify the matter."

"Who on earth would want to do any harm to me?"

"Who? Who, indeed? I wonder," Patricia thought aloud. "I have an idea. It's not a very pleasant idea, but I think it's time I had a word with Harriet."

"Harriet Pettijohn, I mean, Harriet Phenwick?" Nancy said, correcting herself. "I d'clare, you don't think that my best friend in th' whole world would have anythin' to do with this, do you?"

"I'm not so sure, Nancy, but I think it would be wise to have words with her."

Chapter 16

PATRICIA SUMMONED THE BUTLER and sent word that Harriet was to come to Nancy's room.

Disturbed by what Patricia had said, Nancy began thinking back over the past few months. She had to admit that there were certain strange things about her friend that had perplexed her at the time they happened. Now that she considered them, she was certain they were odd. This was disturbing. In her concern, she raised herself into a sitting position, reaching out for a glass of water which was on the table beside the bed and connected with it. As she did she looked strangely at her hands. Feeling was coming back into them where there had been a semi-numbness. After drinking, she returned the glass to the table. While Patricia and Jane Augusta sat in straight-backed chairs as if attempting to interpret one another's thoughts, Nancy made a conscious effort to wiggle her toes. They moved. A scatter of excitement ran through her and she felt herself becoming giddy.

Patricia rose, saying to Jane Augusta that she felt it would be better if the interview with Harriet were to take place in her own parlor. Casting a glance at Nancy, the old woman wondered about the singular expression she wore.

"Is there something troubling you, Nancy?" asked Patricia.

"I—well—I don't rightly know at this point, Miz Phenwick," Nancy said, trying to contain the excitement that was welling within her. She was the type of person who wanted to make a full discovery by herself, not to raise the others' hopes until she was certain of her accomplishment. "I am concerned that you have suspicion of Harriet, but I would appreciate it if you were to talk to her in another room. I don't believe I want to see her and hear that conversation."

"That was precisely what I was about to suggest. Come along, then, Jane Augusta," Patricia ordered, taking her niece by the arm and leaning slightly on her for support.

Patricia and Jane Augusta were situated in comfortable seats in the sitting room on the second floor, which overlooked the now dormant rose garden.

Patricia said, "Jane Augusta, I have written the questions I would like you to drop at your brother Daniel's office for which I desire answers as soon as possible."

"No trouble at all, Aunt Patricia," Jane Augusta replied. "The fact is I was contemplating stopping by Daniel's office on my way home. I don't see Daniel as often as I like. He is busy with his law practice and often preoccupied with important matters." She took the sealed envelope from her aunt.

Harriet entered the room wearing a light blue frock which had a rather gay appearance and a daring cut to its neckline; a sign, thought Patricia, that the girl was beginning to show improvement.

"Miz Phenwick, Miz Ornby-Clark," Harriet acknowledged, "you-all sent for me?"

"I did," Patricia replied.

"I d'clare, I don't quite understand what you-all would want of me."

"If you have a seat, I'll explain my motives, my dear," said Patricia.

Harriet daintily sat in a chair. "I didn't mean to sound impudent, I'm only confused."

"Why are you confused?"

"I d'clare, it's more excitement than anything else. Mr. Phenwick has promised that by th' first thaw we will re-

186

turn to Savannah. I swear I am plum homesick for my kin down yonder. I thought I would be and I sure am."

"Is that the only reason you wish to leave Boston, Harriet?" persisted Patricia.

"I don't much care for th' weather heah," Harriet explained. "This winter has been just downright frightful as far as I'm concerned—*miserable* is a better word for it."

"It isn't that you want to be away from your friend, Nancy, is it?"

"Lawsy, be away from Nancy! Why, I'd be th' happiest person in th' world if she would come with me; but she's bound herself to Mr. Peter Phenwick even as sick as she is," Harriet replied.

"Nancy has been your friend for a long while, hasn't she, Harriet?" questioned Patricia.

"Lawsy, we've been th' best of friends for as long as I can remember," Harriet replied, her eyes widening and a smile coming to lips that did not often smile. "Why, she's closer to me than any of my brothers and sisters. I've got a sister Annabella right next to me in age practically and we're like strangers compared to Nancy and me."

"Harriet, I know there are some unpleasant things in your past. But because of what has happened to Nancy," Patricia persisted, "I must get to the bottom of this affair once and for all. I must ask you some questions."

"Things from my past, Miz Phenwick, why, whatevah could you be talkin' about?" Harriet looked startled, the smile was now gone.

"The first thing I feel I should mention is the name Tom Cleghorn."

"Tom Cleghorn?" For an instant Harriet looked terrified, then she repeated the name. Shattering explosions seemed to go on within her that erupted her emotions, and tears welled in her eyes.

"You do know the name, don't you?"

"Yes," Harriet said after a pause, "I do know th' name. He was a slave on our plantation when I was a little bitty girl. He got sold, then he got sold again. Every so often I'd see him. Sometimes I wouldn't see him in person, but I'd see him in my mind, like his image was hauntin' me. I had a very strong love for that man. Why, he was one of th' kindest darkies I've evah known. At least, he was when I was a little girl."

"Do you recall what happened when he attempted to run away from his last owner?" asked Patricia. "Believe me, when I question you about this, I am not sympathetic with slavery whatsoever, but I need to get this out in the open because it has to do with other things."

A vision from the past flashed into Harriet's mind as if a vague cloudiness was suddenly wiped away and the picture was far too vivid to be anything but severely painful. "I *was* accosted by him when he ran away. I was a twelve-year-old at the time. I loved th' man so much that I ran to him and wrapped my arms around him. He was scared, frightened and he mistook my affection, I reckon. He took me back behind th' bushes and treated me—well—he hurt me. He hurt me by doin'—well—I guess you know what he did to me. Anyway, when I yelled and hollered, he slapped me a couple of times. That didn't hurt like what else he did to me."

"And after he raped you, Harriet," Patricia continued, "what did you do?"

"I ran home and I never told anybody. Pretty soon I was gonna have a baby. By then, Tom Cleghorn had been captured. My daddy asked me what man had been to me. At first, I didn't know what he was talkin' about. I wiped that terrible ordeal from my mind. When he persisted, I told him it was a black man. My daddy went into a rage. He was furious and he said that he would get even with whoever did that to me. He asked me if I knew who it was, and I said yes. Then he asked me if it was someone who was workin' on th' plantation, and I said, 'No, someone who used to.' Right off he knew and he said, 'Was it Tom Cleghorn?' I said, 'Yes, Daddy, I believe it was.' He took me down where they were holdin' Tom Cleghorn in jail and they made me look him straight in th' eye and asked me again and I told them, 'Yes, he was th' one.'

Well, Tom Cleghorn didn't have much of a chance then. They just took him out and hanged him from th' old hangin' tree. They made me watch th' man who had hurt me. I forgot everything about it then till right now. Funny, I remembered bits and pieces, but right this very minute is th' first time I ever seen it clearly in my mind."

"Then Elsworth Grayson sought to revenge the death of Tom Cleghorn, a white man helping a black. Elsworth Grayson, who knew many of their secrets, had hired or in some way had commissioned a black voodoo woman to put a curse on both Nancy and you."

"I d'clare, I don't know what you mean, a voodoo woman."

"Wasn't it Elsworth Grayson who had this done?" questioned Patricia.

"Well, I suppose he did, you know what he tried to do to me. He tried to kill me and he might have."

"He might have hired a voodoo woman to put a curse on you and upon Nancy."

"I don't know about Nancy. She nevah did anything to no one," Harriet returned.

"Harriet, we are certain that Nancy is under a voodoo curse at this moment. That is why she cannot walk, why she is bedridden. Now if Elsworth Grayson, the *late* Elsworth Grayson, did not have a curse put on Nancy, who do you suppose it might have been?"

"I d'clare, I don't know," Harriet said.

"Could it have been *you,* Harriet?" asked Patricia.

"Why, what a question!"

"Is it?" Patricia asked, folding her fingers together and cracking them significantly. "Tell me honestly, Harriet, haven't there been times in your life when you've been envious of Nancy? Perhaps you've always been envious and jealous."

"Why, no! Why should I be envious and jealous of my best friend? Nancy and I, we've been like that," Harriet said with her fingers crossed to indicate their closeness.

"You are despondent because you lost your baby."

"I'm disappointed because I lost my baby by Mr. Phenwick, but I'm determined to have others."

"How do you feel about being a Phenwick woman, Harriet?" quizzed Patricia, now staring hard into the girl's face.

"I feel it a great honor and distinction."

"An honor and a distinction which you now hold above Nancy. A reason for which she might be jealous of you. But might it not be the other way round if Nancy is to become a Phenwick woman? Then she would be continually upstaging you?"

"I don't know what you're talkin' about, Miz Phenwick."

"Don't you, Harriet? I've watched you. You are her friend, but you do resent her in many different ways. That has been apparent in your face and in your actions."

"Very well, I admit I had a little animosity in my heart when I thought of Nancy becomin' a Phenwick woman, too. At first, I thought there was no possibility of it, since who was there for her to marry but Stuart Phenwick and he's still a boy. It nevah dawned on me that she might marry old—I mean, she might marry Mr. Peter Phenwick. At first, when I heard that she was interested in him, I thought she was doin' it outa spite for me."

"Out of spite?"

"So that she could become a Phenwick woman, too. I had some terrible thoughts at one time. Believe you me, I prayed them away. Lawsy yes, I got down on my knees every night for three whole weeks and I prayed to God in Heaven that He take such terrible thoughts away from me. I realized that Nancy is my best friend and she always has been. It was absolutely wrong of me to hold such a notion. I'm terribly sorry. One day, maybe I'll apologize to Nancy, but I can't do it now for fear of what she might think."

"I will ask you one more time," Patricia said sternly, "and I expect a truthful answer. Whatever you tell me,

I will accept. Do you know of anyone who is practicing voodoo in Boston at this very moment?"

"Lawsy, no," Harriet replied.

"Then you did not hire or in any way arrange for a voodoo curse to be put upon your friend?"

"Why, nevah in this whole wide world, Miz Phenwick! That would be th' last thing I would want to do. Oh, lawsy, I don't know why I feel so terrible. I was so happy when I came in here about returning to Savannah. Now I'm just miserable. I want to cry because of th' things I remember and because of th' accusations you've made about me and about th' realization that I had such feelin's toward my very best friend. Oh, I just want to go back to Savannah. I'm happy that Nancy's gonna become a Phenwick woman. I really am happy for her. She'll be a Phenwick woman up heah in Boston and I'll be a Phenwick woman down in Savannah. I mean, oh please, Miz Phenwick, I would just like to leave."

"You mean leave Boston?"

"No, I mean this room before I burst into tears," Harriet practically screamed as her eyes welled with liquid.

"Very well, Harriet, you may leave. I believe what you have told us."

"Thank you, Miz Phenwick, Miz Ornby-Clark. If you-all would please excuse me." Harriet ran from the room.

"What do you make of that, Jane Augusta?" Patricia asked.

"The girl is extremely emotional, Aunt Patricia, and you did badger her a good deal. I am certain that I, under such interrogation, would have broken into tears, too," Jane Augusta admitted. "I seriously doubt that she has any contacts with a voodoo person or that she would be cruel enough to want such a thing to be practiced on her friend."

"I have to agree with you on that, my dear Jane Augusta. However, I still don't know where to turn. Do take that letter to Daniel and ask him to get back to me as quickly as possible."

Patricia remained alone in her sitting room for nearly an hour, contemplating the experience of that afternoon. The logs had been lit in the fireplace, making the room warm and cozy. She was confused, perplexed about how she should proceed in this matter, for she felt it was her duty as head of the household to get to the bottom of the whole affair.

The supernatural had somehow always lingered in the family for as long as she had been a member. She could not help but believe that that was ironically influenced by Augusta Phenwick's strange promise that she would linger over the clan to see that Phenwick ladies were properly chosen. Would voodoo come under that heading of supernatural? It was preposterous to believe, yet what else could this thing be called? The wax dolls, the paralysis in Nancy with no sign of disease or any physical problem that might have caused it, coming on as swiftly as it had. Even if she got to the core of the situation, and it were resolved, what could be the next step?

A light rapping came at the door. Patricia glanced up before she called for the person to enter.

Patricia was alarmed when the door opened and she saw Nancy standing unassisted. Quickly she rose and went to the door.

"No, don't touch me, Miz Phenwick," Nancy said. "I've walked this far by myself. I'm certain I can walk into th' room as well."

"Why, Nancy Cox, what has ever happened to you?"

"I don't rightly know, Miz Phenwick," the girl explained, "but I reached for a glass of water a while back. When I did, my hands could clutch around it and I had no difficulty liftin' it to drink th' water. Then I began wigglin' my toes; pretty soon I could move my legs, and after a while I just clean got outa bed. Of course, I admit there was pins and needles stickin' in my feet at first, but I walked around th' room clinging to first one thing and then another until I realized that I didn't have to. I could walk all by myself. I went to th' window, opened it and had a breath of fresh air. Then I went and

192

changed my clothes, and found that I could move every part of me just like that." She snapped her fingers.

"Why, Nancy, this is miraculous! I thought you were destined to be an invalid for much longer than this."

"So did I, Miz Phenwick. All of a sudden I just began to feel that life was comin' back into my bones, I mean in my toes and all. It really is a puzzlement, isn't it? I couldn't move this mornin', I know that. When Miz Lillian Phenwick was givin' me a bath and preachin' to me all th' while about my sinful ways, she declared that I was gonna be a cripple th' rest of my life, said it would be a wonder if I evah got outa bed. I just kept sayin' to myself, 'I'm not goin' to be a cripple all my life. I'm gonna walk and I'm gonna dance.' And you know what, Miz Phenwick? I have been able to do some dance steps. That's what I was doin' in my room before comin' in heah."

"Nancy, you mustn't overdo. It may be only a temporary thing," Patricia said.

"No, I know it's a permanent healin' 'cause I believe it. You know, when you said th' reason I was affected by that voodoo doll was because I believed in it, I got to thinkin' that was true, that I did believe I was sick. If I just started thinkin' that I was well, I could walk. There was no validity in all that hocus-pocus about a voodoo doll, so there was no reason why I couldn't walk or why I couldn't be my old self again. After all, I have everything in th' world to live for. With Mr. Phenwick comin' back soon, I want to run to him. That's what I want to do. I want to dance with him. I want to hold him, and I want to do all the things that people do together that'll make us the happiest Phenwicks in the whole clan."

"Nancy, I really am delighted to see you change this way," Patricia remarked, "but I have a little fear."

"A little fear, Miz Phenwick?"

"That someone didn't want you to walk again, and I think that person, whoever he may be, is unscrupulous. Once he discovers that you can walk and are up and about, he is likely to do something again to cause you further distress."

"My goodness, how awful, whoevah would want to do that to me?" questioned Nancy.

"Whoever did it in the first place. Therefore, I suggest, until Peter returns, that you remain confined to this house. You may walk around and have full run of the place," Patricia explained, "but it would be wise, if your tormentor is an outside person, that he not know you have improved."

Nancy stared at the older woman, fear beginning to fill her. She began to feel faint. Lightly she sat in a chair, a dazed, incredulous expression deepening in her face.

Chapter 17

DANIEL ORNBY, ESQUIRE, was tall. While not in the least bit stocky, he was not as slender as his brother, Dr. Ted. Both men's features were similar. Daniel had the same thin hooked nose. He possessed a full head of rich dark hair, whereas the doctor was quite bald. In his youth, he had been a favorite of his Aunt Patricia. As the years went on when he attended Harvard Law School, Daniel grew away from Patricia's artistic crowd. When he married Melissa Kessler, whose father's political views were diametrically opposed to Patricia's, an even wider gap existed between aunt and great-nephew.

Daniel always appeared at Edward House without his wife. Both Patricia and Daniel preferred it that way. Still the old lady was never adverse to going to Daniel for advice.

"I received your letter via Jane Augusta," Daniel said after initial greetings were exchanged. Four days had passed since he had received that epistle. "I believe that I have garnered as much information for you as I possibly can."

"Aha, I knew I could count on you, Daniel."

"I must admit I found you asked some rather singular, if not downright perverse, questions," Daniel stated with a slight chuckle. "Since when have you taken an interest in notorious practices such as witchcraft, and for that matter, that barbarous nonsense called voodoo?"

"Is it such nonsense, Daniel? I wonder." Patricia offered a drink and proceeded to fill Daniel in on the details as she had observed them concerning both Nancy Cox and Harriet.

"So your latest candidate for a Phenwick woman has run into opposition, has she?" the attorney exclaimed. "Let me explain that I have found no cases of conviction for witchcraft in Boston courts, at least in the last century or so. There have been rumors of such things among my colleagues, and legends, but nothing concrete."

"No witches' covens?"

"Nothing quite so dramatic, Aunt Patricia," he said with laughter. "There are a few latter-day advocates of what is generally clustered in a grouping called the occult. A few radical groups are assembling to espouse contemporary religious thoughts; but as for witchcraft, I'm afraid this is an archaic subject."

"And voodoo?" questioned Patricia.

"That's a slightly different matter," Daniel informed her. "The fact is with the migration of Southerners, some free blacks, there have been a few reported instances of so-called voodoo. One woman was deported from the State of Massachusetts for allegedly casting voodoo spells. That was two years ago."

"Nothing more recent?"

"Not that I have discovered," replied Daniel. "Yet, you said in your letter that evidence of voodoo practice has been discovered. But that is taking the word of an excitable Southern girl, isn't it?"

"Nancy found a wax doll apparently made in her likeness," Patricia explained. "I didn't see that one, of course."

"Aha," Daniel exclaimed with a large smile.

"I did view the one your own sister Jane Augusta found," Patricia continued.

"Jane Augusta? She found one, too, in the likeness of herself?" questioned Daniel, a disturbed expression erasing the smile.

"No, of Nancy," Patricia replied. "At least the material of the costume was from one of Nancy's dresses. Ted removed the pins from the dolls's legs. Nancy was shown the effigy and the removal of the pins. Shortly after, the paralysis began to leave her. Now she can walk again."

Daniel scratched his head. "Curious."

"Most. I went to you for this information in hopes we might get a lead as to who has created these dolls to torment Nancy," Patricia said. "I thought perhaps there would be evidence of some person or persons in or around Boston who has been dabbling in this form of the occult."

"I don't believe I can be of very great assistance in this matter, Aunt," Daniel replied, nervously picking at his fingers. "However, I should think that your best procedure would be to see who might have a motive or who would want to frighten Nancy Cox or to put her out of the running, as it were, to be a potential Phenwick woman."

"I don't quite follow your meaning, Daniel."

"I should think that was simple enough. Who would want Nancy Cox out of the way or to become a cripple or perhaps in her grave? That is where you must look for your culprit."

"Yes, I suppose you're right. But when it comes to motives, I can think of no one," Patricia observed, "unless I go back to my original premise that there was, and perhaps for many years has been, a deep sense of competition between Nancy and the girl who poses as her best friend."

"This best friend is also a Southern girl, is she not?" questioned Daniel.

"True. But she herself has been ill most of the winter, and has hardly left Edward House," Patricia explained. "After much consideration, I don't see how she could be involved in such a nefarious plot."

"If you like, Aunt Patricia, I will have a friend of mine look further into the matter. He is more into investigating such matters than I," Daniel said. "As a matter of fact, I have an appointment with him this evening.

197

I will mention it to him and see what he thinks. If he has any suggestions, I will get back to you."

The Tooth & Tail Tavern was rarely busy in the afternoon. Only a few regulars came into the place and generally they just remained long enough for one drink, then left to go about their business.

Every day that week at two o'clock, Milford Wartstone had arrived at the tavern and had lingered until six, taking his time with perhaps no more than three drinks as if he were waiting for someone, expecting something.

On Friday afternoon, Milford Wartstone lurched into the bar, his hunchback always causing a murmur of attention which he pretended to ignore. Going directly to the bar, he motioned for a drink. Pomeroy Belcher, who was usually a jolly sort, changed his expression to annoyance whenever he saw Wartstone enter his establishment. He thought that by being cold to him, the man would become discouraged. This was not the case.

"I'll have me usual pint, if you don't mind," Wartstone ordered.

Belcher went immediately to draw the ale and gave it to the man, taking his coin from the bar. He was about to go about his business when the thought struck him. He turned back to Wartstone. "You wouldn't be expecting something in here, would you?" the beefy bartender asked.

"Yes, I am," Wartstone replied, his cold eyes looking from side to side to see if he had been overheard.

"A rather heavy envelope was delivered here this morning," Belcher stated. "The deliverer was a young boy whose face I didn't recognize. He simply said that it was to be left for the man in the black cloak."

"I am wearing a black cloak," Milford said.

"So you are. Would your initials be M.W.?"

"That's right, Milford Wartstone," he answered. "Is it a brown envelope? If so, give it to me. I have been expecting it all week."

The envelope, while thickly packed, was larger than

usually used for letters. Furtively, Wartstone took his drink into a corner where he found a table. Cautiously, he unsealed the envelope and examined the contents. First, he removed a piece of paper with written instructions upon it. Second, he examined the currency inside and found five one-hundred-dollar bills. A grim smile crossed his face as he hurriedly pocketed the envelope with the money. Then, he turned to the paper. Holding it to the afternoon light that was barely streaming in through the window, he read the ominous instructions. Upon completion of same, he let forth an ominous chuckle of malevolent delight. Then he folded the paper of instructions carefully and tucked it into his pocket.

Leaning back in his chair, he grandly sipped of the ale, and watched the others as they pretended not to observe him. The instructions were indelible in his mind already. He would formulate the plot to go with them.

Patricia had sent word to New York for Peter to return when Nancy seemed to be so very ill, the paralysis creeping through her body. A letter came saying that he would leave as quickly as possible, but he had further business to which he must attend before he could return to Boston. A very important matter. He had written to Patricia asking her to do whatever she could to ease Nancy's discomfort. He promised he would return within a fortnight to the girl of whom he could not help but think most of his waking hours. Even at night while asleep, he dreamed of her.

Once Prentise got wind of the suspicion that had been cast about Harriet, he decided to throw caution to the winds and leave Boston before the first thaw, taking Harriet with him. They would go back to Savannah and she could stay with her Aunt Magnolia until their new plantation home was completed.

Patricia, while she had concern for Harriet's health, suggested that Prentise was right in considering leaving early. Her one hope was that the accommodations aboard the ship would be adequate to keep the young woman warm since she was still in a physically weakened condition. That attended to, Prentise made plans to leave before his father returned from New York.

Lillian had kept a close watch over Nancy before her unfortunate outbreak about believing Nancy to be a pawn of the devil. Afterward she continued a prayer vigil in her own home and at the church for Nancy, sending Gus nightly to relay the information that she had prayed during that day for Nancy's soul.

Raymond had been a particularly close friend to Nancy and Arthur a second, each looking in and visiting daily with her. She liked them both. The more she got to know the men, the closer their friendship became. They were sworn to secrecy not to disclose the fact that Nancy was no longer paralyzed.

On the evening that the *Augusta IV* departed for Savannah with Prentise and Harriet aboard, Augustus Phenwick made his usual call to Edward House to look in on Nancy. She had become her usual gay self and no longer appeared to be an invalid. Gus spent only a few moments relaying his usual message that Lillian was praying for her. He was about to leave when he was approached by Patricia.

"Augustus, I would like to have a word with you," Patricia said as she touched him lightly on the shoulder.

"Whatever you wish, Aunt Patricia," Gus replied.

"Good. Come into the library," Patricia invited, leading the way.

Gus closed the door behind them and felt awkward in the grand lady's presence. "Is there something in particular you wanted to speak to me about, Aunt Patricia?"

"I am curious to know if Prentise and Harriet got off all right today."

Gus sighed with relief, a comical smile coming to his face. "The ship got out on time. We went to a great deal of trouble seeing that their cabin was sufficiently supplied with heat. It's not customary, you know, to put a stove in a cabin aboard a ship. We managed to do a makeshift

200

job which should keep the precious lady in comfort for her voyage home."

"What is your opinion of your sister-in-law, Gus?" Patricia asked.

"You mean Harriet?" Gus asked. "I must say I don't feel too comfortable in her presence. She appears sickly to me, especially since she lost that baby. Lillian says that Southern girls have a tendency to be weak. How she would know that, I don't know, but that's her opinion."

"But what is *your* precise opinion of Harriet?"

"As far as I'm concerned she is good enough for Prentise. She will probably be as good a wife as any woman he could find, and he has certainly taken his time in locating one."

"What is your opinion of Prentise, for that matter?" asked Patricia.

"I don't think that's a fair question, Aunt Patricia," he replied. "One should not have a staunch opinion about his brothers, should one?"

"I can't see why not," Patricia answered. "After all, one has a favorite brother or sister usually."

"Then perhaps I'm different, Aunt Patricia. I've never been particularly partial to either of my brothers nor to Joanna for that matter. They have been necessary evils with whom I have had to put up. I don't dislike them, but I can't honestly say I have a real love for any of them. I am pleased that Prentise is opening the Medallion office in Savannah. It will give us a great outlet and perhaps an increase of business. I am equally delighted that Joshua will one day take over the London office of Medallion Enterprises. He has a good head on his shoulders and a sensible wife, if she doesn't pursue a career in the theater. But that is neither here nor there. If she wants to flaunt herself upon the stage as Joanna does, that's her prerogative, I suppose. Were she my wife, I would put my foot down."

"I haven't noticed that you have put your foot firmly down on Lillian over the years, Gus," Patricia observed, trying to contain a smirk that wanted to come to her face.

"Lillian is a very domineering woman," Gus admitted. "She has a mind of her own. I suppose if I had taken a whip to her in our early years of marriage, I could have tamed her as one would tame a wild animal. I didn't have the time for that, nor did I have the time to oversee the raising of my children. Unfortunately she has had a strong hand in that. God knows what they will grow up to be. I can only pray that they will have some of the Phenwick common sense and not be so hysterically fanatic as Lillian is. Ah, but fanaticism runs in the Webb family. She gets it from both her father and her mother."

"I'm sure from what I know of both Stuart and Gordon they will grow up to be fine young men despite Lillian's influence over them."

"That is my prayer, Aunt Patricia. But did you ask me to linger simply to discuss such family matters?"

"In a sense, yes," Patricia replied. "Your father will be returning shortly and with his return, I am certain he will consider marriage as an imminent possibility. What is your opinion of that, Augustus?"

"My father has a mind of his own, too. He has always done exactly what he has wanted to do. I admit I have been close to him at times and at other times I have been at a remote distance—I would say more times than not. We have been apart in our ways of thinking, still I manage to work along with him and we rarely have disputes," Gus informed her. "He is a man of peculiar ways to my way of thinking. But then who am I, Aunt Patricia? I am only the rebellious son, the eldest who never received any particular notoriety for being the eldest, just one of the clan."

"Do you or have you missed that notoriety, as you put it, of being the eldest?"

"I did once as a young man. I felt cheated when Joshua and Prentise went away to England to school and I had to endure the schools in Boston and live at home," Gus said, trying not to sound bitter. "I have always been disappointed with Father's attitude toward Joanna. Oh, she is the star of his eye. Anything she does is perfectly all

202

right. It always has been that way. But with me, no matter what I did, I was criticized. When I rebelled or acted up in any way against his wishes, a whip was taken to my backside. I might add that that whip was spared my brothers, at least as far as my father was concerned. Mother was a little fairer in disciplining when it came to them. I have a feeling that is one of the reasons why Father permitted them to go to England at Uncle Lex's invitation—to get them away from Mother's influence."

"So you have become a kind of martyr brother, have you? The eldest, the neglected. Is that why you married Lillian?"

"I don't really know why I married Lillian," Gus confessed. "She was a whim, a means to an end. I knew Father would never approve of her. I suppose I married her for that reason."

"Did your mother approve of Lillian?" Patricia asked.

"She approved more so than Father did," Gus explained. "I don't think she really liked Lillian very much. I'll confess something else to you, too. I don't like Lillian very much—I don't think I ever did. She was all part of my rebellious attitude. I thought she was a means to an end, not a way of getting even or getting back at Father so much as to prove that I was my own man, that I could make my own choices. And you see what lousy judgment I have. Very well, I accept my fate and I accept Lillian for whatever she is. I try to tolerate her, but it is not an easy matter, Aunt Patricia, now that you've asked. I would never confess this to you under other circumstances. Since you have put me on the carpet, asked me point-blank, I have no other alternative but to tell you the truth."

"I appreciate your candor, Augustus," Patricia said, softly folding her hands together and looking ever so much the matriarch that she was.

"Now would you tell me one thing?"

"If I can, Augustus. What is it?"

"Why have *you* disapproved of Lillian all these years? Why have you not accepted her as a Phenwick woman?"

"I think if you will go back over what you have recently said, you will find the answer to your question. Lillian is a singular type. She is not what I would call a lady of importance and her fanaticism is quite unbearable. I am sorry now that I allowed her to come regularly to my house to look after Nancy. I should have made other arrangements, hired a woman to come in. There are certainly enough in Boston looking for work. But Lillian pleaded so, wanting to do something for the girl, that I accepted her. I felt in her way that she was trying to exonerate herself, to put herself in a better light as far as I was concerned. Instead she made a mess of the whole thing by allowing her emotions to carry her away and become a raving fanatic. I could not allow her in my house again. When I give family parties, which I will only do in the summertime after this, she will be included, naturally, because she is your wife, but they will be outdoor affairs."

"Then you don't like her at all, either, do you, Aunt Patricia?"

"Since we are being candid, Augustus, my answer can only be an unequivocal no. I never have liked Lillian and I don't think I ever will. As to you, I have pity for you. Yet I know that you must be enduring many hardships, putting up with much to live with a woman like that. I feel very sorry for you, Augustus, very sorry indeed."

"I don't really want your pity, you know, Aunt Patricia. I've learned to live with my fate, if that is what one calls it. I accept it."

"You may tell Lillian that it is no longer necessary for her to keep her prayer vigils for Nancy. The curse or whatever it was that caused her to be paralyzed has been taken away and Nancy is strong once again."

"Do you actually mean that she can walk now?"

"She can walk and run and dance," Patricia replied. "She can do all the things she used to do, my nephew, but that is to be a secret for a while. We don't want any recurrence of what happened before, not until your father returns and she is able to run to his arms."

"You are encouraging that, aren't you, Aunt Patricia?"

"Encouraging, Augustus?"

"The marriage of my father to this young girl."

"Do you disapprove deep within your heart? Do you disapprove, Augustus?"

"No, no, I don't believe I do. I want him to be happy in his last years," the man said. "If taking a young girl for a wife will make him happy, he is quite a different Phenwick man than I am. That is all I have to say. I just hope he knows what he is getting into."

"I'm certain he has had sufficient time to think about it. No doubt when he returns, his mind will be well made up, and little time will pass before the wedding occurs unless . . ." She hesitated.

"Unless?"

"I don't want to think about any unlesses," Patricia said. "Thank you for the conversation, Augustus. I'm sorry that over the years we have never had more intimate little chats. Perhaps if I had gotten to know you better, and you me, we might have had a different relationship. But that is water under the bridge, isn't it?"

Augustus nodded, said goodbye and went to the door.

The following Monday, Patricia received a letter. Upon opening it and quickly perusing the contents, she left her room and went to find Nancy. She was amusing herself in the ballroom, practicing dance steps she had learned.

"Glory be, you startled me, Miz Phenwick," Nancy exclaimed. "Actually I was expectin' Mr. Nelson and Mr. Townsend directly to come and show me some new steps they have learned. They promised they would, but I suppose they had other things to do this early in the day. Come to think of it, they said they wouldn't be heah till one. I reckon I just came in to brush up on what they taught me before."

"Nancy, I have good news for you," Patricia announced. "Word has come which I think will make you happy."

"What is it, Miz Phenwick? I d'clare, you got me covered with goose bumps th' way you speak about it."

205

"To put it in a word, my precious Peter, or should I say *our* precious Peter, will be back in Boston tomorrow."

"You mean, tomorrow, Tuesday? Oh, saints above! I d'clare, my prayers have been answered. I hope he nevah goes away from me ag'in for as long as this."

"He's likely to go away and never return, Nancy, he being so much older than you."

"I've thought of that eventuality. Then I would resign myself to th' fact that he was gone to his final reward. But when I know he is just down in New York instead of up heah . . . Why, if'n we had been married, he would have taken me along. He was afraid of th' scandal it might have created."

"I know. I am happy for you. I am pleased despite the hardships you endured here while you remained in Boston. It has given you both time. I am certain the results will be well worth the waiting."

"I know they will be, Miz Phenwick." Nancy reached to take the old lady's hand. "Thank you evah so much for all you've done for me. I hope I will always be as close to you as I am at this moment. I feel very close to you."

"I understand Arthur is helping you to lose your accent, is that true?" Patricia asked, avoiding an emotional reaction to the girl's words.

"I reckon he is. So far it doesn't show much. Maybe d'rectly it will. I'm tryin', but it's those final *g*'s. Why, I didn't even know they existed on words except for spellin' them—I mean spelling them."

Patricia laughed. "I'm glad to see you happy, Nancy, and well and dancing. Furthermore, I'm pleased that you decided not to have further romantic interests in my young men, Mr. Nelson and Mr. Townsend."

"Your young men?" Nancy giggled. "Why, Miz Phenwick."

206

Chapter 18

TUESDAY HAD BEGUN as a gray overcast day. By afternoon it had begun to rain. The precipitation persisted into the night. The servants at Edward House were traditionally off on Tuesday all except for Matilde and Ethelbert, a maid and second butler. The servants' day off coincided with outside activities with which Patricia was involved. This particular Tuesday afternoon, she attended a meeting at the Boston Historical Society. The session was to be special, long, lasting into the evening when a social supper was planned. The supper was designed to entice new prospective associates as well as friends and families of members. Usually the meetings were dull, but Patricia felt it her civic duty to attend.

Nancy remained at Edward House alone with the exception of Ethelbert and Matilde. The dreary day inched with an interminable slowness, the minutes seemed hours and the hours seemed days. Ethelbert served her tea and sweet toast in the parlor at four, came and picked up the serving things at four-thirty and seemingly vanished from the house not to be heard from again that afternoon; nor was there indication that Matilde was anywhere about.

By five o'clock the sky had become dark, only occasionally to be lit by shocking electric streaks of lightning. Ethelbert had built up the fire in the parlor with sufficient wood in reserve to last through the night; but he did not return to tend it. Nancy turned up the flames in four lamps. The light was shallow and created an eerie aura in the dismal atmosphere of the afternoon. She could not get warm, chills striking through her with each flash of lightning and crack of thunder. The rain was coming down with a fury.

Deciding that she would have the servants come in to sit with her until the storm subsided, Nancy pulled the cord that rang a bell both in the kitchen and in the servants' quarters. When there was no response in five minutes, she tugged it again. Still no answer.

After getting no reaction from pulling the summoning cord a third time, alarmed and shaking with apprehension, she decided to go investigate. Just sitting there could fracture her nerves.

Taking a small lamp, Nancy ventured from the parlor into the dark hallway. She held the light high at the dining room door, seeing nothing but the glaring faces of family portraits ominously gazing down at her. It was enough to terrify a perfectly composed person. The effect on the already excited girl caused her pulse to quicken with fear. She hurriedly left the room, moving down the hallway as fast as she dared and going toward the kitchen.

A fire was still beneath the simmering teakettle, but there was no other sign of life in the large kitchen. Nancy would not venture into or beyond the servants' quarters. Instead she went toward the front of the house where the library was to her left and the ballroom was to her right. Gazing from one closed door to the other, then to the huge front door that led outside, a sensation of stark loneliness came over her. She pivoted around to glance at the stairs leading to the dark second floor. Why had not the hall lights been ignited? The servants usually attended to this at the first indication of darkness. A gloom hovered about the hallway.

Some magnetic compulsion seemed to be drawing her toward the ballroom. She had spent many hours in that place practicing her dancing with either Raymond or Arthur or both and felt that it was especially warm to her. She liked the walls covered with mirrors and the several portraits that hung around the large room, including one of Augusta Phenwick.

Entering the ballroom, the small light she was carrying seemed brighter as it reflected in the many mirrors. The room itself was cold. She shivered upon examining her reflection in one of the mirrors. Then she found herself observing the entire room through the glass.

Why did her attention become compulsively drawn to the enormous portrait of the first matriarch of the family, Augusta Phenwick?

As if she were magnetically compelled to it, she moved across the shining ballroom floor until she stood beneath the painting. How lifelike that lovely lady still looked as though she were really sitting there. There was dimension to the canvas. That proud face, those determined eyes still appeared to be alive and radiating through her.

Nancy stepped back and observed the painting from a short distance, believing that she had been standing too close so that an optical illusion had been created. But the more she stared at the painting, the more lifelike it became until it seemed that at any moment the lips would move, the eyes blink and words come forth. The girl was hypnotized by the stately features of that grand woman. Did she imagine the scent of violets?

When the bell chimes were struck, Nancy let out a tiny shriek of alarm, quickly putting her fingers to her lips and spinning about as she stared at the slightly opened door to the ballroom. She waited several minutes, expecting to hear footsteps come to answer the door. There were none. The chimes rang a second time and Nancy ran hastily across the ballroom floor, but hesitated as she reached the door.

This time a knocking was heard against the wooden door. Dare she open it? Dare she turn the key and twist the knob? Perhaps she might open it to an unwelcome stranger. On the other hand, maybe it was some member of the family who had been caught in the storm and had come to find a place of warmth and comfort until the rain ceased. Mustering courage, she went to the door, adjusted the key and opened it.

A boy of about twelve or thirteen was standing outside. He was drenched to the skin, his hair streaming with water down his face so that he was hardly recognizable. Upon seeing her, the boy wiped his hand across his forehead to relocate the fallen hair and to wipe away some of the moisture.

"Are you Miss Cox?" he asked, his voice sounding as if it were about to make a switch of octaves.

"I am, who are you?"

"My name is Charlie. I've come with a message for you."

"A message for me? From whom?" Nancy asked.

"A man down by the Medallion offices gave it to me," he said, "and he paid me handsomely to bring it here immediately. If the price had not been so large, I would have waited till after the storm."

"Thank you," Nancy said, receiving the envelope. Then, looking at the pathetically wet creature standing outside, she was tempted to invite him in to warm himself by the parlor fire. Still he was only an urchin boy. She closed the door behind him.

In the hallway she set the lamp on a table near the door. Then she tore the envelope open to read the message: "My dearest Nancy: My ship has returned to Boston and I will be available to see you within an hour. I will send a carriage around to pick you up and you will be brought to me where we will once again be joined together."

It was signed, "Peter."

She let out a cry of joy. Peter Phenwick was in port! He had arrived at long last. His time away had seemed an eternity to her. Now all those dreadful hours, those tedious days of waiting, the time of paralysis and feeling as if she would not live long enough to see her beloved man again were only fleeting moments which were now gone. Hastily she connected to the lamp and took the stairs to the second floor as rapidly as she could, excitement filling her with anticipation over the arrival of her man.

Penetrating the dark hallway as she did, her small lamp seemed tinier and with even less glow to brighten her pathway. Still she knew the way to her room and she went toward it without giving second thought to the ominous blackness that surrounded her.

Within her room she quickly lit as many lamps as she could, even putting flame to the candles. It was bright. Since she had an hour she decided to put fire to the stove wherein wood was laid.

That hour went by in no time at all and she wondered if she were suitably presentable for her lover. The mirror reflected a beauty that only love could radiate in a person's face. The old luster had returned. The enthusiam for life which had somehow begun to dwindle in those long days of waiting had returned.

Being in the front part of the house, her room overlooked the street. She watched from the window in those last few minutes until she saw the black silhouette of the carriage arrive.

The driver got down from the seat. She could not distinctly see the man. She did not wait for the door chimes to be rung. Instead she flew from her room after extinguishing the lights and carried the small lamp back through the dark hallway. What had become of the servants? Why had they not answered the door? Had they left the house unbeknown to her? They were faithful to Patricia and would never have disobeyed her orders for fear of losing their positions.

When she reached the door, Nancy saw that the black-cloaked driver had returned to the driver's seat. She called out, "Yes, who is it?"

"A hansom carriage come to deliver you to Mr. Peter Phenwick," the driver called, a husky harshness to his voice.

"Will you open the door for me?" she asked.

"I just returned to my seat. It is raining and the door

211

is ajar," the driver called back to her. "You can manage for yourself."

"Very well," she said, closing the door firmly behind her, hearing it latch tight. Then pulling her hood over her hair, her cape tightly about her, she ran down the few steps and managed to get into the waiting carriage. A few moments later she was sitting on the seat as comfortably as she could, her full skirts billowing out about her. Perhaps she would have been wiser to wear fewer petticoats for that occasion in all that storm, but she wanted to look her finest for Peter.

The carriage started with a jerking action, lurched down the driveway and was soon on the cobbled road, bouncing the passenger about from side to side so that she had to hold to the handles on both sides of the coach to keep from jostling about too much.

The lightning continued but was in the distance, somewhat northeast of Boston so that only occasionally the sky was brightened by its glow. The thunder, too, had lost its intensity over the city. Distant rumbling could still be heard.

The carriage went faster and faster through the city streets; the ride became rougher and rougher for the girl. Still she held on with all her strength, only anticipating the reunion with Peter Phenwick.

Soon she could tell by the sound of the carriage wheels they were no longer riding over cobbled streets but bumping over an unpaved road. Water splashed about and the sound of the wheels was that which they make when going through mud. Nancy pulled herself to the window to observe that they were not going toward the wharves at all, but in another direction.

A few moments later they were crossing a bridge over the Charles River. She had the feeling that they were going farther and farther away from her specified destination. Then as if looming out of the darkness, she saw a sign pointing in the direction they were headed. It said, "Lexington."

She cried out, "Driver, driver, where are you taking me?"

The more she hollered, the faster the driver went, the cracking of his whip resounding through the night. She was pitched and jolted about. Fear overwhelmed her, as she believed that instead of going to see her lover, she was being kidnapped and taken out of the city limits of Boston.

How long she had been riding, she had no idea. She only knew the taste of fear, dry in her throat. Trembling, she clung to the carriage straps until her hands ached with the intensity with which she was holding them.

Now it seemed the carriage was catching up with the lightning storm as periodic flashes of electricity lit the sky with a cold blue-white light and a jagged line seemed to be rending the skies asunder. The thunder rolled like an echo of a whip crack. She screamed. Again and again she raised her voice to plead with the driver to take her back to Boston, explaining that he was going the wrong way. In her torment, she perceived that his reply was a roar of maniacal laughter.

After traveling for nearly an hour—she had no concept of time—Nancy again peered through the window just as a flash of lightning lit up the entire sky. As it did, she saw the silhouette of a black mansion in the near distance, atop a knoll and surrounded by a forest of straggly-looking trees. The carriage wheels went over a wooden bridge, she could tell by the sound. Keeping her face to the window as best she could, she saw that the coach was increasingly getting nearer to the old house.

Soon the carriage slowed to a halt and she could feel the weight of the driver as he got down from his seat. Before she could collect her wits and try to make an escape, the door was jerked open. A lantern was hanging beside it. She gazed with horror into the hideously distorted face of Milford Wartstone. She shrieked at the expression of diabolical menacing that he wore and cringed with fear as she became aware of his misshapen figure and his hunched back. His leer, as he gazed up at her, showed

213

several missing teeth, which only underlined his sinister expression.

"All right, come out," he ordered, that terrible voice of his insinuating violence if she did not comply with his orders.

"Where is this place? Why have you brought me here?" she asked. "Why, I d'clare, we're in th' middle of nowhere."

"D'clare all you like," Wartstone returned, "but get down from there before I jerk you out."

Nancy complied, delicately putting her foot on the first step. Instantly Wartstone raised his hands and grasped her about the waist to pull her down. The rain was still falling lightly, but the heavy downpour had either ceased or had not yet reached that area.

Wartstone pulled her face to face with him, his terrible breath causing a repulsive reaction within her. His piercing eyes gave her a sensation of disgust and dread.

"What do you want of me?"

"I should hoist you in and take pleasure from you, Miss Cox," Wartstone replied. "But that is not why I am here nor why you have been brought to this place. So I shall control my animal instincts and deliver you into the house."

Nancy caught only a quick glimpse of the place. The exterior was wooden and apparently unpainted for it looked gray-black. She did notice, however, that the windows were boarded over, most of them, and those which weren't had bars across them. The building was three stories high and the old gingerbread that trimmed it was falling apart. The lightning rod atop the roof was broken. The building looked abandoned.

Roughly Nancy was pulled to the front door. Once it was open, Wartstone threw her bodily into the entranceway so that she fell forward landing on her front side in a sprawled, unladylike position, her petticoats tilted upward. Wartstone laughed sardonically as he viewed her. A moment later he slammed the door closed, himself on the outside as he attached a stout lock to the door.

Trembling, crying, aching with fear, Nancy lay upon the floor for several moments, stunned by all that had happened. Then finding strength from she knew not where, she slowly raised herself to her feet. She attempted to penetrate the dark. Her eyes had not adjusted, and she was like a blind person for a few moments. Then she heard a cracking sound, followed by scampering noise such as a small rodent makes when racing across the floor.

Chapter 19

GOING BACK TO THE FRONT DOOR, she attempted to open it. Nancy found it stoutly locked. Banging her fists against it several times, she cried for the driver to return. As she heard the carriage drive away, she ceased her calling and began to sob. Finally she leaned heavily against the door as she resolutely accepted her fate.

Still she was not a girl to give up easily. Her daring nature was such that she would attempt to find a way out of that old house and walk all the way back to Boston if need be. She refused to remain in such a sinister place.

Inching her way, hands held out to her sides, fingers outstretched, she felt for the wall. When she found it, she moved slowly along until she came to a door. Turning the handle she swung it open and moved into a large room. Fortunately, although it frightened her at the time, a shock of lightning lit the sky and illumination came in through four different windows in that corner room. She could see a candelabra with three half-burned candles in it. She made her way in that direction, holding her hands out until they touched the old candle holder, which was on a dusty table. Her hands swept through cobwebs as she searched in hopes of finding matches. Luck was with her, or so she thought, for she felt a metal box that contained seven or eight matches.

Quickly she struck one and lit the candles. The light dispelled little gloom from the room. In fact, it added more to her apprehensive feeling. What sort of place had she entered? An old abandoned house. Torn curtains were on the windows. She could see bars on the outside of them.

Nancy went from window to window. All were the same, bars covering them. The curtains were torn remnants of what had once been organdy. The floor creaked beneath her footsteps and a dusty, dirty feeling was throughout the room. Air was coming through a hole in one of the windows where the glass had been broken. The room was cold.

Taking candles and matches with her, she left that room, went back into the hallway and ventured into the room on the opposite side. There she found a few sparse objects of furniture broken, some covered with material. The feeling that prevailed was that this house had long since been abandoned, perhaps for years. Rats and other vermin had left their signs. There were places on the furniture that had been gnawed. Where there was fabric, it had been chewed. A foul odor hung in that room. She found it difficult to remain.

She wandered about two other large rooms on the first floor. Checking each window and the door that seemed to lead from what was once a perfunctory kitchen, she discovered them all securely fastened and impregnable. Her horror built as she realized that she was trapped in that old house.

Her next course was to invade the second floor to see if she might find a lamp of some kind or other candles. Also she hoped to locate a stove she could light in a room small enough to hold heat. The stairway was rickety, creaking noisily with each step she took. At first she touched the old banister, but it was so covered with dust that she did not want to hold onto it. The candelabra trembled in her hand, making the shaking flames even more unstable and causing grotesque shadows to appear as she moved.

It was fearfully cold. With her cloak tightly wrapped around her, she was still trembling. Was that from actual cold or was it from fear? In either case her teeth were chattering. She knew she must wander through all the rooms and check all possibilities if she were to survive in that place.

On the second floor there were four rooms which appeared to have been bedrooms and two which were storage rooms without windows. Only one room contained part of a bedstead and a dresser with all the drawers missing. An old lamp was on the dresser. Nancy discovered there was no oil in it. She did, however, find two pieces of candle which she felt might come in handy before the night was over. Then she set the candelabra on the dresser and warmed her fingers by the tiny flames.

Finally, in a fourth bedroom she found two quilts which had been heaped into the corner of it. The pile of material, although it appeared filthy, might give her some warmth. As she touched it, a mouse ran out from the folds of the cloth and she jumped back shrieking with alarm. The rodent gone, she again attempted to pick up the quilt, to discover that it was partly chewed away. The second quilt was not in much better condition. However, she thought if worst came to worst, she could use them for warmth.

As she stood in that room, examining the quilts, her attention was drawn to the sound of movement on the floor above her. Were there other rodents? Or perhaps a squirrel had gotten into the house and made a home upstairs. Or was some person up there waiting for her? That thought terrified her. She held her position, staring from candle to ceiling. Had she heard human footsteps? Was it the sound made by shoes walking above her? Was her imagination running rampant?

Again she negotiated a flight of stairs, one which was in an even worse state of disrepair than that which she had climbed to the second floor. Twice she feared the step board would give away beneath her weight. The terror that scrambled through her at the thought of falling caused her to react with a terrible sick feeling. Yet, something was drawing her upward to explore, to make certain she was quite alone in the house.

There were only four rooms on the third floor which was at the top of the building. Water dripped from the ceiling of one room and completely covered the floor. The second room was empty. Those first two chambers were in the back part of the house. A broken rocking chair was sitting in the first front room. A doll looking like a relic from the days of the Revolutionary War was sprawled in the corner, badly decayed, its arms folded over its head, the body rodent-chewed. Impulsively, she went to examine that piece of material that had once been loved by a child or perhaps several generations of children. Yet it was in such a disagreeable state that she felt herself repulsed by it.

In the last room on that floor, she found some blankets. These, too, showed evidence of rodent use, but they did not appear as badly chewed as those on the floor below nor did they for some reason seem quite as dirty. Two small windows were in that room. Perhaps they were large enough for a person to squeeze through, but it was a straight three-story drop from them to the ground. One's best chance might be to break out the glass and try to jump. Nancy was not that brave.

Going to the corner of the room, she examined the blankets. After shaking them out she took them into the room where the rocker and the doll were. This room also had two windows. It would be a three-story drop from them, too.

She stood at the window for a moment. In a distant flash of lightning, she could see a cleared area which must have been the road and the drive leading to the house. She would place the candle on the window ledge so that someone might see it and be aware of her presence.

Sitting on the floor, since she was certain the rocking chair would not support her weight, she put a blanket down first and wrapped it around her, then she drew the other one above her. How long would the candles last? Suddenly, a thought came to her. Perhaps it would be best if she extinguished two of the candles lest they all burn out at once.

Scampering to her feet, she blew out two of the candles. Before returning to her position, she went to examine the doll, this time daring to pick it up. When she did, her attention did not remain with that doll, but with a piece of wax made in an image of a person that was lying beneath it. The dress material on the waxen image was the same that had been on the other two she had seen, and the front of the skirt was lifted with pins jabbed into each of the thighs. She picked it up, looked at it and quickly plucked the pins from their places.

"I will not believe in voodoo," she screamed, "I will not believe." With that she began tearing the wretched-smelling wax into pieces, ripping the material that composed the dress and tearing the hair from the head. Then gathering them all together, she took a match, went into the room which was saturated with water and put them down to burn.

Her eyes became teary as she watched the wax melt beneath the stench of burning cloth and hair. None of the parts of the waxen effigy completely burned before the fire went out, but she considered that enough was destroyed that whatever power it might have, if indeed it had any at all, was destroyed. Then closing the door to the room with effort, for it was swollen, she returned to the front room where she had left the candle. Wrapping herself again in the blankets, she sat in wait.

Arthur Townsend and Raymond Nelson had had dinner together, after which they decided to stop by to cheer Nancy. Recalling that Patricia went to the Historical Society meeting that afternoon and evening, and would not be returning until late, they thought it would be kind to visit Nancy. Taking a carriage to Edward House and finding it dark, Raymond waited in the vehicle while Arthur went to the door and rang the bell. There was no response nor was there any when he banged his fist on the door. Unable to rouse anyone, he decided that Nancy probably had gone to visit Jane Augusta Ornby-Clark. That being the case, they would not disturb her. They would go instead to the Tooth & Tail Tavern to enjoy a few drinks before returning to their respective homes

The Tooth & Tail Tavern was as usual relatively busy at that hour with many familiar faces present. Arthur and Raymond found a table in a corner where they often sat to observe. While they were devouring their first drinks, Milford Wartstone came lurching into the tavern. He seemed to be wrapped in a flurry of mystery, his black cloak wet and his hat shining with moisture. He removed the cape and hung it near the stove to dry along with the hat. Then he went to the bar and ordered himself a glass of rum.

"Pomeroy Belcher," he said, "were there any more messages for me?"

Pomeroy Belcher wiped the back of his hand across his brow, then over his apron, and said, "I know of none. What brings you into my establishment this time of night?"

"It's wet out and I have been riding."

"I know it's wet out," Belcher replied, "but I've told you before, I don't want you here during my busiest time of the evening. You frighten people."

"So what if I frighten them? They have been frightened before, they will be frightened again," Wartstone stated and downed his glass of rum. He pushed the glass forward and asked for another.

"I told you I didn't want to serve you in here."

"And I said, 'Give me another'."

Milford Wartstone was able to outstare Pomeroy Belcher, who after several tense moments reached over to refill the glass.

Raymond and Arthur had observed the byplay between the two men. They rose from their seats and went to the bar, taking positions on either side of Wartstone.

"Well, well, well, if it isn't my notorious model," exclaimed Raymond.

Wartstone turned to glance over his shoulder. "Hmmph, so it's the fancy-pants artist, is it?"

"And the writer," Arthur said from the other side.

Wartstone barely moved his head to acknowledge that Arthur was standing there. "What do you dandy gents want with the likes of me this rainy night?"

"I was just curious to buy you a drink, Mr. Wartstone," Raymond said, unconsciously scratching at the upper left side of his chest.

"Buy me a drink? Have you a guilty conscience or some such?" asked the man.

"No," Raymond replied, still scratching. "I simply wanted to have a word with you." Then it hit him and he looked down at the fingers that were rubbing his upper chest. "You know, Mr. Wartstone, there was an evening when you and I were drinking and you became extremely chummy with me."

"I don't recall such an evening, but your memory may be better than mine," Wartstone replied, motioning for Belcher to pour him another glass of rum. He pointed with his thumb to indicate that Raymond was going to pay for it.

Raymond nodded his head. "I remember it quite well. You made it a point of asking what I knew about Miss Nancy Cox. I don't recall the precise information I gave you. Fact is, I don't recollect how that evening ended. I do vaguely remember that I took you to my studio to do some quick sketches." Again, he massaged his fingers over his left upper chest. "I have a feeling I'm not the only one who did sketching that evening, Mr. Wartstone. I have a scar beneath where I am holding my fingers for which I cannot account."

"You're intoxicated, man. I don't know what you're talking about," Wartstone sneered.

"There was another time, a few days later, when I again encountered you and you came to pose for me. I was quite sober that time. It was the day before I went on a picnic with Mr. Townsend here and Miss Nancy Cox. You asked me several curious questions and I naïvely told you about the planned outing. I also mentioned that I would be carrying a leather bag with me to hold my art supplies, the

223

same leather bag in which was found a voodoo doll, made in the likeness of Miss Cox."

Wartstone's eyes grew fiery red with anger. His face paled as he suddenly pushed Raymond backward off-balance. Then flying to the stove, he swept up his cape and hat. Flinging the cape around his shoulders, he put the hat on his head before Raymond could get back to his feet. With abnormal speed the man lurched from the tavern, stopping at the door when he ran headlong into Peter Phenwick.

Arthur shouted, "Stop that man, he's accosted my friend."

A general commotion began stirring in the tavern as the other imbibers became curious about what was happening.

"Unhand me, you fool!" Wartstone commanded. "One side or I'll knee you in the groin."

Peter swiftly caught the man's arm, twisting it into a hammerlock, twirling him bodily around and causing him to suffer a sudden shock of pain.

"Now then, what is this all about?" asked Peter.

After Arthur pulled his friend to his feet, he went to where Peter had a strong hold on Wartstone. The others in the tavern had gathered around, pushing close, causing Pomeroy Belcher to become alarmed.

"This man has just accosted my friend," Arthur repeated.

"For what reason?" Peter questioned.

Arthur stared into the handsome man's face. "Aren't you Peter Phenwick?"

"Yes, I am."

By then Raymond had pushed himself through the crowd and stood facing Milford Wartstone. Quickly, as Peter held the man in a firm hold, Raymond explained about the voodoo doll and the curse Nancy believed was on her. He also explained about the voodoo doll that was allegedly planted by Milford Wartstone in the artist's leather bag.

"Did you do such a thing, Wartstone?" Peter inquired.

"I never," the man growled.

Peter tightened his grip on the hunchback, pressing the man's hand to nearly touch the back of his head.

"For God's sake, man, no more! You'll break my blasted arm! I confess I did put that damn piece of wax in his bag, but I didn't do it because I had anything against the girl. My services were hired and I gave labor in fair exchange for coin. A wretched crippled man like me has to earn a living some way. How was I to know what it was all about?"

"Doing it for hire or doing it of your own volition," Peter said, "either way you committed a wrong against an innocent young lady." Peter turned to Raymond. "Do you know where Nancy is now?"

"She's not at Edward House," Arthur replied. "At least, no one answered the door."

"Perhaps she went to Mrs. Ornby-Clark's," suggested Raymond.

"I doubt that," Peter returned. "She was to have waited for me at Edward House."

"You don't know she's not there, matey," Wartstone said hopefully. "You can't be certain she's not."

Peter tightened his grip on Wartstone. "Where is she, Wartstone?"

"Ow! I think you've busted my arm," Wartstone moaned.

"Not yet, I haven't," Peter returned, "but it won't be long before I do."

"You'd better answer Mr. Phenwick," Pomeroy Belcher encouraged, hoping that Peter would carry forth his threat.

"All right, I'll tell you," Wartstone screamed. "Let up, will you! How can a man speak in such agony?" He gasped for breath. "Why—I picked her up at Edward House over two hours ago. But it wasn't my notion. I was paid. I had been given orders."

Chapter 20

NANCY HAD REFUSED to accept the numbing pain that had come to her thighs. She cried out of fear. Whimpering, she tried to rationalize away her feelings of helplessness. Only a few hours before she had been dancing, laughing in anticipation of Peter Phenwick returning to her. That had been such a beautiful dream, and this had become a terrifying nightmare. Her mind was plagued with imps of fantasy, conjuring pictures of fear and distress. Huddling in the corner of the room, periodically looking at the doll's head, she projected desperate thoughts. If only someone could pick them up, and be guided to where she was being held captive. Captive? Indeed, that was precisely what she was. Would the horrible hunchback man return to torment her during the night? She imagined that a man such as he was both mentally and morally depraved; probably a deviate with perverse notions. Was he so ugly that he had to capture young girls, hide them away in such old houses as this and wait until their resistance was completely broken before he returned to take lustful advantage of them? No! She must erase that thought from her mind, too.

After a period of weary sobbing, Nancy felt exhausted. The rhythm of her crying began to lull her to sleep. Her unconscious dreams were fraught with horrible images, more terrifying than her waking experience had been.

A loud noise awakened her. It was as if something had fallen from the ceiling, or an object had been thrown into the room. Her eyes snapped open. She felt she was still experiencing part of her troubled dream. The room was black. The candle had burned out—or something had put it out. Fumbling among her clothing, she found the box of matches and the stub of a candle she had picked up in one of the rooms. She lit it.

The object that had caused the noise was that lump of melted wax and partly burned material and hair that had been the wax effigy of herself. It was no more than two feet from where she was sitting. Somehow she managed to contain a scream of alarm that was screeching through her. How had that horrible lump of foul-smelling mixture gotten into that room?

She stared for nearly five minutes at the object before she was able to muster sufficient strength to rise and kick it away from her, making it skid across the room to the far wall. Her attention then went to the candelabra at the window. The candle had not burned completely down. Fact is, there was at least three good inches of wax left on it. Standing quietly for a few seconds, she tried to determine if a draft were coming into the room. The place was drafty, no doubt about that, since a few of the small windowpanes were broken in other parts of the building, but that room was relatively free of any direct breezes.

Lighting the candle in the holder with the one in her hand, she moved to the other window and stared out into the night. The rain had ceased and in places she could see clear sky and stars. Clouds were moving overhead and twice a three-quarter moon shone through. She could see by the moonlight that there were no buildings near the one in which she was imprisoned. In the very far distance, the region she considered to be Boston, she beheld one tiny light. It was only a speck. Thus she assumed it was too far away to be of any use to her.

When she turned from the window, she was startled to see a ghostlike appearance standing in the doorway, witchlike in attitude and dress. Great bulging eyes glared at her. Nancy screamed. The witch pointed a finger at her, then moved it to the lump of wax she had kicked against the wall.

Before Nancy could shriek a question, the witch's finger moved back to the girl and pointed at her thighs. The creature made the movement of laughter, lightly holding its belly in an obvious gesture. When Nancy looked at her legs, she felt that terrible numbing pain return. She had to move, to prove that her legs were still able to be maneuvered. When she glanced up, the apparition, or whatever it was, was gone. With effort she took the first step, then the second. The pain could not be denied.

Going to the door, Nancy gazed down the hallway, but saw no evidence of any person or thing. Had that experience been part of a dream, too? Had she begun to hallucinate? She closed the door. There was no way to lock it, but she put the broken rocker in front of it.

Back in the corner, where she had been huddled in dirty blankets, she crouched again, massaging her legs as she did. That action reminded her of Lillian Phenwick and the hours she had spent rubbing her paralyzed legs. What were some of the biblical verses Gus's wife had taught her? She tried to remember.

"He that dwelleth in th' secret place of th' most high shall abide under th' shadow of th' Almighty. I will say of th' Lord, He is my refuge and my fortress, my God, in Him will I trust. Surely He will deliver thee from the snare of th' fowler and the noisome pestilence . . ." she recited. Not recalling what came next, she went back and repeated the first part of the verses, considering each phrase as if to glean the meaning of it. Over and over she recited those words. As she did a light began to dawn in her consciousness. "So that is what Lillian Phenwick was tryin' to tell me all this time!" she exclaimed. "It has to do with faith and trust in God. *He that dwelleth in the secret place of the most high* . . . Glory be! I d'clare, I reckon I just figured that out. I dwell! I believe! I will be delivered from th' ol' fowler's snare! I will! I will!"

A new feeling of excitement and confidence came over her. As it did, the pain began to subside in her thighs. She returned to the window and gazed out. Still no sign of anything but empty night. But she was becoming filled with

229

new thoughts as she gazed up at the sky, where more and more stars were beginning to show. "I've never been all that good at bein' religious, God," she prayed, "but once I'm outa this mess, I d'clare I'll get better."

Three thumping sounds thundered against the wall to the adjoining room.

"God? Is that you? I mean *Thee?*" she asked.

The thumps were followed by a diabolical cackle and a weird, irritating scratching noise.

"God?"

A crackly voice said, "Blasphemy! Satan is calling for you!"

Nancy was certain she had heard the voice of a bona fide witch, no doubt the one who had earlier appeared at the door. She stood petrified for several seconds as other strange sounds came from the next room.

Nancy backed toward the window, but was too terrified to turn around to look at the starry sky. Then a putrid aroma came seeping into the room. It seemed to come from the place where the remains of the wax doll were lying. As it got stronger and almost suffocating, she noticed that a fine stream of vaporous smoke was rising from under the door. Quickly she went to it, pushed the rocker aside and flung the door open.

An old battered pan was directly outside from which the obnoxious fumes were wafting. Kicking it with her foot, Nancy guided the receptacle to the room that was covered with water and managed to turn the pan over, suffocating whatever had caused the aroma.

Returning quickly to the room in which she had been and putting the rocker in place, she hurriedly went back to the window and stared up at the starry sky.

"Th' Lord is my shepherd, I shall not want," she recited. "Thank goodness, Miz Phenwick made me learn them psalms. Oh, I just know that whatever this is all about will be over soon and I'll be returned to th' arms of Mistah Phenwick. Lawsy, but I can hardly wait."

"Wait you must, my child," a voice said from the opposite part of the room.

Nancy turned with alarm. Eyes widened as she saw a figure slowly materializing before her. She gasped. While the image became clear, it appeared to have little substance and she could see the outline of the door through it. The room was somehow brighter. Nancy was strangely aware of the scent of violets.

"Who—who are you?" Nancy asked incredulously.

"Don't you recognize me, Nancy? Haven't you gazed sufficiently long at my portrait to know who I am?"

"Why, I d'clare, you look like—I mean, there is a speck of resemblance between you and—and th' picture of—I mean th' one in th' ballroom at Edward House," Nancy stammered. "Do you-all know th' one what I mean?"

"Yes, Nancy Cox, I know. I have watched you and I believe you will make a fine Phenwick woman. Long have I observed Peter. How sorry I felt for him being tied to Helen Barnfather. How the man ever put up with that, I'll never understand. Now you . . . yes, I am pleased with you, Nancy. I believe you will make a beautiful wife for my grandson."

"Your grandson?" Nancy asked.

"Peter is the third child of the only one of my own children who lived. I have always loved my Danny's children, even though I had only pity for poor Rachel. Still it worked out."

"Then you *are!* I mean . . . Miz Augusta Phenwick?"

The vision of Augusta Phenwick smiled gently. *"Let me assure you that I am the only true spirit that you will behold this night. All others will be contrivances of mortal mind. But I will see that you are protected. You may receive a daring thought or two before it is over, but that's only me giving you a little advice from this side. Never mind. It will be worth following. We'll speak again, Nancy. Come to the portrait whenever you like and talk to me. I'll hear. I may not be audible to you, but you'll receive thoughts. You would be surprised how many times Patricia comes. She thinks she comes up with the ideas herself, but I don't mind—as long as they work for her."*

The image began to fade out as it had faded in. Nancy

231

stood, her jaw hanging in amazement. "Miz Phenwick? Do you really reckon I'm right for Mistah Phenwick?"

There was a faint chuckle and a hollow, *"I reckon, Nancy."* Then the vibration was gone.

Slowly Nancy went over to run her hand through the air where she had seen the sight. She felt nothing. Her hand had a strange glowing sensation, which soon disappeared. She backed to the window and turned around to gaze again at the heavens.

"He that dwelleth in th' secret place of th' most high . . ."

Chapter 21

I DON'T KNOW what caused me to stop by, Jane Augusta," Patricia said that evening after returning from the Historical Society meeting and supper. "I just had this urge. Funny, during the after-supper speech—which was as dull as dishwater—I got an image in my mind of that portrait of your great-grandmother."

Jane Augusta giggled. "Augusta?"

"Precisely," Patricia admitted. "Well, the more I tried to put it from my mind, the more it persisted. I thought the silly thing was beginning to haunt me. I suppose, realizing who it was, and knowing that Augusta is part of your name—well, I simply got the notion to stop by to have a cup of tea with you. The food was greasy and I declined most of it. Perhaps you have a cookie or two upon which I can nibble."

As Jane Augusta went to brew the tea and get a plate of freshly baked cookies, there came a knocking at her front door.

"Aunt Patricia, would you mind seeing who that is?" Jane Augusta called from the kitchen.

Patricia had effort getting out of the comfortable chair, but she managed and went to the door. Surprisingly she opened it to her great-great-nephew, Stuart Phenwick, who looked equally as amazed at seeing Patricia.

"Stuart? Well, this is a surprise."

"Me, too. I mean, Aunt Patricia. I expected to see Cousin Jane Augusta." The lad tried not to appear too awkward. However, he always held Patricia in great esteem and wished that he could one day be as close to her as other of her friends were. "I promised Cousin Jane Augusta that I would get some things for her this afternoon, and I'm just getting around to bringing them." He produced a bundle.

"Come in, come in, boy," Patricia scolded. "You'll let the cold air in. That air is damp with the rain."

"Who is it?" Jane Augusta called as she toddled in from the kitchen. "Oh, Stuart. I'd given you up for today. Come in and have some tea and cookies with us. There was no need of you coming out in all this weather. It's a wonder your mother let you come out."

"She isn't home."

"Oh? Of course, it's prayer meeting night, isn't it?" Jane Augusta remarked casually and flipped her wrists to indicate she wanted the boy to join them.

The three sat in the parlor and lightly conversed as tea and cookies were passed.

"Speaking of your mother, Stuart," Jane Augusta said at last, "she was over this morning. I must confess she had me confused. Her conversation was quite disjointed and she seemed to be rambling on. First she quoted from the Bible, then she blabbered something about witches in Salem. Well, I couldn't quite see the connection. Then she mentioned something about Olivia, Josh's wife, and Harriet, Pren's wife. I plain out and out asked her what she was going on about. She said she was concerned because neither young lady had been saved and that they both were sinners."

"I hope you told Lillian that was none of her business," Patricia inserted. "She annoys me with her religious carrying-on."

"I could hardly get a word in edgewise," Jane Augusta replied.

"Mother is like that sometimes," Stuart remarked. "Sometimes she rants and raves like a crazy woman. I pretend to agree with her, but I usually don't."

"Anyway, out of the blue," Jane Augusta stated, want-

234

ing to conclude what she had to say, "Lillian started talking about an old house—an abandoned old house."

"An abandoned old house?" questioned Patricia. "That's curious."

"She said it was a place where witches met to form a coven," Jane Augusta continued. "I asked her how she knew about such a thing, and she said that she just did."

Stuart laughed. "Mother was speaking of an old house that used to belong to her uncle. It's out in the middle of nowhere on the way to Lexington. When Gordon and I were small, she used to tell us that the house was haunted and that was why her uncle didn't live there anymore. The reason she told us about it was that she threatened to take us there and leave us if we weren't good boys and went to church with her. Poor Gordon was about four at the time, too short to sit on the church bench and touch his feet to the floor. One Sunday morning he wagged his legs back and forth. When we got outside, she said she was going to drive him right out to that old haunted house and leave him there for misbehaving. Gordon swore he would never wiggle in church again. He never has either."

"What a cruel thing to do to such a small child," said Patricia.

"Well, it worked, didn't it?" stated Stuart.

"What made her think witches held a coven in that old house?" Patricia asked. "Did she ever mention that to you, Stuart?"

"Sometimes I think Mother is obsessed by the idea of witches," Stuart said. "That is why she wanted me to—" He hesitated. "Well, I might as well tell you. She wanted me to break into this house and find the books written by Rosea Hackleby and destroy them. But I wouldn't do it. However, she got Gordon to come one time when everyone was at Edward House for a picnic, but he couldn't find them. He told me he didn't look very well and felt ill-at-ease in Cousin Jane Augusta's house without her being there."

"Gordon entered my house?" Jane Augusta questioned. "Why, Stuart Phenwick!"

"Mother made him do it."

A curious thought struck Jane Augusta. Was she beginning to pick up some psychic vibration? "Nancy."

"What is that?" asked Patricia.

"I said 'Nancy,' " Jane Augusta replied. "Your mother didn't ever ask you to leave anything in my storage room, did she, Stuart?"

"No. Never. She just wanted me to find those books. The works of the devil, she said they were."

"What is it, Jane Augusta?" Patricia questioned. "You have a strange expression on your face."

Jane Augusta closed her eyes. Her lips began to tremble as images flashed into her mind. "That old house, Stuart, do you know where it is?"

"Yes."

"I just received three distinct pictures," Jane Augusta explained. "The first was a picture of an old house. There was an old doll with its stuffing rat-chewed and a broken rocking chair."

"Mother said that a child used to live in that house," Stuart explained, "but she was taken by the devil, leaving her doll behind."

"The second image I got was that of Great-Grandmother Augusta," Jane Augusta continued. "And she was in that old house, not as a portrait but moving about in it. She seemed to turn to me and beckon. The third picture I received was that of—of all people—Nancy Cox."

"Nancy Cox?" Patricia exclaimed. "Why Nancy? Peter was to have returned before now. They are probably together. That is one of the reasons I lingered instead of going directly to Edward House."

Cryptically Jane Augusta said, "Nancy isn't at Edward House, nor is she with Peter." Her eyes blinked open. "Stuart, did you come in the carriage?"

"Yes."

"Then you will gather up three well-filled lanterns and

236

instantly drive me to that old house," Jane Augusta commanded.

"To *that* old house?"

"You heard your cousin," Patricia stated. "And I'm coming along with you."

The Lexington road was muddy and difficult to drive. But the moon was bright, making the way easy to find. Jane Augusta and Patricia braced themselves in the interior of the coach, holding on as best they could. Neither attempted to speak over the rumble of wheels, although each moaned occasionally when the vehicle hit a particularly rough spot in the road.

In areas the way was broad, but in other spots it was quite narrow. Periodically there were turnoff places in case a faster carriage wanted to overtake and pass a slower one. While a good driver and well-skilled with horses, Stuart had a natural tendency to be cautious. Besides, he had not been convinced of any great urgency to get to the old house.

Hearing a rumbling sound behind him, he turned back to see that a carriage with a team of four horses was approaching him at a swift gait. He looked for a turnoff place on the side of the road.

"Why have we stopped here?" demanded Patricia, sticking her head out the door.

"There's a carriage coming hell-bent," Stuart explained, "and I'm sure he wants to pass us."

The coach with the hatless driver slowed slightly as it passed. Patricia got only a quick look.

"Maybe my old eyes are deceiving me," she said, "but that driver looked a bit like Peter Phenwick."

"He motioned for us to follow him," Stuart commented. "I have a feeling it was my grandfather, too."

"In that case, don't dawdle, boy," Patricia ordered. "Don't worry about jostling us about, go as fast as you can!"

Chapter 22

NANCY HAD NO CONCEPTION of the time she had spent in that upper room. Periodically she had heard strange noises and twice she was alarmed by the twisting of the doorknob. In retaliation she yelled out the few verses she could quote from the Ninety-first Psalm, believing that if there were some evildoer of Satan out to harm her, the quotation would somehow act as a deterrent in a positive way. Whatever charm it had, the annoying force was repelled and temporarily desisted.

Later loud clomping sounds were heard throughout the house, followed by several crashing noises and hurried movement up the stairs. The first impression Nancy received was that someone was searching for something. But why do that while she was in the house? The next thought was that whatever was out there was trying to frighten her, perhaps in some way to affect her sanity.

Over and over Nancy repeated the few verses of Scripture that Lillian had taught her, considering the words and slowly perceiving the meaning contained in them. Mysteriously she took much encouragement from those thoughts.

Then there were long periods of ominous silence. Those were the most frightening moments, for Nancy was completely confused as to what to believe her assailant was up to. At any moment she expected something terrifying to occur.

A thought struck Nancy after a period of interminable

silence. A plot began to curl about in her mind. She was determined not to remain in that old house any longer than need be. It was a daring scheme, but one that might possibly work.

Leaving the candelabra in the third-floor room, but taking the candles from it and the metal box of matches, Nancy stealthily pushed back the broken rocker. One glance at the remnants of the doll and she wanted to return and get it; she thought better of that. Before departing from the room, she lit a single candle. Her other hand free, she used it to feel her way since the light was meager at best.

She did not dare to look in any of the upper rooms for fear she might encounter an unexpected surprise. Rushing immediately to the stairway, she refused to glance back. Not remembering which of the steps were weak, she rationalized that by walking on the extreme side of each instead of in the middle, there would be more support beneath. With footsteps as light as those of a cat, she crept to the second floor.

A clapping sound echoed throughout the house almost as if it had been a shot from a gun. That thought greatly alarmed her.

"He that dwelleth in th' secret place . . ." she muttered.

Was she walking into some sort of bizarre trap? Would someone suddenly leap out at her from one of the rooms on the second floor?

"He is my refuge and my fortress . . ." she continued.

The house became deathly quiet before she put her foot on the top step of the last flight. She moved down two steps, then turned around and held the candle flame to the rickety banister. The wood was dry. It took several seconds for the flame to catch, even then it smouldered. She went down the rest of the stairs. Only smoke was festering at the banister above.

Putting the flame to the bottom part of the banister, she had little luck starting a fire. Quickly she went into the room with the most furniture in it. The rodents had gnawed at the upholstery. Taking a small chair to the base of the stairs, she placed it upside down over the first two steps, the legs toward her. She placed the candle flame to it, and the old material was fortunately dry enough to catch fire instantly. Waiting several seconds for it to get a good hold, Nancy lifted the chair by the legs and carried it to the top of the stairs. By then it was a torch and flames lapped out in all directions.

Scampering down the stairs, she found another piece of furniture and ignited it. This she put at the foot of the stairs.

Remembering curtains in the kitchen, Nancy went there and set them afire. Then she went throughout the other rooms, lighting whatever would burn before she went back to the front room in which most of the curtains were hanging.

She had knocked on the walls and perceived that they were wooden. Her one hope was that the flames would burn through by drying the outer wood. Soon all the curtains, except one that was wet, were ablaze. As they burned she took a piece of wood and jabbed out windowpanes, allowing wind to enter to fan the flames. It was her belief that the walls of the ground floor would go first.

By then the place was becoming an inferno. She went into the one room in which she had not started a fire and proceeded to disrobe, stripping down to her underthings, those which remained closest to her body. Although she loved that particular dress, she put flame to it too, as well as to the petticoats. She kept only her cloak, which she rolled into a bundle, thinking that when her moment of escape arrived, she wanted nothing superfluous that might snag on a finger of flame and turn her into a living torch.

The room with the furniture and curtains was like a furnace. Every step of the stairs was a platform of dancing flames. The heat was becoming almost unbearable. Dare she try to dash through the room and see if she could push through the flaming front wall?

Nancy got so far, but had to turn back, the heat was so intense. Had she trapped herself? Was she soon to be consumed by the flames? She ran to the kitchen. There was no escape route. On her way back through the hallway toward the front of the house, part of the stairway collapsed.

Then a shrill voice cried out from one of the floors above. "Damn you, Nancy Cox! You will die in the fiery flames of Hell!" There was madness in the voice. Hysteria. It crackled with the sound of the burning wood. "There's no escape! No escape!"

Raymond and Arthur were holding Milford Wartstone inside the carriage. Pomeroy Belcher had loaned Arthur a pistol. While the writer was shaky with the weapon, he held it steady on the hunchback.

Peter, in the driver's seat, did not need instructions on how to get to the house. He could see the flames and drove directly to it.

Patricia was badly jostled about in the other carriage, as was Jane Augusta. The old matriarch kept uttering that bruises would heal. Then Jane Augusta's bulky body would come flying at her again.

Peter pulled up a distance before the house. Looking back, he saw the other carriage approaching. A small pond was in front of the house, probably not very deep. He removed his cloak and all loose garments, then threw himself into the cold water. Drenched in an instant, he quickly climbed out as Stuart drew the other carriage up alongside the first.

"Stuart! Down here!" Peter ordered. "Pull off your greatcoat and anything frilly you might be wearing."

Stuart complied without questioning his grandfather's orders. Peter led him to the pond and motioned for him to get in. During a moment of hesitation, the older man pushed the lad into the water, then quickly fished him out.

"All right, boy," Peter ordered, "we're going to try to break in the door."

Patricia and Jane Augusta got out of the carriage and watched as man and boy tried to ram down the front door. It would not give.

Peter motioned toward a burning wall, part of which was smouldering with red coals. He ran back to the carriage and ordered Wartstone and Arthur to give him their cloaks. Moments later he was dousing the garments in the pond.

Sopping wet, Peter gave one cloak to Stuart and kept the other himself. Using them as shields over their heads and bodies, they rushed the smoldering wall, plowing through it.

Patricia, her composure gathered, marched to the other carriage and opened the door. "Arthur . . . Raymond, bring that man out. I want to have a look at him."

"Yes, Patricia," Arthur said, the gun shaking in his hand.

Raymond was the first to the ground. He jerked Wartstone out of the vehicle.

"Why, it's the man in that dreadful picture you painted," Patricia exclaimed.

"He's the one who put the voodoo doll in my leather bag," Raymond stated.

"And he's the one who locked Nancy in that house," Arthur echoed as he crept from the carriage lest an abrupt movement cause his trigger finger to slip.

"You did?" questioned Patricia. She held out her hand. "Give me the key."

"I don't have it," Wartstone snarled.

"Very well, Arthur, give me that pistol," demanded the lady. "I'm a good shot, Mr. whoever you are. It's the key or your life."

Wartstone glared at her for a moment, then slowly reached into his pocket for the key.

"No. You unlock the door," Patricia ordered. "I might add, I would not be impartial to shooting you in the back if you do not comply with my wishes."

Wartstone hesitated only an instant before he went toward the burning house. He did not look back but quickly unlocked the lock.

Peter was nearly hit with a falling beam. He was blinded by the red-hot flames that leaped at Stuart and him. "Nancy! Are you in here?"

243

There was no reply.

Peter pulled Stuart toward the burning stairway. "We'll try one more place. If we don't find her, we'll have to go back or die in the fire."

"I'm already getting weak, Grandfather," Stuart said. "My lungs feel as if they're about to burst open." He coughed.

"Mistah Phenwick!" Nancy called through the snapping flames.

"Over this way, Stuart. Take my hand!"

"I can't see, Grandfather!"

"Put that wet cloak over your head and take my hand!"

Man and boy went toward the sound of Nancy's voice. Peter saw her. He released Stuart's hand and threw the wet cape he was carrying over the flames that danced between the girl and him. She ran across the cloak and into Peter's arms.

The front door was open.

"Look, Mistah Phenwick. We can go that way," Nancy said.

Peter snatched the cloak from Stuart. "Grab the boy's hand, Nancy, and put your other hand beneath the waist of my trousers and follow me. I'll hold the cloak as a shield until we get out."

Patricia was waiting to catch her nephew when he came flying forward. Raymond grabbed Nancy, taking her cloak from her and holding it for her to wrap about herself.

"I'm all right, Aunt Patricia," Peter exclaimed, "only slightly singed. Let me help Stuart."

Confusion followed as Peter went to help his grandson. The boy had stinging eyes from the smoke, but he was all right.

Jane Augusta had been watching the entire affair from a distance, trembling with the cold and wanting desperately to get back into the carriage where she would at least be protected from the wind. She was fascinated by the flames. Her attention was attracted to the third floor where she saw a small head being thrust through a windowpane. A moment later it was plunged through a second and then a third. She could see the figure of a distraught person standing in the window.

"Get me out of here! I'm burning alive!" came the helpless cry. A fourth windowpane was broken and the object used to do it came flying to the earth. It was the doll's head. "Help me! Please! I confess my sin! I repent! Oh, Jesus Christ, don't let me burn alive!"

Stuart, now able to see again, looked up at the flaming building. "That's my mother!"

"Lillian?" questioned Patricia. "Then I was correct! I suspected, but I couldn't put my finger on the precise answer."

"I've got to get her out of there!" Stuart yelled. "That's my mother up there!"

Peter hugged his arms tightly about the boy and held him with all his might. "You can't go back in there. Nobody can. You would never make it out alive."

"Save me! Save me!" Lillian cried. A moment later she disappeared from the window and was not seen again.

Patricia removed her cloak and put it about Stuart. "She lived by hellfire and damnation, boy. And it has at last consumed her. Get in the carriage with Jane Augusta. Raymond will have to drive this carriage back. Jane Augusta, remove your cape. Peter will have to have it if he drives back to Boston."

Peter took the pistol from Arthur and pointed Wartstone toward a clump of bushes.

"Are you going to kill me?" Wartstone moaned. "None of this was my idea, you know. She hired me to do it. It was her, that lady that was standing in the window. I have no trade, so I hire out at odd jobs. Dishonest as it may be, it's still a living."

"I'm not going to kill you," Peter replied. "A court of law will decide your fate. I just want your clothing."

"They won't fit you."

"No doubt," Peter replied. "But they'll help to keep

245

me warm until we get back to Boston. You can wear these wet ones if you like."

A few minutes later Peter was clad in Wartstone's ill-fitting and somewhat odoriferous apparel. Raymond was already at the driver's seat of the other carriage. Peter looked inside. Stuart, with Patricia's cloak about him, was bent over, his head on Jane Augusta's lap, sobbing. Peter patted him gently.

"You did a brave job, Stuart," the older man said. "I'm extremely proud of you, lad."

Stuart reached his hand back for Peter to grasp, then the youth burst into uncontrolled crying.

"We'll go now. Slowly this time," Peter said.

"We all have faith in you, Peter," Patricia returned. "I've got to say this for you, you're getting a daring girl in Nancy. And a very sweet prize."

Chapter 23

"As I said before," Milford Wartstone mumbled, the starch momentarily dampened in the man, "I am a simple man, a cripple. I have no trade, so I hire out at odd jobs. I'm just trying to make a living."

"Tormenting young ladies?" fired Peter.

They were sitting in the living room of Augustus' house, waiting for the constable to arrive. Wartstone had been given three substantial portions of brandy to warm him and to loosen his tongue.

"How long had you been working for my wife?" questioned Gus. His face, while framed in grief, showed certain signs of relief, as if a large burden had been lifted from his shoulders.

"I didn't even know she was your wife," snarled Wartstone. "I never laid eyes on the woman. She answered an ad I put in the newspaper, like I always do when I go into a new town. Naturally, I thought her requests bizarre, but I've done worse things in my life."

"Do you believe in voodoo?" Patricia asked, now comfortably settled in the best chair available.

"Don't know as how I do, and don't know as how I don't," Wartstone replied. "Fact is, I never knew what I was doing had anything to do with voodoo, or anything like that."

"You actually mean to say that you can coldly carry out such acts—" Patricia continued.

"Occupational necessities, missus, if you don't mind,"

247

Wartstone interrupted. "A man has his job, the pay is good, and he does what he is ordered to do."

"And had you no compassion for the victim?" Jane Augusta quizzed.

Wartstone cast a hurried glance at Nancy, who was sitting beside Peter on the opposite side of the room. "Compassion is a word I've never learned. The lady had a job to be done. What happened to her was none of my concern. I don't have much respect for pretty young ladies." He cleared his throat as if preparing to spit. "They've always looked contemptuously on me. All women have, unless they want some special favor from me. Then comes the sweet talk and the cooing. But when they've got what they want, they turn on me in disgust. So I accept my fate. I'm a freak of nature and no handsome prince like the notorious Phenwick men. I accept my place and my fate. Eventually I'll go to another city and apply my wares there—the only ones I know."

The constable and two men arrived and dispatched the curious personage of Milford Wartstone to the mills of justice.

"We should all be going now," Patricia commented, putting her hands to the arm of the chair, but making no further effort to rise.

"Not yet," Gus said with a plea in his voice. "My sons have gone upstairs to weep for their mother. I don't seem to be able to find tears for Lillian. It seems that I should . . ." He shook his head. ". . . but I can't."

Peter rose and went to his eldest son, placing his hand upon his shoulder. "Shall I stay over with you, Son?"

"No need, Father. I'll have to get used to the vacant house soon enough," Gus replied. "I appreciate your concern."

"Had you no idea about Lillian and the twist of her mind?" asked Jane Augusta.

"Hadn't you, Cousin Jane Augusta?" Gus returned. "I believe she confided more in you than she did in me—at least over the last ten or twelve years. Still I have to admit that she has always been paradoxical. I've known her to

248

have quite a mean streak at times. She always said she wanted to get her hands on those books of Rosea Hackleby to destroy them. But I believe she wanted to devour the information in them first. She was a real Christian zealot to the outside world. Even to me and the boys. It was only recently that I discovered she was secretly into the occult. I only became suspicious because she kept ranting and raving about it. Then some crony of hers came to the door one night when Lillian was supposed to have been at prayer meeting. The night before last. My curiosity got up because of the peculiar appearance of that person. I spoke with the minister and he told me that there was *no* prayer meeting the night before last. I waited until she got home, then surprised her in the kitchen while she was fashioning a wax doll. She flew at me in a rage. Little did I know the doll was supposed to be in the likeness of Nancy Cox. I questioned her. For the first time I believe I saw madness in her eyes, they were red and wide and, well, I've only seen two insane people in my life—and they had that same look."

"I had an uncanny feeling that Lillian was too good," Patricia said. "I can't remember when I first got the notion that she was hiding something. She was too zealous, too fanatical. I wonder if such people don't sometimes teeter on the verge of sanity and can be easily swayed to conjure negative devices to justify their own enthusiasm and belief."

"Lillian was always so religious," Jane Augusta added.

"That's precisely what I mean." Patricia glanced about at the others. "Yet, if she were truly a Christian, she could never have had hatred in her heart."

"She always resented not being accepted as a Phenwick woman," Jane Augusta replied.

"She was a Phenwick woman," Gus inserted, somewhat indignantly. "After all, she was married to me."

"Yes, of course, she was a Phenwick woman," Peter said in a soothing voice. "Wasn't she, Aunt Patricia?"

"In name, yes." Patricia rose. "I think it time I be getting home now. Jane Augusta?"

"Oh yes, indeed," Jane Augusta returned. "I'm never up at this hour of the night."

"I'll see that you get home," Peter volunteered.

"No, Father," Gus said, rising. "It'll be no trouble for me to drive them both home. Besides, I want to ride in the cool night air and organize my thoughts."

"I d'clare, I must look a hideous mess, Mistah Phenwick," Nancy exclaimed after the others were gone. "I'd planned to look so pretty and all for you. You must think I look a wretch."

"Nancy, you look beautiful to me," Peter replied. He took a wad of wrapped paper from his pocket. "Love only sees beauty. And I do love you, Nancy. I've had time to consider that, and I do love you."

"Why, Mistah Phenwick, that's downright sweet of you," she said sincerely. "I'll tell you th' truth. I'm certain I'm very much in love with you, too."

"Do you think you could be happy married to a man as old as I am?"

"I don't think of you bein' old, Mistah Phenwick," Nancy replied. "Fact is, I don't think I could be happier with any other man in th' whole world."

"In that case, will you become Mrs. Peter Phenwick?"

"A Phenwick woman?"

The scent of violets wafted through the room, gently hovering over Nancy.

"What is it, Nancy?"

"Violets. But only for a minute. I d'clare, they're up and gone already," Nancy said lightly. "I do like violets, don't you, Mistah Phenwick?"

"Violets happen to be a family tradition." He unwrapped a large diamond ring and slipped it on her finger.

"Oh, it's gorgeous, Mistah Phenwick, simply gorgeous!" Nancy exclaimed. "I rather imagined that violets might be something special in your family."

"I'll tell you about it sometime, my dearest." He took her in his arms. "I love you, Nancy. And I intend for you

250

to be the grandest Phenwick woman of them all, even greater than Aunt Patricia."

"Well, I d'clare, I will have a long way to go."

They kissed and there was no doubt in either of their minds about the deep love they felt.

Again the scent of violets seemed to rush into the room. And was there distant contented laughter? Maybe it was only in Nancy's imagination . . . maybe.

AUGUSTA:

The founder of the family who married the first Joshua Phenwick because she liked the name. Thrice married, the first three of her four children were killed during childhood. Daniel was the only one of her children to survive to adulthood. Later she adopted the two youngest Munsk children, Edward and Jane, making them Phenwicks.

DANNY:

Augusta's weak, emotional son. Husband of Margaret O'Plaggerty, and father of Elias (by Kate Mumford), Alexander (Lex), Peter and Rachel. Now deceased after a wrecklessly traumatic life.

ELIAS:

Danny's illegitimate son, who in adult life was accepted as a Phenwick. He married widowed Patricia Kelburn Phenwick; father of Rebecca.

ALEXANDER (Lex):

Danny's second son, an attorney and head of the family business in London. He married Susannah Phenwick, his foster cousin.

PETER:

Danny's second son, head of the family business in Boston. Widower (Helen Barnfather), he is the father of Augustus, Joanna, Prentise and Joshua.

AUGUSTUS (Gus):

Peter's eldest son. Married to Lillian Webb, father of Stuart and Gordon.

LILLIAN WEBB:

Gus's domineering wife who was never accepted as a Phenwick woman. Mother of Stuart and Gordon.

JOANNA:

Peter's only daughter, an actress, never marries.

Cast of Characters

NANCY COX:

A pretty and vivacious girl who delights in adventure and excitement.

HARRIET PETTIJOHN:

A Southern girl, who experienced a traumatic episode at a very young age and has never been able to escape the shadow of it.

ARTHUR TOWNSEND:

A dashing, somewhat aesthetic writer-poet. He is a handsome member of Patricia's entourage.

RAYMOND NELSON:

Another of Patricia's entourage, he is a painter, whom she has discovered.

MILFORD WARTSTONE:

A hunchback with a disagreeable attitude, who seeks to make his way *any* way he can.

POMEROY BELCHER:

The owner-keeper of the Tooth & Tail tavern.

TOM CLEGHORN:

A black man accused of once accosting Harriet.

ELSWORTH GRAYSON:

Cleghorn's young white friend who sought revenge.

MATHILDE: ETHELBERT:	Servants at Edward House.
STUART:	The eldest son of Augustus and Lillian.
GORDON:	The second son of Augustus and Lillian.
PRENTISE:	The awkward second son of Peter, stiff and formal, he is neither outgoing nor gregarious. Presently betrothed to Harriet Cox.
JOSHUA:	Peter's youngest child. Married to Olivia Pritchard.
OLIVIA:	Peter's beautiful, actress, wife.
EDWARD:	Augusta's handsome adopted son. First husband of Patricia Kelburn, father of Susannah.
PATRICIA:	Widow of both Edward and Elias, she has taken the position of grand matriarch of the Phenwick family. A child by each husband, she is the mother of Susannah and of Rebecca.
SUSANNAH:	Patricia's lovely and talented first daughter by Edward, a concert pianist. Married to Alexander.
REBECCA:	Patricia's second daughter, by Elias. She was married to Johnny Ornby, then to Robert Cathcart. Mother of Kate Phenwick, stepmother of Adriane and Lydia Ornby.
KATE PHENWICK:	Rebecca's daughter.

THE ORNBYS

JANE PHENWICK-
  ORNBY: Augusta's adopted daughter, married to Jeffrey Ornby; mother of Frederick, Johnny and Andrew.

ANDREW: Jane's youngest son.

JANE AUGUSTA: Andrew's eldest child. Widow of Eustace Clark.

DANIEL: Andrew's eldest son, an attorney.

THEODORE
  (DR. TED):   Andrew's second son, a physician.